This second edition (paperback) published in 2020 by
Ottobeast Publishing
ottobeastpublishing@gmail.com

First edition published 2013

Cover design Rebecca Moss Guyver.

ISBN 978-1-912861-09-5

A CIP catalogue record for this title is available from the
British Library.

D1355170

Also by Pauline Manders

The Utterly Crime Series

Book no 1 Utterly Explosive (first published 2012) - 2nd edition (2019)
Book no 2 Utterly Fuelled (first published 2013) - 2nd edition (2019)
Book no 3 Utterly Rafted (first published 2013) - 2nd edition (2020)
Book no 4 Utterly Reclaimed (2014)
Book no 5 Utterly Knotted (2015)
Book no 6 Utterly Crushed (2016)
Book no 7 Utterly Dusted (2017)
Book no 8 Utterly Roasted (2018)
Book no 9 Utterly Dredged (2020)

To Paul, Fiona, Alastair, Karen, Andrew, Katie and Mathew.

PAULINE MANDERS

Pauline Manders was born in London and trained as a doctor at University College Hospital, London. Having gained her surgical qualifications, she moved with her husband and young family to East Anglia, where she worked in the NHS as an ENT Consultant Surgeon for over 25 years. She used her maiden name throughout her medical career and retired from medicine in 2010.

Retirement has given her time to write crime fiction, become an active member of a local carpentry group, and share her husband's interest in classic cars. She lives deep in the Suffolk countryside.

ACKNOWLEDGMENTS

My thanks to: Beth Wood for her positive advice, support and encouragement; Pat McHugh, my mentor and hardworking editor with a keen sense of humour, mastery of atmosphere and grasp of characters; Rebecca Moss Guyver, for her boundless enthusiasm and brilliant cover artwork and design; Judith Maria Wiesner, book and paper conservator, for the generosity of her knowledgeable advice; David Withnall for his proof reading skills; Andy Deane for his editing help; the Write Now! Bury writers group for their support; Sue Southey for her cheerful reassurances and advice; and my husband and family, on both sides of the Atlantic, for their love and support.

CHAPTER 1

'No, Storm! Wooah… stop!'

Matt tried to focus. If he let go, he'd never get the dog back and Tom would kill him. If he held on, then he'd be dragged across what looked like an abandoned vegetable plot and towards a railway line. He regarded Storm's hind-quarters with distaste – haunches curving as muscular buttocks flexed and paws pushed hard, straining to move forwards. Squit, he thought and closed his eyes to shut out the image.

The lead jarred, cutting into his palm. Matt pulled back, missed his footing and lost control. Helpless, he launched headlong over rough earth and shrub-sized weeds.

'No!' he shrieked as a raspberry cane thwacked against his shin and thorns ripped through denim. 'Bloody Tom,' he howled as pain shot beyond his leg. He gasped for breath. His stride failed. 'Shit!' he yelled and let go of the lead. It was over.

Matt watched, heart pounding as Storm disappeared into the distance. He should have known. When had anything associated with his older brother not ended in trouble? He thought back to the phone call.

'Hey, Matt – I need a favour. I've acquired a canine. Kind of valuable in the sniffer dog world…. You still there?'

'A dog? Yeah, yeah, Tom I'm listenin'. So when you say *acquired*, you mean…?'

'Not your problem, mate. Thing is - I'm going away for a week or so. Need you to take care of him.' And there the conversation ended. That had been three days ago.

When Matt saw the dog for the first time he'd expected a bull terrier. A Staffy. A fighting dog. Something to make Tom look well hard. So why a chocolate Labrador, he wondered. Matt knew he shouldn't have said 'yes' to taking the dog, never more so than now, as he screwed up his eyes against the April sunshine and scanned the distant foliage. 'Storm! Storm! Where are you?' But desperation replaced authority and his tones fell flat.

Something dark and brown moved through broken slatted fencing. 'Hey, wait! Storm!' Matt kept his eyes riveted on the shape ahead. He worked his way forwards, lifting each grubby trainer high as he forced a path over matted foliage. Sweat broke in beads on his forehead and trickled down his plump face. This was pure hell. He hated physical exertion and he felt cross. It should have been a short walk, he reasoned; a quick stroll with the dog around fields backing onto his mother's modest bungalow, his home in Stowmarket. He'd lived there for all of his nineteen years, but here he was crashing through undergrowth, lost and a dog missing.

Ahead, the ground fell away and the railway continued over an embankment. It seemed to loom high and long, plunging him into shade and blocking his path. He reckoned Storm couldn't be far away now and his spirits rose as he paused to catch his breath. That's when he noticed a short narrow tunnel beneath a brick span. 'When the hell did that get there?' he moaned, but of course the answer was obvious as he walked through. The old bricks were stained and encrusted; moisture had soaked and loosened the mortar over many decades. He guessed it had been built as a passageway for livestock and farm workers to pass under the embankment, as old as the railway itself and long since fallen into disuse.

'Storm, Storm!' he yelled, now through to the other side. Water had collected in the dip and an expanse of soft mud blocked his path.

'Not such a clever bastard after all,' he muttered, staring at the paw prints leading towards trees and an overgrown path. For a moment he was Sherlock Holmes scrutinising the ground. 'Observe, Watson,' he said in his best imitation voice. 'It must be our dog. Those marks are where he's dragged the lead through the mud.'

Matt pressed on, watching the foliage for movement or a glimpse of something knee-high and brown. The track led him away from the railway line and he walked slowly, concentrating all his attention on the search. He hardly noticed the barbed wire choked by brambles and hawthorn, or the old orchard surrendered to nature. Occasional birdsong broke the silence closing around him, but the only thing he registered was a complete absence of Labrador. Soon he felt as if he'd left civilisation behind. Anger and frustration evaporated as the path petered out. Fear began to grip his stomach.

A few more steps and he broke from the cover of small trees and shrubs. A fence blocked his way and beyond he saw rough ground, deserted. Now what should he do, he wondered, then swore under his breath. Something caught the sunlight. 'What the hell?' Plastic sheeting curved high, arching over a structure. Was it a frame? A polytunnel? 'Storm, Storm!'

'Who's bloody there?' A harsh voice cut through the air as footsteps pounded on dry clumpy earth. A man appeared, sweating and gripping a metal pole.

'I, I've… lost my dog, Stor….' The name died on Matt's tongue. Only a strangled yowl emerged as he looked at the middle-aged man. Instinctively he dropped his gaze, not wanting to make eye contact or stare at the ponytail escaping from the baseball cap.

'It's private here, now get off this land! Scarper, you little shit!' The man narrowed his eyes. They looked like black pebbles beneath the cap's peak. Shade played over his leathered skin.

Matt stepped back. 'Me dog Storm… 'e ran off. 'Ave you seen…?' Anxiety brought out his Suffolk accent and he struggled to find the words as his breath came in short gasps. 'A brown Lab. Lead still hangin' from 'is neck.'

'So it's your bloody dog!' The tones were rough, but the man lowered the metal pole a fraction while he coughed, cleared his throat and spat on the ground. 'You oughtta take better care of 'im, mate. Nice dog like that.'

'You've seen 'im?'

'Yeah, friendly. Reckoned he'd been tracking a rabbit or summut – judging by the way he's been sniffing round 'ere. Caught 'im easy. I've tied 'im up.' The serpent-like hair moved as he indicated the direction with a nod. He frowned and studied Matt's chest. 'Interesting tee-shirt, mate.'

Matt glanced down. It strained across his ample belly and patches of sweat darkened the green fabric. Matt grinned. He'd found the dog, and relief now loosened his tongue. 'It were me brother's. Yeah, 'e got tickets for the Eagles' tour… 2008. The O2 arena.'

'I can see. Kind of retro taste - but what's that written on the front?'

4

Matt squinted at the large *O* and a small *2* printed on his tee. He felt the fabric sticking to his moist skin as he hunched his shoulders to look. The title of one of the tracks snaked over the front like a winding road and ended with a single word written in the middle of the large *O* and almost filling the front of his chest. *WEEDS,* except the *S* had been a casualty to the washing machine.

'*Waiting in the weed*?' Matt read.

'Yeah, reckoned it said weed.' The man fell silent, lingering as if waiting for Matt to say more.

'About me dog… could I…?'

'Yeah, sure.' The tone changed. 'Wait here. Don't move a step. If I think you've so much as even blinked by the time I come back, I'll lay this metal across you. Understand?'

Matt understood.

He gave Matt one last look, and then swung the metal pole. Matt flinched as it slapped against the palm of the man's free hand. Thwack!

'Won't even breathe, mate.'

The ponytail rearranged itself like a sidewinder as the man turned on his heel.

Matt knew he had to wait if he wanted to get the dog back, but that didn't stop the fear rising in his throat. He watched the man stride towards the polytunnel, metal pole swinging with each step. Should he leg it while he still had the chance? He was deciding what to do when the sound of clawing and panting filled the air.

'Here he is,' the man spluttered as he reappeared, stumbling towards the fence and pulling against the dog as it strained at its leash. The soft brown ears were flattened back, the eyes wild. Specks of spittle clung to fur. 'Sure you weren't after some-'

The man didn't finish as Storm bounded forwards.

'Hey, good boy, Storm.' Matt grinned as the dog pushed under the broken fencing. He wished he had time to enjoy the welcome but he felt too threatened by the man.

'Good boy!' He patted the solid brown body as it circled around his legs. A soft muzzle thrust up at his face and chest. Saliva merged with *WEED* on his tee-shirt. Matt grabbed the lead. 'Thanks mate.'

'It's OK. The dog's pleased to see you.' The man coughed and readjusted his cap. 'Sure you're not wanting any...?' He looked pointedly at the green cotton with the large *O* stretched across Matt's chest.

'Eagles?' Matt finished for him, baffled by the question.

The man closed his mouth and narrowed his eyes.

'Not eagles?' Matt rubbed at his forehead. 'Ah! Now I get you. Dope! Grass! Yeah, I can get hold of that kinda stuff in town.' When the man didn't seem to react, Matt continued, 'Even down the 'Cademy.'

'Utterly Academy?'

'Yeah. Did me trainin' there.'

'Sure.' The man nodded slowly. He didn't smile.

'Still go back for the release days. I'm an apprentice carpenter.'

'Then I'll know where to find you if there's ever a whisper you've talked.'

Before Matt could say another word, the lead wrenched at his arm. 'Sorry, mate. Can't stop!' He spun on one muddy trainer. The dog was strong and Matt had no inclination to hang around. 'Should've put me tee on back to front,' he muttered as his foot left the ground.

Storm tugged again, jerking him. There was nothing Matt could do. He started to run. It was either that or fall flat on his face. He felt the man's eyes boring into his back. Sensed the threat.

With a yell Matt leapt onward, jumping and stumbling, dragged by the dog. Adrenalin powered his flight as sunlight flashed through the trees. For a moment he became a comic-strip hero, transposed from the Suffolk countryside to a jungle of his imagination. Captain Fantastic pursued by a monstrous winged beast. An eagle – and then he tripped on a jungle creeper. Reality had pulled him up short and nearly bust his ankle.

'Bloody brambles,' he gasped.

•••

The dog panted. Matt's ribs ached. His ankle throbbed. He bent over as he tried to catch his breath. He closed his eyes, hoping to shut out the memory of a man with sidewinder hair and a metal pole. He'd survived the Suffolk wilderness and he'd made it back to Tumble Weed Drive on the Flower Estate, but at a price - his nerves were shredded, his muscles in spasm.

'Shit, Storm. What the hell got into you back there?'

The four-legged creature at Matt's side pushed a wet nose at him and wagged its tail. He shook his head. 'I s'pose you wanna come out with me this evenin' an' all.' Matt knew there wasn't going to be an answer.

Matt leaned against the front door with the peeling paint and fumbled for his key. He guessed his mother was out, probably on her afternoon late shift at the local Co-Op. At least he'd have the place to himself and there'd be no one to grumble at him about the dog. He staggered down the bungalow's gloomy hallway, elbowed his bedroom door open and collapsed onto his bed.

Matt fell into a dreamless sleep. Earth, superheroes, life; nothing existed for several hours. He experienced no tangible thoughts, no memories, no emotion. Instead he inhabited a vacuum until something nudged and thrust at his face, prodding him back into consciousness.

'Ugh!' He wiped at his cold wet cheek. 'Houndin' hell, Storm. Ugh!' He pushed the insistent muzzle away and blinked, trying to focus on his phone. 20:00. He'd been out of it for hours.

Matt struggled to sit up, his muscles aching and burning with the effort. He rubbed the sleep out of his eyes as he stood, swaying on his stiff ankle. It twinged a bit but he reckoned if it wasn't swollen then he was OK for pubbing. He'd already arranged to meet up with his mates later that evening and he'd be damned if he'd let anything else mess up his day. Without Storm, the Easter weekend would have stretched on forever, but now he needed the company of his mates and he'd been looking forward to finishing Easter Monday with a skinfull down at his local. They'd all agreed a pint or three would be essential by the end of the long Easter Weekend. But how to get to the Nags Head without any pain?

'Sorry mate, but me body won't allow me to walk. And you aint comin' on me scooter!'

Two brown eyes searched Matt's face, trying to make sense of his words.

What lay behind that soulful expression? He didn't even know if Storm was the dog's real name, or what he'd been trained for. Tom had implied he sniffed things out, but that could mean anything from explosives to drugs, tobacco to cash. And what about bodies trapped in earthquake rubble or hunting and tracking people? There were even obscure things such as sniffing out cancer. The list was probably endless. Matt reckoned you could train a dog to do tricks as well. Ride a scooter? Anything was possible in a comic-strip book.

'No, you're stayin' here tonight.' He ruffled the fur as he ran his hand over the broad flat head. 'Don't s'pose you've been chipped?' It set Matt thinking. Microchip information might reveal who the real owner was, explain what Tom was up to and why Storm's nose had led Matt into such a dangerous wilderness. In Tom's world, knowledge was power and Matt fancied a slice of it.

Twenty minutes later Matt slammed the front door. He'd left the dog behind, now settled in his bedroom and fed, watered and curled up on one of Tom's old tee-shirts.

•••

'Hey! Matt! Over here, mate.'

Matt looked across the crowded main bar of the Nags Head. Glasses clinked while drinkers' voices ebbed and flowed. A large LCD screen flickered high on the wall as a white snooker ball struck a yellow and then inched up close against the green cushion. Matt glanced up at the 2011 World Snooker Championship images, beamed live from the Crucible Theatre in Sheffield. He grinned and waved to his friends and then pushed towards the barman, grinning again as he ordered a pint of lager. It dripped from his glass. To his way of thinking it left a gloriously sticky trail on the old floorboards as he shuffled to where his friends sat in the snug area.

'Hi, Chrissie. Nick.' He slumped onto a bench, thrust his legs under the table and gulped at his drink.

'Are you OK? You look kind of…. Are you limping?' Chrissie's forehead creased. She looked cool and fresh in her loose linen jacket.

Matt peered at his friends over the rim of his glass. How should he answer? How much to tell? He'd shared a workbench with Chrissie for the best part of his first year at Utterly Academy and despite her being over twice his age, they'd become firm friends. 'It's kind of complic…, it's a Tom thing.'

'That you're limping?' Nick grimaced. 'Whatever has he done to you now? Roughed you up a bit?' He upended his glass, draining it in one long gulp. 'Anyone want another?'

Matt glanced down at the green cotton stretched taut across his chest. He hadn't thought to change his tee before setting out for the Nags Head. He was tempted to raise his arm and sneak a furtive sniff when he caught Chrissie's eye.

'There's a paw print on your shoulder. Does Tom turn into some kind of werewolf after dark then?'

'That'll be Storm.'

'Storm?' Chrissie and Nick asked in unison.

While snooker balls chinked against each other on the huge screen in the main bar area, Matt recounted his day.

'I can't think where you wandered to. Beyond the railway line, you say?' When Matt nodded, Nick continued, 'I've never walked out that way, but maybe that's the whole point. Sounds like you were in the middle of nowhere. What the hell did you stumble onto?' Nick cradled his empty glass. 'And another thing; you can't take him to work with you. How'll you manage?'

'Got this week off. Easter, aint it?'

'But what about the dog? Poor Storm.' Chrissie's voice rose. 'I mean if Tom stole the dog, well the dog'll be missing its owner. Pining. It's cruel. And anyway, why'd Tom want a sniffer dog?'

'Give it back, Matt. Don't mess about. If it was worth stealing then it was worth microchipping. Hand the dog in somewhere. They'll be able to trace the real owner. Now, anyone for another?' Nick stood up.

'Ginger beer for me,' Chrissie said, as Matt handed over his empty glass.

'Land Girl? Or are you sticking with the Carlsberg?'

'Carlsberg, mate.' Matt watched his friend weave a path to the bar. He was easy to track; Nick's height put him head and shoulders above most of the drinkers now intent on the snooker. For a moment Matt let his thoughts run on and then shrugged. It was simple for Nick to say what he'd said. He'd never had to deal with Tom. 'You know what Tom's like,' he whined to Chrissie.

'Hmm, usually ends badly for you. Drugs - not a good place to be. Steer clear, Matt. Mind you, I don't think there's much of a problem at the Academy.'

'There aint. But if you go lookin' you'll always find.'

'Well don't go looking. You go scratching around and you'll come up against people like that bloke with the ponytail. Just stay away from Tom's henchmen. You don't want any more trouble.'

Matt frowned. Only a few months ago one of Tom's so-called friends had wanted him to case out something to steal from Utterly Academy. But this was different. The

Ponytail was just some weirdo with an iron bar. A hippy with violent tendencies. He had no reason to think he had anything to do with Tom. Chrissie's warning seemed overly paranoid. He looked up as Nick approached.

'Hendry's playing Selby,' Nick said, nodding towards the big screen in the main bar. He put two glasses down and headed back to collect the third.

'Looks like we've lost Nick to the snooker,' Chrissie murmured, as she sipped her ginger beer. 'I know what you're like, Matt. Don't go poking your nose into Tom's business. Just steer clear.'

'I reckon there'd be no harm seein' if I can trace Storm's real owner. I've got a week to myself. Where's the risk?'

Matt watched Chrissie open her mouth to answer, but a cheer went up in the main bar. It seemed to side-track her.

'Sounds like that frame's over,' she remarked and then smiled as Nick returned.

'I was just thinking, Matt,' he said, as he slumped down. 'One of my mum's friends has a daughter who's a veterinary nurse. Maybe she could help you out.'

'Is she…? I mean, d'you know what she's like?'

'I've no idea. I was thinking more of her microchip scanning abilities. I'll ask Mum.'

'Thanks, mate.' Matt swigged at his glass. 'A bird in uniform,' he muttered under his breath. But what sort of uniform did veterinary nurses wear, he wondered. Perhaps the Easter break had more potential than he'd supposed.

CHAPTER 2

Chrissie eased the sharp yellow bonnet onto the Wattisham perimeter lane. The exhaust growled as she accelerated away.

'*And on a lighter, more gastronomic note....*' The news reporter's voice blended with the TR7's droning engine. '*Truffles! Who'd have thought you could find black truffles in Suffolk.*'

Chrissie flicked the indicator switch and slowed to turn into Ron Clegg's bone-breaker of an entrance track. She leaned forwards, jolting against the seatbelt. '*An English bull terrier with a very special nose has....*' The ruts and potholes swallowed the radio's resonance as Chrissie drove on. '*Last October* - crunch! - *a bumper cache* – ping! - *owners are hoping* – thud! - *this coming autumn....*'

The track joined concrete and Chrissie drove smoothly into the courtyard. The April morning sun cast watery rays but it was still too early to feel the heat of the day. She almost shivered as she parked in front of the old barn workshop. '*The owners....*' Chrissie killed the engine and the voice cut out.

Echoes of the reporter's words spun in her mind. '*The owners...,*' and that was the whole point, she thought as she gathered up her bag from the passenger seat. Somewhere near Lavenham, there were owners of an English bull-terrier, so proud their story had featured on the local radio. Their dog had a valuable nose which, according to the reporter, could bring in a cache of black autumn truffles worth one pound a gram. Granted the work was seasonal, but what of Storm? Could he sniff out something even more valuable? Chrissie shook her head. As far as she knew it probably meant drugs, and addiction provided a perennial market. That made him precious. No, Storm's real owners would be missing him. Searching for him.

Chrissie slammed the car door. It was time to get on with the business of the day. She glanced up at the notice on the front of the barn, *Ron Clegg - Master Cabinet Maker and Furniture Restorer*, and then pushed at the old wooden door. Outside, her vibrantly yellow TR7 reflected the pale sunshine. Inside, scents of wood and oils greeted her nose.

'Morning, Mr Clegg,' she called.

She knew she'd been lucky, landing this apprentice placement after a difficult first year at Utterly Academy. And as if to confirm it, her life had started to settle. Now, instead of waking each morning with an emptiness pulling at her mood, she felt a kernel of peace, and it had allowed an optimism to creep into her soul.

'Morning, Mrs Jax.' Ron sat at his workbench, a mug of steaming tea in his hand.

She flung the soft leather, hobo style bag onto a workbench and flashed him a smile. She could have sworn he was trying to keep a straight face. 'Everything OK, Mr Clegg?'

'Of course. But I sense you're in a rush, Mrs Jax. There's time for a mug of tea, you know. Did you have a good Easter?' He shifted on his stool and settled his tea back on the bench. His movements were slow and Chrissie watched him release the mug stiffly, as if his fingers were painful. He exuded stillness.

'I'll put the kettle on. Yes, Easter was nice, thanks. And you?' She instinctively touched her hair as she

14

remembered the wind-blown hike with Clive. Oh my God, she thought as she ran her fingers over her matted blonde thatch. Earlier that morning it had been a neatly layered bob, but she'd driven with the hood down and the airflow had whisked it into a frenzy. She tried to flatten and tame it, hoping she'd disguised her movements as if absentmindedly touching her head.

Ron didn't answer. He smiled and then continued, 'We've been asked to give an estimate for repairs on a pedestal table out Stanningfield way. Water damage – a vase knocked over or something. Anyway, the veneers have lifted.' He paused for a moment and then added, almost as an afterthought, 'It might be good experience for you to come as well.'

'Really?' Chrissie felt her cheeks glow with pleasure. This was praise indeed. Ron was always careful with his words, obscure with his direction and sparing with his compliments. So if he suggested she should come, he meant she was doing well. 'That would be great. Do you want me to drive you in the TR7, Mr Clegg?'

Ron closed his eyes for a moment before replying. 'I think we'll take the old van, if that's all right with you, Mrs Jax. It might....'

'Look more professional?'

'I was going to say that your car seats are only about eight inches higher than the footwell. My hips - I'd never get out of your TR7, Mrs Jax.'

Chrissie laughed. 'Nick and Matt do call it the Yellow Wedge, but I think they were referring to the shape of its bonnet.'

•••

Ron Clegg drove the van while Chrissie sat in the passenger seat. She was perched higher than in her TR7 and able to gaze far across fields of winter-sewn wheat, now green, about a foot tall but still too young to have developed grain-laden heads. Like a cine film, the view rolled past her window.

'We can either take the main route through Lavenham or cut across from Hitcham. Any preferences?'

The mention of Lavenham reminded her of that morning's radio programme: truffles; super-nosed dogs; and by association, Matt's problem. 'As long as I don't have to map read, cross-country sounds nice.'

Ron glanced at the clock on the dash. 'Hmm, maybe we'd better take the A1141 to get there on time. Then we can cut back via Hitcham. Doesn't that nice detective inspector of yours live somewhere out that way, Mrs Jax?'

'Clive? Yes, Lavenham. It feels as if his home is in the middle of nowhere. It takes him forever to get to Ipswich. Not quite so bad for Bury.' Chrissie didn't say more. It wasn't that she had any secrets, but Clive was a relatively new development in her life. She hadn't been looking for a lover or partner, quite the opposite in fact. When she first met him, she'd still been grieving for her husband Bill, who'd died two years before. But over the past six months, the relationship had grown.

Now she feared if she spoke of Clive too much, it would sound as if she thought him permanent. Fate might be tempted and he could be plucked away or lose interest in her. Either way, it would break her heart again. They drove on in silence. She found the movement and engine noise lulled and soothed her.

'Watch out for a turning somewhere on the left.' Ron's voice collided with her dreamy thoughts.

'There?' Chrissie pointed, trying to pull herself into wakefulness. 'Wow!'

Ron swung the van into a well-kept drive. For a moment Chrissie imagined she was looking at the Suffolk equivalent of the Hansel and Gretel gingerbread house. The thatched roof swooped low to overhang lime-plastered walls bathed in pink. Small windows peered out, pushing up into the thatch which overlaid them as if with a marzipan drape. 'Wow,' she repeated.

'Very pretty. You can't beat Suffolk Pink. Come on; time to get some work done, Mrs Jax.'

Chrissie followed Ron across a lawn peppered with clumps of late flowering daffodils. A porch cast shade across the low front door and Chrissie hung back, drinking in the atmosphere as Ron knocked and then spoke to an elderly man.

'Good morning, Mr Hinton.' Ron smiled and then added, 'This is Mrs Jax, my apprentice.'

Chrissie stepped into what had once been a narrow passageway. Along one wall, the wattle and daub infill must have been removed, because the upright beams stood naked. The old wood stretched up like bars of a cage, completely exposed, shrieking age and character. The whole effect created a sense of space and allowed her to see directly into the adjoining room. She supposed her face must have reflected her surprise.

'Come in, come in, my dear.' The voice came from a lady sitting in a chintz-covered armchair. One leg stretched in front, propped up on a stool and encased in plaster.

'This is my wife,' Mr Hinton explained, leading the way through a wide gap in the skeleton wall. 'I'm afraid she's had a bit of an accident.'

'It wasn't an accident, dear. When someone deliberately drives a 4x4 at you, well accident is the wrong word.' Her voice gained a sharp edge as she spoke and for a moment the polite mask slipped. Chrissie picked up the flash of anger and outrage.

'Yes, yes, darling. I know. Now try not to upset yourself. I'll just take Mr Clegg and his apprentice through to the dining room to look at the table.' Mr Hinton spoke quickly as he led the way through a stripped pine doorway.

'The table is just through here. We didn't know what to do with it. Obviously we removed the vase and mopped up the water, but... it had been like it for several hours and....'

'Ah!' Ron let the sound escape as if he'd been punched in the stomach. A craftsman's *cri de coeur* at the sight of lifted, twisted veneer.

Chrissie bit back the *Oh my God*, on the tip of her tongue. 'It's....'

'A bit of a mess,' Mr Hinton finished for her.

'But it had been beautiful. Very unusual.' Chrissie traced the pattern of flowers and leaves with her finger, trying not to catch at the irregular wood.

'Yes, it's a family piece, from my wife's side.'

Chrissie stepped back while Ron examined the table more closely. What a shame, she thought. She could hardly bear to look at its ruined surface. Averting her eyes, she couldn't help but notice some black and white photographs hanging in minimalist frames from the beamy dining room walls.

'They're my wife's; she usually takes colour,' Mr Hinton murmured.

Chrissie dragged her gaze away from the black and white still of a stricken elm, leafless and dead against a winter backdrop. She frowned. What was he talking about?

'The photographs – my wife took them,' he explained. 'She's a photographer. In fact that's how she came to break her ankle.'

'Oh, I see.' Chrissie didn't think she saw at all.

'She was out walking, and as always, she had her camera with her. She says you never know when the right shot will come along. *Be prepared*, that's her motto.'

'So what happened, Mr Hinton?'

'She stumbled onto some illegal hare coursing. Well, not literally. That's not how she broke her ankle. No, she took a photo of them.'

'And that's how she broke it?' Chrissie was having trouble following Mr Hinton.

'Kind of. They didn't want her taking photos. They yelled at her. You know, the usual foul-mouthed stuff, and then drove a 4x4 straight at her. She managed to jump out of the way… into a ditch and crack, her ankle went. Dreadful business. I suppose it could have been worse.'

'It sounds terrible. She could've been killed.'

'Yes, but she doesn't see it that way.' Mr Hinton fell silent and gazed at the pedestal table. 'She always has her mobile with her, so luckily she was able to phone for help. She also got a snap of the number plate!'

'Good for her!' Chrissie remembered the flash of anger and outrage she'd picked up from Mrs Hinton. 'So did the police trace the 4x4 and the driver?'

'You must be joking! False number plates.' Mr Hinton directed his attention back to Ron. 'So what d'you think? Can you do anything with it?'

Ron seemed to deliberate for a moment. 'Some of the veneers are unusual. They may be difficult to match exactly but I should be able to get it back to pretty much how it was before the water damage.'

Mr Hinton laughed. Chrissie thought it somewhere between derision and anger. No humour.

'The vase was only on the table because a kind neighbour thought some flowers might cheer my wife up after the 4x4 incident. Bloody hare coursers!'

Ron shook his head.

'So how much will it cost and how long do you think it'll take you?'

Chrissie found she was mildly embarrassed now that price was being discussed. Her natural inclination was towards accuracy and she waited to hear Ron's estimate.

'Anything up to five hundred pounds. Difficult to be precise but I hope it'll be less than that. I need to look through my veneers. If I've got enough of that dark cherry, it'll work out cheaper.'

Chrissie frowned.

'If I have to buy in new veneers it'll cost me more than my old stock.'

Mr Hinton nodded but Chrissie wasn't so sure she followed Ron's business reasoning. Surely he should charge at current stock prices? Perhaps it was time she dismissed the accountant's part of her brain, but it was difficult sometimes to let go and leave that part of her life in the past.

'Tea? Coffee? I'm sure my wife will want to hear what you've to say about the table… and the final word is hers, of course.'

Back in the sitting room again, Chrissie settled into the chintzy sofa while Ron ran through a breakdown of the work required to restore the table top. Mrs Hinton nodded at intervals before finally saying, 'Well, that sounds reasonable to me. Just keep us informed if the costs look as if they're going to spiral, won't you.'

Ron smiled. 'Do you want us to take the table with us now?'

'You might as well. Every time I see the damage I think of those hare coursers.' She paused, as if lost in thought.

Ron spoke quietly, breaking the silence. 'They're thugs – they'll have come up from London. No one from round these parts would've driven at you like that.'

'Definitely thugs, I'd say!' Mr Hinton came in carrying a tray of coffee.

•••

Chrissie sat with a mix of Mrs Hinton's photo printouts on her knee; a combination of shots taken with her camera and mobile phone. The van seemed to rock and sway as Ron drove back along the country lanes and she knew if she looked at them for a moment longer, it would bring on a churning in her stomach. She hadn't been too surprised when Mrs Hinton insisted on showing them to her, but she hadn't expected to be given copies.

'Why do you think she wanted me to have these, Mr Clegg?'

'I expect Mrs Hinton wants as many people as possible to see them. The more the better. It increases the chances of someone recognising those thugs and their dogs.'

'But she's already given copies to the police.'

'Yes, but she's still very angry. All they've come up with anything so far is a false number plate and a dead end. She didn't strike me as the type of person to give up on it.' He smiled at her. 'You know the type!'

Chrissie glanced down at the blurry picture of the 4x4 on her lap. It was easy to sense the speed of the off-roader. It was implied by the tilted image and the camera's unclear focus. It contrasted with the sharp detail of the other shots: a man peering at something through binoculars, a large hound-like dog bounding across a field, and then a sequence of the hare – inches from the dog's nose. 'I can see why it's illegal. What's in it for those thugs? Are they just bloodthirsty, or something?'

'Betting, Mrs Jax.' Ron slowed to take a sharp corner. 'There'll be more than one dog and they bet on which dog will get the hare first. The fastest dog.'

Now Chrissie understood why the man had been looking through binoculars, but before she'd formed her next question, Ron seemed to have anticipated it.

'They choose East Anglia and Lincolnshire because it's mostly deserted. And it has an added advantage - it's pretty flat. Swathes of countryside, miles from any main roads. If you're betting, then it's easier to track the dogs if you can see a reasonable distance.'

Chrissie pictured Storm. The stolen dog with a valuable nose. 'Do they use Labradors?'

'No. Greyhounds and lurchers. Dogs built for the chase. Sight hunters, not scent hunters.'

Chrissie looked at the photo of the dog again. Big chest. Powerful and strong. Bred for speed. 'What happens to the hare? Is that a stupid question, Mr Clegg?'

Ron didn't answer for a moment. 'If the dogs catch the hare then they'll kill it, no question. I suppose it adds to the excitement. A kill at the end. If you're that kind of a person, then you'd say it was a natural way for a hare to die. Large amounts of money exchange hands when something's illegal.'

'So: betting, risk, excitement and a kill – all in all, a good day out, if you're into country pursuits, and lack empathy and a sense of fair play. Oh yes, and a disregard for the law, wouldn't you say, Mr Clegg?' Chrissie tried to imagine the sort of person who'd be attracted to those elements. People like Matt's brother Tom came to mind, and there were plenty around like him. She shook her head. What was Tom mixed up in? And more to the point, what was he likely to get Matt mixed up in? Last time Tom had demanded a favour, they'd all got dragged into the drama. She shivered as she remembered the fire. At least with a chocolate Labrador, it was unlikely to be hare coursing.

And poor Mrs Hinton? Chrissie pictured the photographer, elderly, spirited and with a leg in plaster. Would there be justice for her? She made up her mind to speak to Clive.

CHAPTER 3

The thought struck Nick with the suddenness of an early morning wake-up call. He hadn't phoned Matt. He'd promised to give him the contact number for the veterinary nurse. He'd even remembered to get the details from his mother, but then it had gone clean out of his head. For all he knew, Matt might at that very moment, be fighting off the attentions of a lively chocolate Labrador and the thought made him inwardly grin. Nick glanced around to see if anyone would notice if he sent a text. Dave, one of the other carpenters from Willows & Son, was talking to the owner of the manuscript and book restoration business, and the assistant was busy looking through a ledger, seemingly unaware of Nick.

The room was large and open plan, and the voices echoed off the flat prefabricated ceiling. It had the feel of an industrial unit, but the patina of something ancient and antique, with books and manuscripts strewn on large wooden tables stretching across the width of the space. He sent the text and then caught a glimpse into a room beyond. Almost without realising, he moved towards the doorway, all thoughts of veterinary nurses momentarily forgotten.

'Can I help you?' The assistant's tone was sharp, almost accusatory.

Nick immediately felt guilty. His cheeks started to burn as he turned to face her. 'I… I'm sorry. I couldn't help wondering what that room is used for.' He flashed her a smile as he indicated the open doorway.

'Through there?' Her face was expressionless as she studied him. He could almost feel her piercing eyes as she appeared to drink in every detail from his work trainers to his short dark hair. It made him uncomfortable and he shifted his weight from one foot to the other. He imagined she examined the manuscripts with the same intensity.

'That's where we wash and dry the manuscripts.' She spoke precisely but her tone had softened. 'I didn't think Mr Santo was having any work done in there.'

'No, not as far as I know. I was just interested. All these old books and prints. It's fascinating – what you do here.' He smiled again, and this time he sensed she thawed a little.

'Well, if you're really interested I'll show you.' She inclined her head a little. He assumed an invitation to follow her through the doorway and happily fell in behind, stepping into what appeared to be a huge laundry room. Not with washing machines and tumble dryers, but with large flat sinks and drying racks. The air felt cool and there was a smell he couldn't immediately recognise.

'It's awesome. Those sinks....' They seemed to dominate the room, the shiny stainless steel shouting clinical laboratory when viewed against the whitewashed walls. He guessed it would be difficult to make porcelain sinks that large. They'd weigh a ton. 'Wow!' He let the word escape slowly as he gazed around.

'Maps, manuscripts, prints... pages from old books. They come in all sizes, you know.'

He could tell from her tone she was pleased with his reaction, and he dragged his eyes away from the drying racks and back to her face. It was difficult to guess her age exactly. Late twenties, he reckoned.

'They have to be soaked flat, you know,' and she smiled in a neat kind of a way.

'Lia!' Mr Santo's voice rang plaintively through the doorway.

'I'll be with you in a moment,' she called and then added quietly, 'Better be getting back. Looks like the tour is over.'

Nick followed Lia. He was secretly disappointed. She was definitely older than his preferred age range for girl-friends. His ideal was closer to his own age, nearly twenty-two. And she wasn't particularly glamorous, but he'd been attracted by her calm self-assurance and when she'd thrown down the gauntlet, he'd picked it up, intrigued.

'I'm Nick, by the way. Apprentice carpenter. Perhaps you can explain it all more when everyone isn't so busy.' He spoke to her back as she led the way to Mr Santo, who was still deep in conversation with Dave.

'There you are, Nick. I wondered where you'd got to,' Dave said, as he glanced up from some plans. He smiled weakly, sighed and turned his attention back to Mr Santo.

Nick looked at Mr Santo more closely. His overall impression was of a globe. There wasn't a wisp of hair on his shiny scalp to break the roundness. Even his body shape seemed designed to fit his name. It hinted of a jolly Santa, but with a large circular "O" replacing the angular "A" at the end of the name. He spread plump fingers in an expression of appeal to the heavens.

'Lia! Lia, my dear. The height of these work tables – you're happy with them?'

They all three scrutinized Lia's face for any sign of unhappiness with the height. For a fleeting second, Nick wondered where the power lay in this manuscript restoration business.

'They're fine. Just make sure there's space to get my knees under when I sit at it.'

Nick instinctively turned his attention to her knees, or more accurately, her legs.

Dave's voice cut through his imaginings. 'They'll be the same height as your current work tops. Of course, some of this we can make off site and assemble here, but these are large, heavy units and we'll have to do some of the construction here. I mean – there are three and you want drawers and shelves in their bases. Will that be a problem? A disruption for you?'

Everyone waited for Lia to speak but when she didn't, Mr Santo nodded and said, 'I dare say we'll cope, won't we Lia?'

'Yes, Mr Santo,' she said sweetly.

•••

Nick stepped up into the van and scooped the plans off the passenger seat. Dave had already started the engine and was beginning to ease the Willows & Son van out of the parking area.

'Mr Abramo Santo - sounds Italian, don't you think?' It was more of a thought than a question. Dave's mellow tones contrasted with the sharp clicking of the indicator.

Nick fastened his seat belt. 'Bucklesham. I don't think I've ever been out here before.'

'Convenient for Felixstowe, I suppose. Interesting though – I think I'm going to enjoy this job. Large pieces of solid wood. No chipboard! It'll be a good exercise for you to work out how much wood we need to order in. Yes, see if you can figure it out, Nick.'

'Thanks, but can't it wait till we get back? I don't think I can read these figures while we're driving. It'll make me feel sick. Sorry, Dave.' Nick closed his eyes to shut out the vision of leafy hedges whipping past the van's window, seemingly rotating with each twist and turn of the road. There were few things he regretted about pursuing his ambition to train as a carpenter, but Dave's driving had to rank high on the list.

'You seemed quite taken with Mr Santo's assistant.'

Nick opened his eyes. He glanced at Dave and caught him looking sideways at him, studying his face. 'For Christ's sake, Dave. Watch that car!' A silver-grey Fiat came from nowhere, straight at them.

Dave swerved and Nick's stomach lurched. 'They're on the wrong bloody side of the road. Probably straight off the ferry.'

While Dave negotiated the next few corners Nick thought about Lia. Her name sounded as if she could be Italian as well. For a moment he pictured Kat, his current girlfriend with the riot of long curly toffee-coloured hair. Both girls appeared strikingly different, but putting looks aside, each exuded an unhurried calmness. A kind of measured deliberateness; qualities that no doubt lent themselves to manuscript restoration or, in Kat's case, target rifle shooting. So where had it started to go wrong with Kat, he wondered. There'd been a definite cooling off when he'd failed to show up on bonfire night, but that hadn't been his fault. God, it had been months ago. He'd nearly died in a fire, and she'd taken the huff because he'd lost his mobile, couldn't remember her number and didn't phone her.

'You OK, Nick?'

'Yeah, sure.' Nick let his mind wander on as the van rocked and swayed. They'd patched it up, of course, him and Kat, but deep down he'd felt betrayed, let down.

'Not feeling queasy?'

'No, no.' Something more was expected and he dragged his mind back to the present. 'No I'm fine, Dave. So what kind of wood? Oak?'

The conversation turned to the practicalities of the job and Dave talked about European oak, North American oak and then European oak again as he drove back to the Willows workshop. 'You see, Mr Santo has specific requirements. We couldn't use the Northern Red... not with its high tannin content.'

'Why not?'

'If the wood gets wet the tannin sometimes makes it look bluish, and we wouldn't want anything leaching into the manuscript paper.'

'Couldn't we just make sure the oak surfaces were properly sealed?'

'Yes, but I think we'd be better off with the European – and of course there's Eastern European available now. That'll be cheaper.' And so they talked, as Dave turned off the A14 and headed for Needham Market.

Ping! Nick reached for his mobile. 'A text,' he explained as he read the screen. 'Just checking it isn't anything important.' The message was brief. Typical Matt Speak. *Thanks mate. Will meet Kerry this pm.*

'And?'

'And what?'

'Is it anything important?'

Nick shook his head. The text message read as if he was running a dating agency, not a dog repatriation service, and he smothered a grin as he imagined Matt.

'So what's so funny, Nick? Come on, I like a good joke.'

Dave was one of his trainers. An established carpenter at Willows, middle-aged and good humoured. But he was unusual in that he liked to talk, not only about carpentry and cars, but about anything. Nick wondered how much to say. 'Do you know much about dogs, Dave?'

'Not a lot. I can make a dog kennel. Why? You got a dog now?'

'No, it's just a mate of mine. He's been asked to look after a... mutt for someone, but he thinks... well what do you do if you suspect the dog's been stolen?'

Dave slowed as he indicated and turned off the main road. 'Police? He could go to the police, or maybe the RSPCA? What are we talking about? A fighting dog?'

The tyres scrunched over gravel and rough concrete as Dave coasted past the main Willows workshop and into the parking area for the vans, behind the one-storey building. A single word seemed to burn in Nick's ears. *Police*. 'God, not the police again,' he muttered as he climbed down from the van.

'Right then, Nick; put the kettle on for a coffee and we'll look at these plans.'

Nick watched Dave's stout figure disappear through the works entrance doorway. He should have been right behind and carrying the drawings for him, but the mention of the police somehow froze Nick. It produced a physical response: a tightening in his chest, an urge to breathe fast, a buzzing in his head, a-

'Stop it,' he hissed, breaking into a wheeze. He needed to calm down. There was no reason to have a panic attack. The business with the police was over; months ago. They'd believed him in the end. Accepted he hadn't started the fire, even praised him for his initiative when all the evidence was out in the open. But it was difficult to shake off the memory of an interrogation, of how they could behave when they thought he was a terrorist. It distorted his view of things.

Nick let the weak sunshine wash over him, its cool warmth soothing his mind. There was nothing to fear. After all, it was only Matt and a dog. Just the connection with Tom was the problem. He needed to get on top of his anxiety, slow his rapid breathing.

He forced himself to focus on a pebble in the concrete while he shut out the memories. 'It's the here and now that matters,' he whispered on a long, single breath. It was time to make the coffee and look at the plans with Dave.

CHAPTER 4

Matt gazed at the Utterly mansion building. It seemed to reach up into the sky. From Matt's angle, its finials spiked and impaled wispy clouds, while beneath, red blocks ran in stripes, forming patterns through the background of yellowy-white clay brick. They'd been fired in local kilns in Edwardian times, and now made Matt think of straps, as if constraining and holding the building down. By contrast, the newer additions looked like cheeky upstarts with flat roofs and prefabricated constructions. The Easter break was under way and Matt wondered if he'd made a mistake. He'd banked on the Academy being open, but he'd been the only student parking his scooter and there weren't many cars in the car park.

He'd had to get away from Tumble Weed Drive. Storm was driving him crazy. Every time he'd moved, the dog had leapt up. Matt didn't do hyperactive and this was proving to be one hell of a canine roller coaster. In the end he'd shut the dog in his bedroom with a bowl of water and a handful of kibbles. He reckoned he had about two maybe three hours, and then if he wasn't back home again, his bedroom would be earthquake / war zone territory. He pushed at the main entrance door. It swung open and he stepped into the cool still air.

FOOD FAIR. Matt read the notice slowly. *Exhibitors please register in reception*. He smelt the air, but there weren't any scents of Suffolk Harvest Cake or St Edmund's Buns. The building felt deserted. He read the notice again. *Saturday 10:00 am – 4:00 pm*.

'You appear to be several days early.' A familiar voice floated down the main staircase from somewhere above and behind his head.

He swung around. 'Rosie!'

The library assistant smiled down at him from half way up the stairs. 'I thought I had the day free – and then I get a call from Mrs Wesley.' She paused, and then spoke with a mock crabby voice, 'Can you pop into the library for me?' She gazed at Matt for a moment. 'Pop in! On my week off?' and then in the crabby voice again, 'Can you look through Sir Raymond Utterly's old collection and see if there are any cookery books... Victorian, Edwardian... they'll create some interest, a bit of PR for the Academy. We,' and now she reverted to her own voice again, 'meaning me, can *man a stall*! I ask you!'

Matt felt surprised. Rosie was always friendly but it was rare for her to say so much to him. They were usually in the library at the time, so he figured that was probably the reason. 'But you're... didn't you say on holiday?' and then he felt his cheeks burn as a thought struck. Perhaps she was chatting him up.

'She said she'd give me a day in lieu.' Rosie almost spat the words.

'In the loo? Mrs Wesley said...?' Matt watched as a grin spread across Rosie's face.

'Don't give me any ideas!'

Matt ran a hand through his dark sandy hair, hoping it would cool his head. 'So... are you...? Where you goin' now, then?'

'The library, but it's not open, not officially. Why are you here, Matt?'

'I was hopin' the library....' He let his voice trail away and dropped his gaze.

'Oh, all right then. You've got half an hour – then I'm locking it up again. OK?'

'Thanks, Rosie.' Matt started to climb the stairs. 'What's with this food fair, then?'

'Don't ask me. I'm only the library assistant.' She strode ahead, wisps of auburn hair escaping from her loose ponytail and framing her head. 'Come to the food fair... and then sign up for our car maintenance course.' She tossed the words into the air like heavy pancakes.

Matt thought for a moment as he caught his breath at the top of the stairs. 'I could help you man the stall, if you like?'

Rosie slowed her pace as she reached the library doors. She looked back along the corridor at Matt and then scrabbled in her handbag. 'That's very sweet of you, but.... Ah, here they are.' She pulled out a bunch of keys and turned her attention to the lock. 'The place feels funny like this – no students, just the occasional member of staff and of course, security.'

'But I'm here. I'm a student.' Matt followed Rosie into the library.

So what'd happened just then? She'd called him sweet and then failed to jump at his offer of help. Mixed messages. The only sure thing he knew, as Tom would say, was that birds were complicated. He sighed. So, he had thirty minutes. It was time to head for a computer.

While Rosie unlocked a block of glass-fronted bookshelves, Matt settled at a computer screen. It didn't take him long before he was reading about pet microchips. The companies appeared to have sprung up like weeds, each developing and promoting their own brand of chip and then designing scanners to only read the microchips specific to their individual brand. Matt thought it was a bit like cattle rustling and expecting a blind man to read the branding marks, distinguishing between them by feel alone. A deeply flawed process and open to abuse. It needed the stronger players to dominate the scene. Natural selection, he remembered they'd called it at school, and the phrase *dog eat dog* sprang to mind. He tried not to smile.

'Let's hope this Kerry bird has a universal scanner,' he muttered and thought back to his phone call to the veterinary surgery earlier that day.

'Hi! It's Kerry; you asked to speak to me. How can I help?' The conversation had opened well and Matt found himself trying to guess her age from her voice.

'I've... well I'm in a... bit of a kind of....' He'd stumbled over the words, the nervousness bringing out the Suffolk in him. He'd tried again. 'See, I've got this dog an'....' His tongue stuck to the roof of his mouth and his language tangled.

She'd eventually coaxed the story out of him, and they'd agreed to meet at the end of the afternoon. All he had to do was get Storm to the branch surgery, somewhere beyond Barking Tye.

'Waggin' hell! An' how do I get 'im out there?' He still didn't know.

Matt turned his attention back to the computer screen. AAHA, he read. He'd found a website for looking up universal pet microchips. All he needed was the sequence of numbers and letters on the microchip, and then he might discover who owned Storm. He sat back and closed his eyes.

'You're not dropping off, I hope.' Rosie's voice drifted across the library.

Matt straightened up and watched Rosie as she turned the pages of an old book. 'Found somethin'?'

She glanced at him and smiled, a kind of triumphant grin. '*Mrs Beeton's Household Management: A Complete Cookery Book.*' She read out the title, lingering over each word. 'It's not the original, of course, that was printed in 1861 – but Sir Raymond has done us proud. This is a good example. A newer edition... *Ward, Lock & Co. London, 1930*. One thousand, six hundred and eighty pages!'

'Wow!' Matt didn't know what else to say. He thought for a moment. 'Any Suffolk stuff in there?'

'I've found a recipe – Mrs Beeton's Suffolk Pickle for Hams. I'd already searched on the internet, so I was reasonably hopeful. Hmm, I need to think how to display this. Mrs Wesley'll have an opinion.'

'So, you goin' to make it, then?'

'You must be joking. Where would I get saltpetre nowadays?'

Matt shook his head. As far as he could remember, saltpetre was potassium nitrate. He'd enjoyed chemistry at school. He'd remembered the names, collecting them in his memory like other people memorised dinosaurs, or football players. Trouble was, he never knew what to do with the information and none of his teachers had known how to inspire a clumsy boy with a photographic memory. He was just considered weird.

Rosie snapped the book closed. 'Well you've got ten more minutes, and then I'm locking up the library.'

Matt sighed. There was just about time to look for reports of missing sniffer dogs. He set to his task. An article on the BBC News Suffolk website immediately caught his eye.

'That's a turn up for the books,' he muttered as he read on. It seemed the Suffolk police had appealed to the public for unwanted gundogs simply for their sniffer skills. Give to us rather than rescue centres, was their message. But dogs and cats seemed to go missing on a daily basis and most of the websites were aiming to rehome rather than re-unite with the owner. 'Hmm....'

'What're you smiling at?' Rosie stood behind his screen. He hadn't heard her pumps on the old wooden floorboards.

'Oh hi, Rosie.' The surprise made his face burn up again.

'You're embarrassed! What are you looking at?' With one stride she was next to him. '*Pet dog on drip after eating cannabis*,' she read out. 'Honestly, Matt. Haven't you got anything better to do?'

'I-I....'

'Come on, log out. Time's up! I want to lock up now.' She shook her head slowly, but he couldn't help noticing what might have passed for a faint smile.

•••

Matt stood in front of his bedroom door. On the other side something hurled itself at the hardboard panel. The surface seemed to bend towards him as it absorbed the impact.

'Storm! Bloody calm down.' The dog knew he was there and Matt's voice only seemed to rack up the excitement further. He turned the handle and pushed.

A meteor of chocolate fur struck him mid-chest. Sparks flew as the momentum carried him backwards. Less than a second and Matt was over. He lay sprawled on the floor with Storm astride him, a voluminous tongue licking his face. 'Gerroff, Storm!' He pushed at the muscular chest and neck. The dog took it as play and barked in his face.

Licked and buffeted, Matt sat up. Any plans to put Storm in a backpack and ride with him on the scooter, were out the window. 'No way,' he moaned and the dog wagged its tail. 'How the hell do I get you to Kerry?'

Matt extracted a mobile from his pocket and keyed a text. *Can u give dog and me lift 2 c Kerry 5:30?* Storm nudged his elbow and then thrust a wet doggy nose at his lips. *Urgent* Matt tapped, pushing the dog away. He'd secretly hoped Kerry might be a bird to chat up, but now, from his position on the floor, he no longer cared. Priorities had changed. He didn't mind if Nick was there, he needed his help with transport. Dog sitting had become a nightmare.

By the time Nick picked them both up several hours later, Matt had changed into a fresh tee-shirt. He'd also had a chance to think through his plan. Knowledge was power and might be a useful lever on Tom, but the way things were going, Matt couldn't see how he was going to survive the rest of the week, let alone put pressure on his brother. If the dog was microchipped and the owner traceable, then perhaps repatriation was in order. Urgently.

He helped Nick fold down the old Fiesta's back seat to make room for Storm. Luckily there were no problems persuading the dog to get in the car; in fact he jumped in, ran through the extended boot and would have settled in the front passenger seat had Matt not sat there, slightly twisted and with his hand on the dog to keep him in the back.

'Thanks for helping me out, mate,' Matt sighed five minutes later as they drove through Stowmarket.

Storm eventually lay down and they travelled in silence, apart from the panting. The journey had a kind of finality to it. A sense of pathos and doom as the miles were eaten up.

'You OK?' Nick asked as they neared their destination. He slowed to take a sharp corner out of Barking Tye. 'Interesting tee-shirt, by the way. Didn't know you were a tweeter - sorry, twitcher.'

Matt glanced down at the tight cotton encasing his chest. The seat belt cut across the design, but there was no disguising the bird-tracks, printed in red on a black background. *RSPB Minsmere* was written in discreet lettering along one shoulder.

'Yeah, reckoned it'd impress this Kerry bird.' When Nick didn't say anything he added, 'You know, show I'm serious 'bout animals.' Matt ran his hand over the stretched image of a bird's footprint, widened by his ample girth. He was pleased with the effect, an impulse buy after a school trip many moons ago. Trouble was, he'd been a few sizes smaller when he was sixteen.

'Yeah, I expect she'll notice all right.' Nick turned into a small forecourt. 'Here it is.' The building could only have been a few years old. A functional, single-storey, brick take on a portable cabin design. 'Come on, let's get this over with. You get him in while I lock the car.'

Matt wondered how long it took to lock a car as he slipped the lead around Storm's neck. 'Come on, boy. In we g-g-o-o-o.' Matt lurched towards the door, sidestepping and hopping in an attempt to stay upright. He reached the doorway one pace behind a flurry of paws and claws. Then he was through and moving at speed over slippery, wipe-clean flooring.

'Sit!' A voice rang through the air with icy authority.

Storm stopped mid stride and dropped to his haunches. Two steps behind, Matt faltered to a standstill. He looked across the reception area and into the eyes of someone dressed in green tunic and trousers. Matt opened his mouth to say something, thought better of it and closed his mouth again like a goldfish.

'Storm? Is this Storm?'

Matt nodded. The building felt deserted and he couldn't see anyone else at the reception desk. He hoped he was gazing at Kerry.

'OK. Bring him through. It's Matt, isn't it?' She led the way. 'Just walk slowly and he'll calm down.' She sounded friendly, her voice soothing.

Storm tried to pull forwards, his claws skating on the flooring.

'Heel!' Her command pierced like a bullet.

Matt flinched. After their phone conversation he'd imagined a cartoon nurse from one of his old comic-strip books. A bird in uniform was supposed to be sexy, but the green loose-fitting cotton-polyester wasn't his idea of suggestive. Still, Kerry had a nice voice and smile, when she wasn't shouting orders.

'He seems quite obedient,' she said as she waited in the consulting room. Her expression seemed to relax as she watched Storm, and then she held up her hand. Storm immediately halted. 'He's been well trained by someone. So what've you been doing to get him so excited? Tit-bits and scraps? He needs plenty of exercise, you know.'

'I'm... I....' Matt remembered the slices of pizza. He hoped his burning cheeks didn't give him away.

She eyed up his tee-shirt. 'So, you're better with feathers than fur? You've probably already guessed I'm Kerry. Come on, Storm, let's be having a look at you.'

Matt watched as she patted the dog, ran her small hands over his back and tummy, looked in his mouth and ears and then reached for a hand held scanner.

'He's been microchipped. That's good.' She frowned as she passed it over Storm's shoulders again.

Matt let his breath escape slowly. 'So what does…?'

'I'll look it up.'

Matt waited, trying to see the computer screen as she keyed in the scanner sequence, but the letters were too small. 'So what… what's it show?'

Kerry took her time before answering. 'Seems he's probably been trained by the police.' Small creases deepened on her forehead. 'I guess it'll be the Suffolk Police Dog Section. They're based near Ipswich.' Her voice was even, no hint of surprise, but her frown spoke volumes.

'What? Are you sayin' he's police?'

'Hey, there you are.' Nick bustled through the doorway, car keys in one hand and pocketing his phone with the other. 'Thanks for agreeing to see the dog, Kerry.' Nick flashed a smile. 'Did I just catch something about the police and Ipswich?'

'Yes. Seems Storm may be a canine cadet.'

Nick seemed to freeze.

'But what's me brother doin' with…?' Matt shook his head as he looked at Nick, but he didn't focus on his friend. Instead, a trick of his imagination conjured up Tom, angry and accusing. He'd wanted a lever on Tom but this was more like a crowbar. He blinked and the fantasy Tom vanished to be replaced by Nick's round face staring back, pale and tense.

'You can't keep him, Matt.'

'I don't want to, mate.' Matt turned his attention back to Kerry. 'I think I said before, Tom'll kill me if 'e finds out I've….'

'But the dog should go back, Matt.' Kerry spoke quietly. 'Look, if you're worried about the police, I can return the dog. I know someone there. I can say something about him being found and how we scanned him. Your name need never come up. The police've invested a lot of money in him. Trained him. He's a young dog with a long working life ahead. Think about it - you can't care for him or give him the stimulation and time he deserves.'

'And neither can Tom,' Nick added. 'Or whoever Tom's holding him for.'

'Exactly. And he'll be a valuable sniffer dog, I expect.' Kerry patted Storm.

Matt knew Tom's anger would be terrible, but as he tried to weigh it up against another week of Storm, his own stiff muscles teamed with an aching shoulder and painful ankle. His body was inwardly groaning. Another week and he'd be a broken man. And anyway, hadn't Kerry just said the dog should go back? The temptation was too great.

'You're sure no one'll know 'bout me?'

Kerry nodded.

'An' you'll take the dog?'

She smiled. 'Of course. You can leave him with me now, if you like.'

'OK, then.'

'You're sure, mate?'

'Yeah. Come on Nick. Let's go.'

'Before you change your mind,' Kerry murmured.

Matt turned and hurried for the door. His eyes seemed to burn and his ears buzzed. Behind him he heard Nick say, 'Thanks… thanks, Kerry.'

CHAPTER 5

Chrissie stood at her kitchen sink. Water gushed from the tap as she gazed through the window, the kettle momentarily forgotten in her hand. What had the text from Utterly Academy said? It had arrived just as she was tidying up at the workshop before coming home. She pictured the words, mouthing them as she recalled the message. *Mr Blumfield would like to see you in his office at 1:45pm on Monday May 9th*. But that was ages away, well over a week ahead.

'Ah-h-h!' Cold water poured over her hand as the kettle flooded. She snatched at the tap and the torrent dwindled to a drip.

To be honest, the text had surprised and unsettled her. It was the last thing she'd expected. Not only had it been sent at the end of the working day, more surprisingly, the Academy was still enjoying its Easter break. Maybe the secretary had overlooked some earlier instruction, and then suddenly remembered and sent the text while at home or even on holiday. A flash of conscience, or something? The office staff took their job very seriously, so it could be the explanation.

But was it just her or did Mr Blumfield want to see all the first-year apprentices? He was, after all, the carpentry course director. Her problem was that she still didn't know, despite immediately phoning Nick after she'd read the text. He'd sounded a bit distracted and said he was about to see a veterinary nurse with Matt and the dog. However his answer had been clear. He hadn't been asked to see Blumfield - and neither, as far as he knew, had Matt. She'd hoped for reassurance. There'd been none.

'Oh no-o-o,' she groaned. She was going to have to stew on it for the rest of the week, have to wait until the Academy was back in full swing. And even then she might still be unable to find out what it was about until Monday week, the day of the appointment.

Chrissie switched on the kettle and reached for a mug. The yellow one with *Club Triumph* printed on the front. She smiled. Clive had been so pleased when he'd found it on an internet site. To honour her TR7, he'd said. But the thought of Clive didn't distract her for long. Instead, her anxious mind strayed back to Blumfield, and then Nick and Matt's dog. The sense of foreboding weighed heavy as she dropped a tea bag in the mug and poured on steaming water.

Ding-ding! The tone was faint.

She hurried back into the hallway for her bag. It was where she'd flung it down when she arrived home from work ten minutes earlier. Her fingers immediately recognised the mobile's familiar shape as she rummaged inside, and a second later she had it in her hand and read the small screen.

Dog situation resolved. Storm turns out to be a police dog. Kerry will return him. Promises to keep Matt's name a secret. Nick.

'Good God!' She read the text again. 'A police dog? And who's Kerry?' She shook her head. On the face of it the message was reassuring but light on detail. She scooped up her bag and headed for the kitchen. It would be easier to think with a mug of tea.

Chrissie gazed at the tiny space for inspiration. By a miracle of kitchen design, she had managed to squeeze in units and a scrubbed pine counter. The result was crowded but cottagey and she was lucky there'd been just enough room for a narrow table. She settled at it now, pushing her laptop to one side. So why would Matt's brother have a police dog? Weren't they usually German shepherds? She sipped her tea. The more she thought about it, the more she realised she didn't know the first thing about dogs. Take the hare coursing. Greyhounds and lurchers, Ron had said, but what was a lurcher?

'Of course, Mrs Hinton's photos!' The printouts were still in her bag. Hadn't she just thrust her hand past the sheets of paper as she'd delved for her mobile, her mind intent on the text message?

A few moments later and she'd retrieved the printouts. She ran her hand over the paper, smoothing out the folds as she pressed them against the pine table top. She'd intended to look at the dog, captured bounding across the field, but instead she found her eyes drawn to the 4x4. There was something wrong about its lines, an irregularity at the back of the vehicle and onto the roof. Chrissie pulled the image closer. What was she looking at? Would it help if she scanned the printout into her laptop, and then blew up the image? She glanced at the shelf above the table. The printer sat neatly in a gap between some cookery books. She'd always thought if she developed a greater interest in cooking, then she'd have to relocate it. But so far there'd been no contest. The printer stayed.

Chrissie stretched up and slipped the printout into the machine's scanner unit. It only took her a few seconds and she'd woken her sleeping-mode laptop and activated the scanning command. She sipped her tea and waited.

Brrring brrring! The ringtone startled her from her thoughts. She grabbed her mobile.

46

'Yes?' she said before it could ring again.

'Hi! Chrissie?'

She recognised Clive's voice immediately. 'Hi.'

'Are you busy? You sound kind of….'

She heard a background hum and guessed he was in his car. 'Are you driving?'

'I wish. No. I'm trying to get this report finished, but it's proving very tedious. Thought I'd phone you instead.'

Chrissie pictured Clive for a moment and smiled. She'd have liked to say something about the 4x4 photos, but it wasn't the moment and he'd probably say she was interfering in police business. Without really thinking she sighed.

'Are you OK?' Concern mingled with the background hum.

'Well….' She hesitated, but before she could stop herself, it was out in a rush. 'I've had a text from the Academy. Out of the blue. Blumfield wants to see me and it seems no one else has to see him. So why only me?' She listened as the hum disappeared and a silence sat on the line. She imagined him with his hand over the phone.

'Sorry, Chrissie – just had to answer a query.' The hum was back.

She didn't say anything, wasn't going to repeat herself. He was busy.

'Look… think it through, Chrissie. What is it that's different about you?' She could almost hear him smile as he paused to take a breath. 'And I don't mean you're not a fellow. Didn't Blumfield give you a project? Single you out? That moth-eaten tree trunk. You told me about it, ages ago.'

'Moth-eaten?' Was he referring to Blumfield, she wondered. 'D'you mean…?' The penny dropped. 'The totem pole?'

'Yes, the moth-eaten tree trunk.'

Chrissie laughed. 'You may be right. I'd forgotten about that. He probably wants an update on how the totem pole is progressing. You really are a detective!'

She listened to him chuckle. 'See you on Saturday,' and then the line went dead.

Chrissie held the mobile for a moment longer, her thoughts still connected to Clive and not quite ready to break the thread. She watched the screen fade. 'Bloody totem pole,' she muttered.

The project had been doomed from the start. Conceived with a millennium grant, it should, according to Mr Blumfield, have been the flagship of Utterly's carpentry department. That was in the year two thousand, eleven years ago, but somehow it never got off the ground. And Chrissie walked straight into the trap. 'I must've been mad,' she sighed as she remembered how, ten months ago, Blumfield talked her into taking it on. It would be something to carve during her apprentice year. Perhaps she'd been flattered, or maybe she just couldn't resist a challenge. Either way, she should have known better. She shook her head as she pictured it now: discoloured, marked off into sections, partially carved at one end, bullet holes and shattered wood at the other. 'Oh God,' she moaned as she rested her head in her hands.

If it hadn't been for Nick and Matt's help, the totem pole couldn't have got this far. And that wasn't saying much. She needed to speak to them. Now.

•••

Chrissie grabbed her jacket from the back of the chair. Her laptop screen told her she'd successfully scanned Mrs Hinton's printouts, but there was no time to look at them now. Not if she was going to get to the Nags head to meet Nick and Matt. And then she had an idea. A memory stick! Matt would probably call it a USB drive or something techy, but whatever its name, a few seconds later she'd copied the files onto it. Stuffing the paper and memory stick into her bag, she gulped down the rest of her tea, now cold, and then she was out through her front door and hurrying for her car. She only started to unwind as she accelerated out of Woolpit and turned onto the A14. The speed seemed to clear her mind.

The Nags Head appeared reasonably quiet when Chrissie pushed at the pub's door less than ten minutes later. She spotted Nick and Matt almost immediately. They were at the bar, propping it up in a dejected, hangdog kind of way. For a moment she wondered if Matt had undergone an ornithological mugging. Red bird tracks criss-crossed his black tee-shirt and his dark sandy hair looked dishevelled, despite its shortness. At least she couldn't see any evidence of a seagull bombing. Nick looked up from his pint. She smiled and hurried across to join them.

'Thanks for coming to meet me,' she said.

'No problem. We needed a drink anyway. What'll you have?' Nick turned to catch the barman's attention. 'Your usual ginger beer?' he asked over his shoulder.

'Yes, thanks.'

They made their way into the snug bar area and sat at a small pine table. 'So what's the plan for the totem pole?' Matt asked.

'Well, we've got… eight weeks. Maybe more, if I can persuade Blumfield.'

'An' that's a plan?' Matt frowned as he gulped down some lager.

'No. I was trying to underline the urgency. We need to put in more hours, that's what I was trying to say.'

'Bloody funny way of sayin' it, Chrissie.' Matt stared at the floor.

'What's got into you, Matt? Cat bitten your tongue, or something?' The words were out before she could stop them. 'Sorry, that was–'

'Unhelpful,' Nick finished for her.

'Sorry, Matt.' She sipped her ginger beer. 'Come on; tell me about this microchip and what's happening to Storm.' Chrissie glanced at Nick. He looked pale, no trace of a smile. She waited, careful not to interrupt as Matt and then Nick recounted what Kerry had said. When they finally fell silent, she spoke softly. 'It'll be OK, I'm sure it'll be OK.'

'Yeah, like the totem pole'll be OK.' Matt directed his words at his glass.

An air of melancholy descended. Chrissie felt the weight of the atmosphere at their table. Even the sound of midweek drinkers ordering at the bar, laughing and clinking glasses in the background, seemed miles away. The moment stretched on and Chrissie knew she had to break the spell to burst the bubble. Now was the moment for the memory stick and printouts, she decided. 'I've brought something I want to show you.' She rummaged in her handbag. 'See what you think….'

She pushed the glasses to one side, and laid the sheets of paper on the table.

'What the hell?'

Chrissie smiled. She knew she'd caught their interest as they bent nearer to see the images, their eyes scrutinising and searching the printouts. She told them about her visit to the Hintons. 'So, do you notice anything about that 4x4?'

Matt frowned and looked more closely.

Chrissie was on a roll, all thoughts of the totem pole and Storm temporarily forgotten. 'I thought I was looking at something attached to the back of the vehicle. Maybe also something on the roof, but – I'm not so sure now. What d'you see?'

Nick shook his head.

'I thought if I scanned the printouts onto a stick for you, maybe you could do something with it.'

Matt grinned as he watched Chrissie delve into her bag and produce something slim enough to pass for a cigarette lighter. 'Here!' She handed it to him.

'Thanks, Chrissie.' He looked at the stick for a moment as if by just holding it he could look into its files. She knew, if nothing else came of it, the challenge would at least help him get through the next few days.

'Have you shown them to Clive?' Nick asked.

'No. I've only had them a couple of days, and anyway, Mrs Hinton said the police already have copies.' She paused to gather her thoughts. 'I just thought there might be something else to help identify that vehicle, seeing as how the number plate was false. And I needed to be certain before I said anything to Clive.'

'Yeah, Chrissie. I'll 'ave a look at it for you.' Matt gazed at the stick. 'Only a few more days till Utterly's runnin' again an' the library's open. You comin' to the food fair on Saturday? You'll still be able to sing with the band in the evenin' Nick.'

Chrissie laughed. 'I didn't know there was a food fair. Trust you to know about it, Matt.' She stood up. 'My turn, I think. Same again?' They handed her their glasses and she headed for the bar. By the time she returned with beer and lager slopping from the overfilled pints, they'd hatched a plan.

Nick and Matt would come to work on the totem pole at the Clegg workshop more often. At least that was their intention.

CHAPTER 6

Saturday, the day of the food fair, had dawned and Nick drove his old Ford Fiesta into the Academy car park. His dark blue paintwork looked tired and dull against the BMW alongside. He glanced around. Some vans had pulled up near the main entrance, encroaching on the disabled parking area. With names like, *Suffolk Rare Breeds Sausages* and *Doris's Jams & Pickles*, he guessed the exhibitors were out in force.

He pocketed the Fiesta's keys and dodged past a couple pushing a child in a buggy. A trickle of people headed for the entrance and he followed, enjoying the sunshine and smell of onions and burgers from a van already trading. He wished Kat was with him. It would have been fun to show her around the Academy, share samples of local creamy cheeses or slices of Ipswich Almond Pudding. Pity, he thought as he stood in line to pay for a ticket.

The mansion building's entrance hall had been transformed by trestle tables with bright throws and covers. Nick stood for a moment, soaking up the atmosphere as visitors nudged past him, eager to reach the stalls. The smell of caraway seeds wafted across from a tray of Suffolk Buns, several feet away.

'Hey, Nick! Over here.'

Nick looked towards the familiar voice and waved. What's Matt doing behind one of the stalls, he wondered. A few steps closer and it was obvious. The Utterly Library stand.

'Hi.' He glanced down at the display. 'That's clever. Printouts of Suffolk recipes from Mrs Beeton, and... the library's own edition.' He smiled at Rosie. He'd never particularly taken much notice of her in the library, but then he hadn't spent much time in there.

'Great, aint it?' Matt edged closer to Rosie. 'Kat with you today?' He focused beyond Nick, and searched the crowd.

'She couldn't make it. Rifle shooting - a national qualifying competition up in Birmingham.' He didn't say he hoped she'd be back in time to hear him sing with the band, didn't want to sound needy. 'You never said you were manning a stall, Matt.'

'He's not,' Rosie said, as she taped a flyer for the library services to an upright support.

Nick flashed her a smile. Nice eyes, he thought. Kind.

'But he's been good enough to keep me company for a while.'

'Well, I'm going to look round the rest of the food fair,' Nick said, as the aroma of freshly cooked dough, cheese and tomatoes hit his nose.

'Hmm… pizza,' Matt murmured.

Nick led the way, Matt close on his heels. He wove a path down the main corridor, pushing past visitors clustering around stalls groaning with homemade chocolates, jams and pickles. It didn't take them long, and then they were out into the gardens.

'Thank God!' Nick said, as the crowd thinned away. They headed for a large marquee filling the central lawn area. Forty minutes later and Nick felt sick. Too many tasters of sweet then savoury and then sweet again.

'Shouldn't have had those Suffolk Swimmers, mate,' Matt said helpfully.

Nick tried to dismiss the memory of the dumplings, bobbing in gravy. 'Think I need some air.'

Matt grinned. 'Well I'm doin' another circuit in here.'

Nick watched as Matt turned back to join Chrissie, still where they'd found her near the coffee stall.

Outside again, Nick headed away from the marquee with its bustle and noise. He needed some space and he hoped by walking his stomach might ease. He strode past the walled garden with its Edwardian brickwork, and then out beyond, only slowing his pace as the grounds became less formal. This is peaceful, he thought as he stepped over clumps of pale-yellow cowslips and late-flowering wood anemones. A fleeting glimpse of something caught his eye. It seemed out of place but he couldn't be sure. The trunk of a large oak blocked his view. He moved forwards.

A leg, or rather a pair of denim clad legs lay in the rough grass. If there'd been two pairs of legs he'd have moved on and hurried away, embarrassed he was disturbing a favourite student activity. But these legs belonged to one person and they were motionless. Nick stood and listened. No sound, just occasional birdsong.

'Hello,' he called, and when no answer came, 'Excuse me… hello?' He lingered a moment and then crept nearer.

With each step, he saw more. The soft curve of denim clad buttocks. The top of a pair of jeans. Then a glimpse of skin, creamy white and with shadows cast in the hollow of the back. Another step and then the bottom of a sweatshirt, pink and with the edge rolled where it had ridden high.

Nick paused. 'Hi. Are you awake?'

Whoever it was lay on their front. There was no answer, just stillness.

Oh God, he thought. This isn't right. He forced himself to concentrate. Any sign of breathing? He waited for what seemed like an age, but he wasn't sure. Had his eyes tricked him? Had he seen a slight movement?

He bent closer. The head rested on its side. Shoulder length hair snaked over the face, the pale skin almost iridescent between the dark strands. 'Are you OK?'

He'd seen enough to guess it was a girl. He reached out to give her a shake. Her sweatshirt felt cold. 'Oh shit,' he whispered. His pulse raced as his breath came in gasps.

He forced himself to push her hair to one side to see her face. Even her skin felt cold as his fingertips skimmed across her cheek. He gazed down. Her pale lips were parted, her mouth slightly open. Her eyes, closed. He even noticed the dark spot, a mole on her upper lip. She could have been asleep. Except for the stillness. And then the mole moved. He saw it had legs, a pair of wings.

Nick's heart flipped in his chest. 'Oh my God!'

The fly buzzed up at him and away.

•••

Nick couldn't understand how he'd managed to erase the memory of what happened in the first few hours after finding the girl. Her image returned to haunt him often enough, but when he thought back to the ambulance and police, there was just a blank where there should have been memories. A protective blur seemed to have wrapped his mind unevenly in cotton wool.

'You called the emergency services… an ambulance,' Chrissie explained as they sat in the Quay Theatre at six o'clock that evening. The band was setting up and Sudbury seemed light years away from the Academy and its grim find.

'Yeah, mate,' Matt chipped in. 'Then you phoned Chrissie. An' I was standin' with her... an' we came an' found you, mate.'

'I know I couldn't bring myself to touch her. Stuff like... mouth to mouth... chest compressions.... And that fly.' Nick shivered. 'But I don't remember phoning anyone.'

He looked beyond Chrissie and held up a hand, spreading his fingers so Jake, the lead guitarist would see.

'Be with you in a moment,' he called, 'Five minutes.' Nick hoped they didn't notice the waver in his voice. He feared the emotion might creep in and stifle the sound, choke him if he let it.

'Mouth to mouth and chest compression wouldn't have made any difference, Nick.'

'How d'you know, Chrissie?' He dropped the pitch. There'd be less tension in his voice that way.

'Rigor mortis. She'd been dead for hours.'

'Yeah. Already a stiff, mate.'

'Oh God,' Nick wailed. 'Do they know who she is – I mean, was?'

'I heard someone say she was a student at the Academy, but I don't think I've ever seen her around. Are you sure you'll be all right to sing this evening?'

'I'll have to be. The band were well chuffed to get this gig and I can't let Jake down. As it is, their regular singer's off with tonsillitis. I promised last week I'd stand in for him.'

'Their singer's always off with tonsillitis.' Chrissie smiled at Nick and added, 'At least for important venues. I think it's a cunning plan. You were a real knockout when you sang here in Sudbury last year. I think Jake's engineered it. You know they want you as their regular singer, Nick. And don't blush. No false modesty now!'

'Yeah mate, you'll be great. Course I could help out. Only got to say the word, mate… only got to say the word.' In the background the bass guitarist played out a funky rhythm.

'Thanks, Matt, but I'll be OK.' Nick smiled at his friend. He knew him well enough to understand the offer was genuine, not an attempt to distract him with humour. Unfortunately, Matt's singing-range barely stretched to an octave and the few notes he had, sounded as tuneless as a jar of turps.

Nick gazed up at the half-circle windows in the warm red brickwork. They were set too high in the old building to see anything but sky. He could only imagine the River Stour flowing past outside, and the thought of its silent water was strangely soothing. Nick decided he'd channel his feelings into his performance. After all, didn't actors draw on their past experiences to simulate emotion, make their lines seem real? He just needed to control his breathing. He still had an hour or so before the evening's gig. Plenty of time, he told himself.

There was another question he needed to ask. 'How long had she been lying there, do you think?'

'She was well dead when you found her, mate.' Matt took a breath, ready to say more.

'Probably overnight, or since early morning,' Chrissie cut in, 'but they take temperatures and work it out, don't they. There'll be a post mortem. It'll be on the news and in the papers soon enough.'

Jake's lead guitar cut across the bass funk and swooped up and down a jazzy scale.

'But why was she dead? I mean, she's our age.' Nick blinked, trying to dispel the memory of the pale face and the dark snaking hair. 'People our age don't just die without warning. At least, they don't fall asleep and not wake up.'

'Yeah, that's a wrinkly's trick. An' they weren't servin' them Suffolk Swimmers yesterday, so it aint goin' to 've been them.' Matt belched.

Chrissie shrugged. 'You read of youngsters just suddenly dying, say in a gym lesson, and then it turns out there was an underlying heart problem no one knew about – a time bomb waiting to go off.'

'Dumplin' hell!' Matt touched his chest and frowned.

Nick glanced away from Matt's plain black tee-shirt and up at the small stage. The keyboard player seemed to be having trouble with some leads. It would be a few more minutes before they'd want him for the sound check.

'If you hadn't walked out that way, Nick, it could have been days before she was found. Only last week it was Easter and the place has been deserted since then. No one's back till Tuesday. Remember it's the Mayday Bank Holiday on Monday. Just think how her family would've felt if they'd had to wait another three or four days to find her.'

'Yeah, by then she wouldn't have looked as if she'd been sleepin', mate. See, it's been warm... an' several more days in this....' Matt pulled a face. 'An' there's lots of foxes round there.'

Chrissie shot a stern look. 'Shut it, Matt. That's not helpful.' Up on the stage the keyboard burst into organ pitch, cut out and then crackled before morphing into piano tones.

Chrissie had a point though, Nick thought; the girl could have lain there, undiscovered for days. If it hadn't been for the Swimmers, he wouldn't have walked so far into the grounds. He closed his eyes and listened to a chord sequence. This time the girl's face didn't appear. Maybe the music was going to help.

'Come on, Nick. We need you for a sound check.' Jake's voice boomed as he spoke into a mike.

'Right with you,' Nick shouted. He turned to Chrissie. 'You guys didn't have to come here with me. I'd have been OK, you know.'

'Would you?' Chrissie's voice blended with the keyboard.

For the next thirty minutes Nick sang snatches of the set while the band practised the intros and harmonised on choruses. At first the lead guitar was over dominant, then the keyboard, but finally the balance between drums, bass, lead and keyboard complimented the volume setting for Nick's microphone. Sound checks complete, they ran through the order for the set.

'*I'll Be Dead Before the Dawn*.... I don't know if that's a good idea, Jake.' Nick's voice faltered. 'You know what happened today and....'

Jake stepped on the effects pedal, soared up to some high notes, then slid his fingers down the strings. The keyboard surged in, followed by bass and drums. Nick opened his mouth and his voice came, at first a little hesitant, then vibrato. The reedy tenor morphed into full tone, and he sang. The music filled his mind. There was no room for images of a pale face and dark snaking hair.

'*Dead, cold dead before the dawn*,' he sang.

'Sounds good to me,' the bass player said as he drew out the dying note. 'What were you going to say Nick?'

'Nothing....'

'We could swop it round with *Jeany Jean*... or leave it where it is,' Jake said as he propped his guitar against its stand. 'What d'you think, Nick?'

Nick had been concealing his panic attacks since the previous summer. They'd developed after he'd spent over twenty-four hours being interrogated by the counter-terrorist police. He hadn't blown up a car, but they'd thought he had. Since then, any reminder of the interrogation was usually enough to quicken his pulse and breathing, make him sweat and his head spin. He'd never thought he'd be the kind of guy to lose control, but finding the dead girl had shocked him. Shocked him deeply. It threatened to tip him into the spiral.

However, in the Quay Theatre that early evening, he'd discovered something about himself. He had a natural sense of breath control when he sang, and when he sang it tamed his panic.

'No, leave the order as it is. I'll be fine, Jake.' He jumped down from the stage and headed for Chrissie and Matt. 'I'm fine now. Don't worry. Why don't you two go up to the bar area? If Kat arrives, she'll find you up there.' He checked his watch. 'Only half an hour before we're on.'

As it turned out, Kat didn't make it back from the rifle shooting competition in Birmingham until after the interval.

CHAPTER 7

Matt rolled sideways. The duvet wrapped itself around him. He rolled again. In his dream he was Captain Fantastic, caught in a barrel and hurtling through white-water rapids. The falls at the edge of the world were ahead; behind, a monster with a ponytail. His world was vivid with primary colours and outlined in black, the staple of comic-strip imagery. His ears filled with the sound of rushing water as the barrel turned again. And then he was falling.

Thwack! Matt landed on his bedroom floor 'Uhh,' he moaned, still somewhere between sleep and consciousness. Something cold pushed into his cheek. He opened one eye and tried to focus on the steely metal pressed hard against his face. He rolled onto his back. Reality dawned as water hissed in the toilet cistern on the other side of the wall. He'd fallen out of bed and his head was half in the dog's bowl. 'Bugger!' Storm may have gone but his things were still strewn around the bedroom, waiting until Tom returned.

Matt closed his eyes. He could have drifted back into sleep, but the walls inside the bungalow were too thin to muffle the sounds. The bathroom lock shot back and his mother trudged along the hallway.

If only he was Captain Fantastic. And as he thought about the monster chasing him in his dream, realisation struck. His subconscious must have been playing games. This wasn't about comic-strip heroes or a mythical creature with a ponytail. This was about a man. The memories came flooding back: his walk on the wild side with Storm, the polytunnel, the baseball cap, the serpent-like hair.

'Hell!' Now he was wide awake. It was Tuesday already. He sat up, sending the metal bowl skimming across the floor to clang against the faded blue of his bedroom wall.

He rubbed at his eyes and glanced around the room. A pile of discarded clothes lay where he'd dropped them: the black cotton tee-shirt, worn for several days and smothered by blue denim, a grey towel heaped to one side, and trainers cast away to capsize.

'Oh God,' he moaned as he saw the black tee and remembered the food fair. He'd chosen to wear that particular tee because it was plain. He hadn't wanted anything like *weed* printed on his chest in case he bumped into Ponytail again; but then the man hadn't been there, leastways not that he'd noticed.

Today, the 3rd of May, might be different. The Academy opened its doors and the term would begin in earnest. Matt reckoned it was just the day for a dope peddler like Ponytail to visit. Normally it wouldn't have concerned him, except today was also the last day of his holiday. He'd planned to use it for a visit to the Academy library. Tomorrow, Wednesday and he would be back at Hepplewhites, the carpentry firm in Hadleigh.

Matt reached for the black tee-shirt. He pulled at the cotton fabric, liberating it from the mound along with a discarded sock. He held it up, catching the odour of stale sweat and beer. No, the black wouldn't do, not if Rosie was in the library. He flung it back into the heap. Something else caught his eye. Chrissie's memory stick. It lay on the denim, amongst the pile but freed from the jeans. He'd already worked on it, but that had been before the weekend and before Nick stumbled on the dead girl. Since then, everyone's life had taken a jolt.

He drew his duvet close and, still sitting on the floor, grabbed the memory stick. It only took a few moments to pull his laptop from under the bed and boot it up. He settled with his back resting against the side of the bed, the computer balanced on his knee. He clicked on the now familiar file and slowly looked at each photo again. He'd wanted to check radiator grills and Land Rover profiles, read about hare coursing and modifications to 4x4 off-roaders, but his Wi-Fi pay-as-you-go dongle needed topping up. All that would have to wait for the library computers and the Academy internet connection.

He frowned as he looked for the hundredth time at something on the edge of one the photos. Could that be *Jumbuck*? The first few letters were out of shot, but *mbuck* could be the end of the name, *Jumbuck*, a Proton pickup, not particularly common in the area. The 4x4 in centre shot was plainly a Land Rover Discovery, the number plate false, Chrissie had said. There was something else, though. It had niggled at him. He remembered seeing a picture once of horse racing at Higham. The punters had been sitting on the roofs of their 4x4s, watching through binoculars as they picnicked and enjoyed the afternoon. Could that strange outline at the rear of the Land Rover be some form of step? Something to make getting up onto the roof easier, or just to stand on?

Matt shook his head. There had to be something in the shot, an identifying mark, he reckoned. He concentrated on the hubcaps for a moment.

The front door slammed. Footsteps thudded down the hallway. Matt tensed and closed his laptop. Anxiety gripped at his stomach.

'Hi, Mum.' Through the wall the voice sounded much like his own, but brusquer. 'Matt in?'

Matt sank further into his duvet. If he could have fitted, he'd have squeezed himself under the bed. 'Shite!' He hadn't expected Tom to come round. He'd supposed there'd be a call and then he could have said, *the dog's gone*, using his mobile. He'd banked on distance separating him from Tom's anger. Why couldn't he have phoned before landing at Stansted?

'One, two,' Matt breathed as the footsteps continued.

'Three, four–'

The bedroom door burst open.

'Matt! Storm?' Tom stood in the doorway. He was taller than Matt and slimmer, but with the same dark sandy hair and stubby nose. 'What the hell…?' His voice died as he scrutinized the room.

'H-hi, Tom. W-when d'you get back?' Matt tried to suppress the wobble in his voice, but he knew it showed. The old behavioural patterns were starting to play out again: his fear, Tom's dominance, the little kid and big kid of their childhood.

'A couple of hours ago. Where's Storm? Where's the bloody dog, Matt?'

'I wanted to t-tell you.' Matt gulped. ''E did a runner. Wednesday night.' He watched his brother's face blanch beneath the faint tan.

'What d'you mean? You let 'im go? You stupid little shit. So where's 'e now? 'Ave you got 'im back?'

'N-no. It weren't the first time, Tom. 'E kept boltin'. Pulled the lead out me hand. Last time I found 'im beyond the railway line. Y'know – out the back from here. Miles away… with that ponytail bloke. The one with the polytunnel. Grows dope, I reckon.'

'So 'ave you checked there again?'

'Y-yes.' Matt felt his face burn and sweat break on his forehead.

'And?'

'Swung a metal pole at me. Told me to piss off.' Matt met his brother's stare and managed not to look away this time. What he'd just said was true. Displaced in time and deliberately misleading, but true. He held his gaze.

'You mean… he's got the dog an' won't give 'im back? An' you've done nothing?'

Matt looked away.

'Answer me, you little shit!' Tom leapt forwards. With the speed of a snake's tongue, he lashed out. 'So he's got the dog?'

Matt sank further into his duvet. Pain streaked through his nose, blocking all thought. His eyes watered, his lip felt numb. He bit back the sob.

'Well?' Tom turned away. 'Not so clever now, are you, Matt? You always were a pathetic bastard. I s'pose I've got to sort it out for you, have I?' Tom paced the room.

'So you reckon Sobell's got Storm. Yeah – that makes sense. But if this gets back to Dard… shit, from what I've heard, he aint going to like this, aint going to like this one little bit. You stupid bastard, Matt. Can't you even look after a dog?' Tom spun around, took three strides and landed a kick.

Matt lay curled in a ball, wrapped in the duvet, and with his laptop between knees and chest. Tom's boot caught him on the back of his thigh. He bit back the cry before it escaped. Tasted the blood on his lip. He knew from his childhood it was best if he stayed silent. The bully in Tom would only get worse if he heard him whimper.

'For God's sake, Matt....' Heavy footsteps headed back across the bedroom, then paused. 'I s'pose I'll have to fix this mess.' A door clicked. 'Bye, Mum. Phone you sometime.' Tom's voice sounded muffled, distanced by the wall and duvet.

Matt didn't move for a while. He consoled himself with a thought. At least Tom had gone and he knew Storm was missing now. He rolled over and stretched out his legs. Muscles twinged at the back of his thigh. He pushed away the duvet and gingerly touched his nose. He let his fingers explore the shape. It felt pretty straight, but when he touched his lip it was swollen. He ran his tongue along the inside, felt the rough cut where it had split against a tooth.

'Shoot,' he breathed.

•••

A couple of hours later and Matt pushed his helmet on. The chin guard skimmed along his nose as he manoeuvred it down. 'Y-ouch,' he yelped. Chrissie's memory stick was already in his pocket and the Piaggio Zip waited on its stand. A matter of seconds and he was on the scooter, accelerating away from Tumble Weed Drive and the bad memories.

It didn't take him long to reach the Academy, and soon he had climbed the main stairs, limping with each step up to the first floor. While he paused to make way for students hurrying to catch the afternoon sessions, snatches of conversation drifted up from the main hallway below. *It's tragic* and, *seemed OK when I last saw her* mingled with, *she was in my art group* and *did you know Anne Blink? She was only seventeen.*

'Oh God. So her name was Anne Blink,' he mumbled.

Ahead, the canteen doors beckoned, but Matt didn't go in. He felt sick. The memory of the dead girl was still fresh. She was the first human corpse he'd seen and he'd been shocked. He hadn't felt grief. How could he when he didn't know her? But he'd been taken aback to see her lying there, and surprised by how normal she'd appeared, almost as if she was sleeping. He'd seen plenty of lifeless hedgehogs and small birds before, stepped over them on pavements and in gutters, and he'd found the sight of them disturbing. A dead girl was different, much worse. Not that he'd stepped over her, of course, or that she'd been in the gutter. When he'd stood with Nick and Chrissie, waiting for the ambulance and police to arrive, he'd felt a surge of emotion, something between sadness and apprehension. It made him feel weird and now, hearing her name, he felt it again.

'Hi, Matt!' Rosie let the canteen door swing behind her as she stepped into the corridor. She cradled a pack of sandwiches and bag of crisps close against her fitted cotton blouse. 'I'm afraid they've finished serving the cooked lunch, if that's what you're after.' She stopped mid-stride and stared at him. 'Your face…. Are you OK?'

Matt covered his nose and chin with a casual movement of his hand. 'Walked into a door,' he mumbled, hoping he'd said it the way Al Pacino might have delivered the line. He smiled but it was trapped behind his hand and his lip hurt.

Rosie frowned. 'Well, if you can make it to the library, I'll open the door for you. I'll try to keep it away from your face.' She led the way. 'So sad about that student, Anne Blink. The Academy's in quite a buzz about it.'

Matt didn't know what to say. His feelings were more complicated than just plain sad and he didn't understand why. He'd never met the girl when she was alive, hadn't even heard of her. Only death had brought them together. He wanted to say he felt as if he ought to have known her, everyone else seemed to. Guilt joined the mix of emotions and gripped at his stomach. He settled for, 'Yeah.'

'I don't know anyone who's my kind of age and has actually died. It shakes you. Makes you aware of your own mortality, don't you think?'

'Yeah.'

'A kind of misplaced grief... for ourselves, apart from anything else.'

Matt was out of his depth. 'Yeah.'

He liked Rosie, liked it when she spoke to him, but she'd lost him with the misplaced grief bit. Besides, he was getting tired holding his hand to his face. 'Yeah,' he repeated for good measure. 'Don't suppose anyone knows why she died?'

'No... and you can put your hand down. It doesn't look too bad.'

'How'd you know?' He lowered his arm.

'Didn't... but I wanted to, and now I've had a chance to look at you. Your lip looks sore. A bit of a bruiser, but at least your nose is still straight. And you're limping. That was some door.'

Matt grinned but the split in his lip burned and pulled. The pain cut through his smile and he winced. He hoped he'd looked sexy. Like Al Pacino.

He hobbled to a computer station, out of the way and in the corner. Emotion threatened to overwhelm him. Tom's anger had been terrifying and he knew the business with Storm wasn't over. Remembering the dead girl made him feel weird again, and to top it all, the back of his thigh pained, his nose felt blocked and his lip stung. He slipped the memory stick into the USB port and clicked on the computer. Within seconds Chrissie's photo file was up on the screen. He Googled *Land Rover Discovery*, and moments later he was looking at the official sites.

'Bloody car's been accessorised,' he muttered, as he recognised the front lamp guards and the protection bar over the radiator grill. *Rear access ladder*, he read from the shopping list. Well, that explained the rear profile, but the wheels? He looked again. And then he saw it. 'Tyre valve cap,' he breathed. You could buy them in sets of four, Land Rover branded. So that's what he'd noticed on the photo. Now that was unusual. Not many owners would have gone to that expense, he reckoned.

Matt concentrated on the number plate. It appeared real enough, and of course it was. He guessed it was the copy of a legitimate number plate, belonging to another Land Rover Discovery with the same specifications.

'Clever,' Matt breathed. An automatic number plate recognition camera was unlikely to pick up anything suspicious. The database records would confirm the valid tax disc and car insurance, but they'd belong to an identical Land Rover Discovery. Why should the computer know there were two similar cars driving around with the same registration number, one of them a phoney? When the police finally checked, they'd have knocked on the door of the innocent and unsuspecting, genuine owner. As Matt saw it, the hare coursers were effectively hiding behind the legitimate identity of someone else's 4x4.

'Bloody identity theft,' he mumbled. It was ingenious, but if they were that smart, then he reckoned they'd have known to ditch it for another false number plate by now. He committed it to memory, just in case.

Matt clicked forward to the next photo, the one with a man peering at something through binoculars. Mrs Hinton's shot had caught him in profile, and the focus was good. No movement artefact. He made the face larger, but most of it was blocked by a hand, wrist and binoculars 'Looks fuzzy now,' he muttered, but he'd spotted something on the hand. A ring. He increased the magnification again.

'You OK over here?'

Matt hadn't noticed Rosie walking past him with a couple of books. He looked up, startled. 'Oh hi, Rosie.'

She paused, and glanced down at the computer. 'Are you very short sighted, then?'

Matt frowned. What was she on about?

'Your screen. Whatever it is, it's… over magnified.'

'Oh yeah, see what you're gettin' at about the short sight.' He started to smile but the pain in his lip made him flinch. He stifled the wince and thought of Al Pacino. Then he had an idea. 'What's it look like to you?'

'Is this some kind of game? Because if you're trying to get me to look at something rude, Matt and then have a laugh when I think it's a ring or something… well, I'll get you banned from the library.' Her face coloured up.

'No! No, honest.' He clicked to restore to normal size and the photo of the man holding the binoculars filled the screen. 'I reckoned a ring, too. But what d'you think? Am I seein' a disc on it… or somethin' like a gem?' Matt hadn't expected her to get huffy with him.

'Magnify it up again and I'll have another look.' Her face was still flushed as she avoided eye contact and concentrated on the screen. 'No, I don't think it's a coin. I'd say it's more like a gem or a stone. Is it kind of red? Why am I looking at this, Matt?'

'Some illegal hare coursin'… an' someone got hurt. A friend asked me to look at the photos.'

'Are you sure it was a door you walked into, Matt?' Rosie turned on her heel and, without waiting for an answer, strode away.

'No, it weren't me, Rosie. I aint into hare coursin'.'

His words appeared to fall unheard onto Rosie's momentarily deaf ears.

'Bugger,' he muttered.

A few students straggled into the library. The mid-afternooners, as Matt secretly dubbed them. He watched as they asked for help, competing with each other for Rosie's attention. Matt guessed they probably needed to hand in assignments, judging by the reams of paper they loaded into the printer. He slumped further into his chair, despondent as they monopolised her time. He decided he might as well look for recent reports of hare coursing in the area. He reckoned he'd be safe. She was unlikely to come over again for a while.

Matt trawled through the internet for nearly forty minutes. It seemed East Anglia and Lincolnshire were hotbeds for coursing. 'There's hundreds of 'em,' he sighed. He hoped to find something; any similarity with a sighting elsewhere, or some tiny fact he could link with Mrs Hinton's photos. He even located a report headed *Woman Breaks Leg as Hare Coursers Mow Her Down*, but it didn't tell him anything new. It had the same photo he'd enlarged on his screen and essentially the same facts he'd already learnt from Chrissie about Mrs Hinton's ordeal. 'Bloody waste of time,' he muttered when he finally gave up, none the wiser.

There was just one more thing he wanted to check before packing up for the day. Anne Blink. He keyed in the Academy's membership number for the Eastern Anglia Daily Tribune site, and a moment later he was reading one of the day's headlines: *Student Found Dead in Utterly Academy Grounds in Stowmarket.*

Anne Blink, a seventeen-year-old student on the art and design foundation course at Utterly Academy, was found dead on Saturday April 30th. So nothing new; he'd already learnt most of this as he'd limped up the main staircase. He skimmed on. *Last seen at Stowmarket's Sapphire nightclub on Friday night.* Matt nodded. Sapphs, as it was known by the students, was a favourite venue on the Friday night Stowmarket scene. It followed she might have been drinking in there. He read on. *Samples have been taken for analysis.* Why couldn't they just say what they meant? *Awaiting toxicology* was almost certainly code for drug testing.

There wasn't much more in the article, other than to state the obvious. It seemed as yet, no one knew how or why Anne Blink had come to die in the Academy grounds. The *post mortem and tests might give an answer*, but Matt knew he'd have to wait weeks before the findings were reported in the paper. There'd be nothing more for him today. He sighed and logged off, disappointed. The weird feeling had returned to his stomach and he knew better than to risk going back to Tumble Weed Drive too soon in case Tom was after him. Perhaps it was time to ride over to the Clegg workshop and help with the totem pole carving?

CHAPTER 8

It was Wednesday, and Chrissie sipped her tea as she gazed at Mrs Hinton's pedestal table. It no longer represented a straightforward repair project, it symbolised far more: illegal hare coursing, Mrs Hinton's injured leg, her photos, even Matt and his research into the prints.

In the end Ron had decided the water damage to the table was so extensive they'd get a better end result if they took the whole veneered surface off, repaired and then re-applied it. That had been over a week ago.

'Thank God it's only a small table,' she muttered.

'If it had been a dining table....' Ron shook his head.

'Well maybe some of the surface would have escaped and we'd have been able to leave the undamaged bits.' Chrissie set her mug down on the workbench and ran her hand over the base wood of the pedestal table top. She'd sanded off all the old animal glue and lightly scored the surface, ready to help key the new glue for the restored veneer. 'Seems really complicated.'

She remembered how Ron had applied some special film to the damaged veneer and then using an iron, warmed the wood to soften the old animal glues that held it. She'd watched him prise the veneered top away from the base wood with a spatula, and then held together by the film, fix it to a temporary ground board. She guessed the real artistry was about to begin as he replaced, repaired or pressed flat each water-damaged piece so that it fitted exactly against its neighbour. Finally he would be able to glue the completed jigsaw back onto the table top base that Chrissie had prepared.

'It'll be weeks before we take it back to the Hintons,' she said softly.

Secretly she wanted an excuse to speak to Mrs Hinton. When Matt, limping and bruised, had come over to the Clegg workshop the evening before, he'd given her an update on his progress with the photos. Now, fired with curiosity, she wanted to ask more details about the accessorised Land Rover and the Jumbuck, mostly out of shot. She hoped there might be some other photos, possibly considered too poor to pass on, but she knew the longer she waited, the more Mrs Hinton was likely to forget.

'You look impatient, Mrs Jax.'

Chrissie gazed across the barn workshop. Wood dust seemed to hang in the air as late afternoon shafts of sunlight cut through from the windows.

'I just feel....' She let her shoulders drop. 'I don't know, I can't do anything for that poor girl who died in the Academy grounds, but I feel – well I feel it must be possible to do something for Mrs Hinton.'

'We are, Mrs Jax. We're repairing her pedestal table.'

'No, I don't mean that. I mean, about the people who drove at her. Broke her leg.' Chrissie focused on her mug of tea.

'That's what the police are for. But you can bet the locals will be watching out for those coursers. No one'll turn a blind eye now someone's been injured.'

'Are you so sure, Mr Clegg? The police don't seem able to do anything when false number plates are involved.'

Chrissie thought back to the conversation with Clive. They'd walked through woods near Ickworth House on Monday, the Mayday Bank Holiday, and then stumbled on a delightful pub in Horringer. She'd felt warm and relaxed.

Whenever she stayed over with him in Lavenham, he had that effect on her. She remembered sipping her glass of Pinot Grigio as they waited for their lunch order and thinking how calm and kindly matter-of-fact he was, as he downed a half pint of the Adnams on-tap and talked about death.

It had been only two days after the incident of finding the dead girl, or rather The Curious Incident of the Girl in the Night-Time, as Chrissie now labelled it, playing on Sherlock Holmes' words and the title of Mark Haddon's book. Except of course, Anne Blink had been found in the morning. Chrissie had been trying to distance herself from the shock and sadness of it all. It was too easy to imagine the terrible grief and heartache for the girl's family. After all, she'd been through something similar when Bill died and she knew she had to stop herself from reliving it.

'So what are you working on now?' Clive had asked, changing the subject. He ran a hand through his short auburn hair and smiled as someone from the kitchens set down his plate of venison sausage and mash.

'Water damage on a beautifully veneered little table. The Hintons, out Stanningfield way. You may remember they were victims of some hare coursing.' Chrissie watched as her steak and ale pie was placed in front of her.

Clive nodded slowly. 'It was quite recent, if I remember rightly.'

'Yes. Sprightly lady, though of course her leg's in plaster now. What I can't understand is how she could've taken photos of the whole thing and you police still can't catch anyone.' Chrissie cut into the pie. Rich gravy oozed out.

'Well, the vehicle had false plates, Chrissie.'

'But surely there's something you can find out? Don't you have some kind of data mining software to trawl through the computerised records? You know, for previous sightings. Track car journeys?' Chrissie felt animated.

'You mean the national ANPR data centre?'

Animation turned to irritation. 'The *what* centre?' Beef from a hot-spot in the pie steamed on her fork. She eyed it up.

'Automatic Number Plate Recognition. The ANPR data centre.'

Chrissie recalled how Clive had looked at her for a moment, all hints of a smile wiped from his face. He seemed to make a decision.

'Firstly, Chrissie, the crooks will've switched the plates as soon as they could after the photos were taken. Secondly, the ANPR data centre will still show movements for the vehicle with the genuine number on it... so the point or place where the crooks switch isn't easy to identify. Thirdly, the vehicle was probably stolen in the first place, its number plate changed, maybe a re-spray, and no chance of matching against the reported stolen register. And fourthly, I'd need authorisation from the chief to get a data trawl through the ANPR data centre, and weighed against the cost, there isn't enough to justify that.'

Something about his tone told her the matter was closed, not for discussion in a pub on Mayday Bank Holiday. She'd smiled and smothered her frustration. The same frustration she now felt in the Clegg workshop at the slow pace of the table restoration.

Ron stood up stiffly and pushed his stool back. 'Time to get on with some work, Mrs Jax.'

For a moment Chrissie imagined he'd read her thoughts.

'Best leave it to the police,' he added as he selected a scalpel and reached for the sharpening stone. 'You've enough to worry about with that totem pole. Now – to get a really sharp point on the tip of this blade, I rub the back of the blade along the stone... like this. It needs to be needle sharp to mark out and cut the veneers.'

'Oh God! The totem pole,' she moaned.

'If your friends don't walk into any more doors, you'll get it finished.'

An image of Matt with his swollen lip and bruised nose flashed into Chrissie's mind. God, Tom was a bastard, she thought.

'Now, for the rest of the day, Mrs Jax, I think you should concentrate on carving Cromwell.'

They'd previously agreed Chrissie should concentrate on Cromwell's head. Matt would construct some aeroplane wings and the side extensions of an admiral's hat - mainly because he could use flat pieces of wood and attach them later to the sides of the totem pole. Nick, the best carver, was going to work on the Spitfire's body and Nelson's head. The seat of learning, with a crest to represent the universities in East Anglia was still up for grabs, so to speak.

In preparation for this carving marathon, the cedar trunk had been hauled into the barn workshop. It rested on blocks, sad and tatty, and stretched along the length of the barn. Dark lines marked it off into segments. Chrissie sighed as she gathered up her practice Cromwell, some chisels and gouges and settled on a low stool close to one of the sections. She'd previously drawn Cromwell's head on the totem pole. Front, rear and side views. The wart was the only distinguishing feature, and it was going to be huge.

'You'll need a handsaw, Mrs Jax.'

She wondered how he'd known she'd forgotten to bring one over.

'Remember to make a series of straight saw cuts down to your outline.' The words drifted across from Ron's workbench. 'And work from each side, not just the front.'

'And then chisel away the dead wood?' she finished for him.

'Good – you're learning, Mrs Jax.'

•••

Monday the 9th came round soon enough. Too soon for Chrissie's tastes. What had the text message said? 'Oh God,' she sighed as she remembered. *Mr Blumfield would like to see you in his office at 1:45pm on Monday May 9th*, and now the day had dawned.

She dressed in a short sleeved blouse with some embroidery on the collar. A pair of light-grey jeans hugged only at the hips. She hoped she struck the right mix of smart but practical. A carpentry apprentice, not an office worker. Female, but not so girly as to be in a skirt. She lingered in the old entrance hall, gazing at the noticeboards and tried to kill time before the dreaded 1:45 pm meeting. It was better than pacing the corridor outside his office on the first floor.

She barely registered the flyer for the Needham Market Raft Race 2011. The notice called for entries. The race wasn't until the last Sunday in June. Ages away. She moved on and looked at the next poster, the out-of-date advert for the Utterly Food Fair. A notice appealing for information had been pinned onto its photo of a huge Suffolk Gold cheese. It seemed incongruous as it asked for sightings that might help the police track the last movements of the dead student, Anne Blink.

Chrissie shivered. She didn't want to think about last sightings or be reminded of how Anne had looked in her final cold sleep. Anxious and tense, Chrissie turned her back on the boards. Students were everywhere, jostling on the stairs, dodging the canteen doors as they swung, and all single-minded in their last-minute rush for lunch. Deep in her own thoughts, she walked on past the library. What had Clive suggested the previous Monday as she ate her steak and ale pie? She smiled as she remembered.

'If you think that chap Blumfield will get a kick out of wrong-footing you,' he'd said, 'then... it may help if you treat the interview like an imaginary game of chess. Think of each verbal exchange as if he's moving the pieces on the board, as if he's building up his attack strategy. You'll see what he's trying to do, and by keeping cool and staying logical, you'll outmanoeuvre him. It's what I do when I'm trying to trip up some criminal.'

She'd almost laughed at the comparison with a criminal, and even now, the smile threatened to break into a grin as she strode on.

She stopped outside an office. *Mr Blumfield, Director Carpentry Department*, she read. A quick check of her watch. 'It's time,' she sighed and knocked.

Chrissie pushed at the solid door, hardly waiting for Mr Blumfield's 'Come in,' to die away.

'Ah good, I'm glad you could make it, Mrs Jax.' He beamed from behind his desk and gestured vaguely towards an elegant Mackintosh style chair, an overambitious project from a previous year. 'Sit down, please sit down.' As the smile faded, crease lines remained where age had stamped its mark.

Chrissie smiled and hid her nervous impatience. All these niceties were just delaying tactics. Why couldn't he just cut to the chase and say why he wanted to see her? She decided to make the opening move. 'The millennium project is going well, Mr Blumfield. The totem pole is starting to look like one.' She tried to block out the image of the cedar trunk, forlorn and tatty, stretched out on blocks in the workshop like a body in a mortuary.

'That's wonderful. I must drive over and see.'

'The totem pole?' Oh no, Chrissie thought, as her heart missed a beat. If this was a chess game, then Blumfield had opened with an attacking knight, and leapt over his line of pawns.

'Of course. What else would I be driving out to see, Mrs Jax?'

Chrissie felt her cheeks burn. 'It's coming together well.' She groped for words. 'Another few weeks and Cromwell's head will be carved above the wavy water lines.'

'I promised it would be ready before the end of this summer term. I'd hate to be disappointed.' For a moment Mr Blumfield frowned, distracted by the bishop she'd unwittingly moved on the chessboard. 'Wavy water lines, Mrs Jax?'

'Yes, to represent the water. The Broads and the drainage of the fens.' She fell silent. He still hadn't indicated why he'd asked her to come to see him.

'Of course… wavy lines for water.' He paused, as if to gather his thoughts. 'I phoned Ron Clegg, the other week. I keep a regular contact with all the apprentice supervisors…

and I couldn't pin him down about progress on the totem pole.' His forehead started to glisten. 'I've known him a long time. We're old friends and I can tell when he's... well I got the impression he was obfuscating. Vague in the extreme. I wondered if he was trying to protect me from the truth.'

'The truth?' Chrissie's stomach churned with anxiety. Mr Blumfield seemed unstoppable. She felt helpless moving a pawn to protect the bishop.

'Yes, Mrs Jax. The truth being that really there's been very little progress with the totem pole.'

So this was why old Blumfield had asked to see her. Chrissie tried to keep her face expressionless, despite the stab of fear. Blumfield had taken her pawn. The man had effectively called her a liar. She couldn't let that pass. She had to fight back and bring her queen out. 'Considering all the setbacks, I'd say it's on schedule. Well, a schedule of sorts, Mr Blumfield.'

'Yes, there was that trouble with the terrorist. I'll grant you that. But it doesn't alter the fact you haven't much time left and it must be completed by the end of July. It's a deadline.' Mr Blumfield seemed to move his own queen with deadly intent. 'It would be such a pity if the one female apprentice in our carpentry department was about to let us down.'

Chrissie bit back the words. She wanted to remind him that the totem pole project had already languished for ten years without progress before it was given to her. It therefore seemed illogical to say a few weeks late would be a catastrophe, unless he was looking for an excuse to see her fail. She tried to calm her thoughts, blink back a tear at the injustice.

'It strikes me, Mr Blumfield, that I am doing more for this carpentry department than anyone else. I've been asked to rescue the ten years late millennium project for you. Surely I should be helped and supported, not threatened.' She warmed to her theme. 'It was you who asked me to take it on, not the other way round. It is the carpentry department's project, after all.'

As she watched him frown and his face colour up, an idea sprang to her. 'Has anyone else entered a team to represent the carpentry department at the Needham Raft Race this summer, Mr Blumfield?'

'No, but... have you, Mrs Jax?'

She made a lightening decision and nodded. It was the *check mate* moment for her and she sensed victory. He was in retreat.

'Well, I must say that's splendid, Mrs Jax. I hope you didn't misunderstand me when I talked about letting down the carpentry department. You must ask for help if you need it.' He smiled, a kind of benevolent smile as if it was his gift to give all the help in the world, should she need it.

'Thank you, Mr Blumfield.'

She watched as he stood up. She knew from experience it was his way of saying the meeting was over.

'Well, that was a fruitful discussion, don't you think, Mrs Jax? There is just one thing, though. Isn't Cromwell a bit controversial? Wasn't he born in Huntingdon? That's... well, it's beyond Cambridge. May not be so appropriate for our totem pole, eh?' He rocked on his feet, so that for a moment he appeared taller than his five feet five.

Chrissie blinked as she took on board the implications. Was she carving the wrong head? She felt as if a pit had opened at her feet. She was sinking, but Clive's words came to her in the nick of time. This was a chess game. Blumfield had simply shifted his queen to safety and threatened her bishop in the same move. She calmed her mind and inspiration came.

'If you don't like the idea of Cromwell, I can change it to John Constable, Mr Blumfield. I can lose the wart and add a paintbrush.'

'Splendid, Mrs Jax.'

•••

Afterwards, as Chrissie recounted the meeting to Nick and Matt around the coffee dispenser in the canteen, Matt shook his head.

'That aint fair, Chrissie. I looked up some stuff, remember, an' Cromwell owned land in Ely. Don't that make him East Anglian?'

'Yes, Matt. I just get the feeling Blumfield didn't want Cromwell on the totem pole.'

'Well, let's face it, one carved head looks pretty much like another. It doesn't make any difference to us whether it's Cromwell or Constable, apart from the extra letter. But why did you have to say we'd entered a raft at Needham?' Nick downed the remains of his coffee, much as he'd have tossed back the last of a pint of beer. 'You must have been out of your mind, Chrissie.'

'Yeah,' Matt chipped in. 'So who's goin' to be on this raft then?'

Chrissie didn't know what to say. She had to admit she hadn't thought this one through. She shrugged. 'Maybe if we put up a notice... you know get some of the first years to help? Ask people on the apprentice release day?'

'I'd say we've been utterly rafted, Chrissie.'

CHAPTER 9

Nick pulled into the Willows car park behind the main workshop.

'*And now for the eight o'clock....*' The newsreader's voice drifted around the Ford Fiesta. '*The tragic death of a student found dead in the Utterly Academy grounds....*' The words cut like a burning knife into Nick's thoughts as he manoeuvred the car. He stopped and reached for the ignition key. '*Traces of Rohypnol, the so called date rape....*' He froze. In his mind he could see the girl, still and silent, as if sleeping. He didn't recall her clothes looking torn or disarrayed. Nothing to suggest she'd been raped.

'*Substances found in her blood included methamphetamine, commonly known as crystal meth....*' Nick frowned. No one had mentioned drugs before, not seriously. The word on the street, or in this case the corridors of Utterly, hadn't suggested she was a druggie, certainly not a regular user.

'*May have been slipped a cocktail of drugs....*' Nick opened his window further. A light morning breeze cooled his face. '*Police are appealing for anyone who saw Anne Blink on Friday or the early hours of Saturday morning, to come forward....*'

'Oh God,' Nick whispered. He'd been right. Teenagers didn't just fall asleep and die. Drugs were more common than obscure heart conditions. And the phrase, *been slipped a cocktail of drugs*? Did it suggest a prank or something more? A malicious act? Intentional harm?

Nick closed his eyes, the engine still running. The words, '*More local news from Radio Suffolk,*' rang out in the background. He pictured her again, the dark shoulder length hair cast across her face and the pale iridescent skin, unreal, like china. And the fly.

His chest felt tight. He needed more air. He groped for the door handle. 'Sing,' an inner voice whispered. 'Sing. It helped before.'

Nick bit back the gasp, shut his mouth and forced the breath out through his nose. It sounded like a hum. He tried again. First the hum and then, opening his mouth, it became a reedy note. A long note on a longer breath. The image of the snaking dark hair started to fade. He drew air in again, but this time more slowly. He opened his mouth and sang, concentrating on the melody. The girl's face disappeared.

'*Jeany Jean….*'

Thump! The roof of the old Ford Fiesta shuddered.

'What the hell d'you think you're doing, Nick?'

Nick opened his eyes and closed his mouth.

'Switch the engine off, for God's sake. And that radio. This is no place for a mobile disco. You're at work now.' Dave stood with his arm resting on the roof of the car. He stooped so that his face was on a level with Nick's. 'You OK, lad?'

Nick grabbed the ignition keys. 'Yes, I'm fine, Dave.' His cheeks burned.

'Well, you don't look OK.' Dave studied him for a moment. 'The boss had a call yesterday from Mr Santo. Says he's thinking of asking us to do some work on his house – a bespoke built-in wardrobe or something. But he wants to see the manuscript bench units completed first. I need you working, not playing air guitar in the car park. There's a lot to be getting on with.'

Nick nodded and got out of the car. There was no point in explaining. Why should he expect Dave to understand? He hardly understood it himself. He'd never thought he'd be the kind of guy to lose control, but then he'd never imagined he'd find a dead girl in the Academy grounds. And if that hadn't been horrific enough, now it sounded as if the police were going to be involved. He started to hum.

He followed Dave through a side entrance and into the one-storey building. Nick didn't stop to make a morning mug of tea. He felt too unsettled. The office-like sitting area, with its filing cabinets along one wall and an uneasy mix of plastic stacker and fabric covered chairs, was almost deserted.

'Morning Mr Walsh,' he muttered to the foreman.

Nick pushed at a scuffed and abused door. It swung open and he stepped into the large modern workshop, laid out with space at one end. The wide, roller shutter door leading to a small goods delivery area outside was bolted down. When open, the workshop always felt cool and airy.

Still uneasy and hot, Nick headed for some neatly stacked wood. He'd spent most of the previous week feeding it through a thickness-planer and cutting it into lengths for the side panels and frames. He picked up a front rail and idly examined the dovetail joint. Dave must have cut this yesterday, he thought. He'd used a mechanical cutter, a bit like a specialised router, but with a complex jig and blades. 'Thank God I didn't have to cut it by hand,' he sighed. 'Nice result.'

'Yes, dovetails for the front rail, mortise and tenons for the frame,' Dave said as he picked up the plan drawings. 'So, did they teach you anything useful on the release day yesterday?'

'No, not really. S'pose I shouldn't say that, but I learn more when I'm here.'

Dave laughed. 'Well, let's hope you can remember how to construct a drawer then. These are going to be wide and shallow.'

'To hold large sheets of paper? Manuscripts?' For a moment he pictured Lia, Mr Santo's assistant. He recalled how she'd measured her height against a bench. Nice legs.

For the next few hours Nick immersed himself in his work. He started to relax. Thoughts of the dead girl faded. The police wouldn't be interested in him, he reasoned. He was no more important to their inquiries than a dog walker stumbling on a dismembered limb in a bin liner. It was pure chance. He'd just happened to wander beyond the walled garden. He let his breath out slowly, making a low hum and shifted his thoughts on.

'You know I've been volunteered to build a raft for the raft race,' he said as he examined a piece of wood.

'On Needham Lake?' Dave looked up as he marked off a measurement on a drawer rail.

'Hmm… and I haven't the faintest idea how to make one.'

'With anything that floats, I should think. Plastic bottles, metal drums, tractor inner tyres, polystyrene foam – you name it; it's all been done before, Nick.'

'Hmm….'

'And remember, most people just worry about the raft sinking and perch too high on it. This is a race. You don't want the crew sitting too far above the water when they're paddling. It's inefficient. Have to be able to power the thing.'

'This isn't a rally, Dave. No V8 engines, you know. Just me and three others paddling.'

Dave's eyes seemed to focus on something distant.

'Yes, paddles. You'll need paddles, not oars... and don't make it too wide.'

'Hmm....' Nick tried to imagine tubby, middle-aged Dave on a raft. 'I wonder where you get those large plastic drums from.'

'And it's important how you keep the drums together. Tell you what, Nick - we can make some preliminary sketches when we have our lunch break. Now come on, time to concentrate on these manuscript bench units again.'

By the end of the day Nick felt he'd made some head-way, not only with the manuscript drawers but also with the *Chrissie has landed us in it again* project. Dave made a detailed plan for the raft during their lunch and tea breaks, and now at least Nick had an idea of the materials he'd need to build a floating prototype. A draft announcement appealing for materials, volunteers and crew lay folded in his pocket. If Chrissie thought it OK, then he planned to smarten it up and pin it on the Academy notice board as soon as possible. He was trying to stay chilled, but he knew it wouldn't be long before the raft race was upon them. As if the totem pole wasn't bad enough, he thought.

Nick felt reasonably cheerful as he unlocked the old Ford Fiesta. He slipped an Adele disc into the CD player and selected random track order. Guess the intro, he liked to call it as he hummed to the first song and started the car. Great voice, he thought. At least with the radio off he wouldn't risk hearing the news.

Brr brr, brr brr! He pulled his mobile out of his pocket. 'Hi, Kat.' He smiled as he waited for her to speak.

'Nick? Hi. Are you finished at work yet? Not totem poling it again?' Kat's voice was even, the tone flat.

Something in her manner made him feel uneasy. 'I'm in the car and just about to drive home.' The butterfly died in his stomach. 'We are still going out for a drink tonight, aren't we? Are you OK?'

She didn't answer.

Adele's voice wove melodically in the background as *Rolling in The Deep* played on. Nick switched off the engine. 'Kat, are you still there?' He frowned.

'Yes, I'm still here.'

Nick closed his eyes. What was he supposed to say, he wondered. She was there but not speaking. She was OK but patently not all right. Was he supposed to guess what the problem was? Did she think he was telepathic? Nick sighed. He didn't know if he wanted to cope with this, not after a full day's work and certainly not before tea. His experience with Mel in Exeter had taught him to run scared of fluctuating female hormones.

He pictured Kat's toffee coloured hair. 'You're not usually like this, Kat. Come on, say what's wrong. How am I supposed to know?'

'I heard from the coach today. He thinks there's too much competition. He doesn't think I'll make Team GB for the women's 10 metre air rifle class. He says I'll have more chance if I change to the 50 metre event.' Her voice faded.

'Well, that's OK, isn't it?'

'No, it's not OK, Nick.'

'Do you want me to come round?'

CHAPTER 10

Matt closed the front door carefully, trying not to make a sound. Down the hall, the muted tones of the ten o'clock news seeped from the living room. He'd been trying to keep a low profile; going to ground, as he liked to call it. A split lip and bruised nose were a good enough reminder of Tom's last visit, and true to the best comic-strip special agents, he was in no mood to repeat the experience.

'*And now for the regional news….*'

Matt crept on, still that special agent.

'*Police have been piecing together the last movements of Anne Blink, the student found dead on Bank Holiday Saturday in the grounds of Utterly Academy in Stowmarket.*'

Matt caught his breath. He'd wanted to reach the safety of his room, but this stopped him dead in his tracks. He had to see the news item, and reached for his imaginary door-piercing night vision glasses. His fingers touched the familiar shape of his mobile. He pulled his face into the sexy sneer he'd practised. Everyone knew any half decent special agent carried his equipment disguised as a mobile phone.

'*CCTV footage shows a man approaching her outside the Sapphire nightclub on the Friday night. So far this is the last sighting of her alive.*'

Matt pushed the living room door. 'Shoot,' he murmured as he stared over the back of the sofa and past his mother's head. She grunted as she caught her breath between snores.

'*You can see on the recording; his back is to the camera,*' the commentary continued as the footage played.

'*They appear to talk for a moment. Then he walks with her to a car, half out of shot, and opens the car door for her. He doesn't get in; you can see him still on the pavement as the car drives off.*'

Matt gaped at the screen. The jeans and pink sweatshirt were the same, of course, and Anne Blink looked taller than he'd imagined, but could he be sure? The man? His stomach flipped.

'*The police are appealing for the man and the driver of the car to come forward, as they may have vital information....*'

'Shit,' he mouthed. 'That's Tom.'

Matt didn't wait to hear more. He turned on his heel and hurried to his room. It couldn't be, he reasoned. Tom was out of the country at the time. He'd only got back on the Tuesday. That was four days after the CCTV footage, and Matt had the scars to prove it.

Beep-itty-beep! *Beep-itty-beep beep*! Matt, pulse racing, grabbed his mobile and answered before it jingled again. 'Hi.'

'Matt? Glad I caught you. You're proving, what shall I say... yeah, elusive.' The voice grated.

'I've been workin', Tom.' Matt swallowed. His throat felt dry as he glanced around his bedroom. The duvet hadn't helped him last time, he remembered.

'Well, I still aint found that dog.'

'Storm?'

'Yeah, what other dog would I be talking about? They tell me Mr Dard aint amused, and Sobell aint singing. You sure that Sobell bloke's got him?'

'I don't know, Tom. It's me best guess.' Matt thought for a moment. 'How'd you know I was in? Are you watchin' me?'

'Nah, I got better things to do with me time. Now as I see it, Mr Dard'll reckon if Sobell aint got the dog, then you've got it.'

'But I aint got Storm. Honest.' Matt's voice leapt an octave.

'It'll be better for you if Mr Dard thinks it's Sobell who's holding his property. There is just something else, though. Have you seen the news this evening?'

Matt could hardly speak. The camera had only caught the back of the man, but Matt had spent most of his life watching Tom's back. Every movement, every nuance was frighteningly familiar. His heart was beating so fast he thought it might burst. 'W-w-what you s-sayin'?'

'Just wondered if you'd seen the news item about that dead girl. You know, the one they found at your academy.'

'N-n-no. W-why?'

'Well, it's your academy, thought you'd be interested. I was away at the time... remember.'

'I r-remember.'

'Good, 'cause if your memory's working OK then I can get on with telling Mr Dard's people you aint got his dog.' The line went dead.

Matt hugged his stomach and collapsed onto the bed. What the hell was going on? Why couldn't Tom just leave him alone? But then he'd always had an unkind streak, sometimes bordering on the cruel and usually with a psychological twist. Matt always assumed it was just a brother thing. He knew Storm couldn't be found, the trail would go cold and the problem would then go away. But the TV footage suggested something else. A darker side to his brother. He tried to stop his stomach somersaulting and think logically. If Tom had been away on holiday, then he couldn't have been the man approaching Anne Blink. Or could he?

Sleep didn't come easily, and by the time daylight broke, Matt was exhausted. He'd spent most of the night fighting monsters without faces, just the backs of their heads visible. He could have cheerfully turned over and slept another twelve hours, except for one thing. Tom. It would be just like him to appear. He might drop in early morning at Tumble Weed Drive to keep up the psychological pressure. Matt threw off the duvet. It was time to get up.

An hour later and Matt braked as he turned into Hepplewhites of Hadleigh. Tom would never think to pursue him while he was at work, he reckoned, and as long as he kept his mobile switched off, he'd be safe.

Matt parked his scooter on the concrete, as close to the green door into the office as he dared. He guessed it irritated Janet, and he smiled. Stowing his helmet in the under-seat compartment, he pulled out a raft race sponsorship form and ambled into the office.

'Mornin', Janet.'

She didn't look up from her computer. 'Hope you haven't parked that scooter right outside my door, Matt.'

'Me Piaggio?' He rolled the Italian across his tongue.

'Yes, your scooter. What's this?' She looked up from her screen as the sponsorship form floated from Matt's hand and down to her desk.

'Needham Raft Race. Utterly carpentry students are enterin' a raft. Thought you might like to sponsor it.'

'Will you be on the raft, Matt?' She was about to say something more, but his chest seemed to distract her.

He followed her glance and swept a plump hand over the front of his tee-shirt, smoothing the cotton fabric. He grinned. It was one of his more recent finds in a Stowmarket charity shop. 'Yeah, course I am.'

'Is that a promise?' She nodded, indicating the writing on his chest. 'Because if it is, I'll sponsor you if you reach Greenland.'

Matt frowned. 'What you sayin', Janet? Is that a pound then?'

'Yes, if you do what is says on the tee-shirt.' She narrowed her eyes as she read out, '*North Atlantic Drift*. Bit of a stretch from Needham Lake, don't you think? What's *Ocean Colour Scene*?'

'They're a band.' He was about to say their singer collected scooters, but something in Janet's eyes stopped him. 'An' it's the name of their album. So, I'll put you down for a pound, shall I, Janet?'

'You can make that two pounds,' she muttered, 'if you don't come back.'

Matt waited as Janet picked up a biro. She wrote slowly, her hand like a claw as the early morning sun caught the varnish on her nails. Blood red, like talons.

'Thanks, Janet. You're me first sponsor.'

'My pleasure.' She spoke slowly as she handed back the form. 'Now get yourself into the workshop and stop wasting my time.'

Matt grinned as he walked out into the sunshine. He didn't understand Janet. She'd declared war the first time he'd stepped into her office, and that had been months ago. There'd been countless truces and offensives since then.

Matt remembered Alan saying once that her mood depended on Mr White, the boss, but Matt didn't entirely see it. What he saw, that morning, was the first signature on his sponsorship form. Now he'd have something to show the others at the Nags Head that evening. Maybe the old bat wasn't so bad after all, he thought.

Tom, Storm, the dead girl; they all seemed from another world as he ambled alongside the converted stables. He stuffed the form into his pocket and pushed at the workshop door.

'Morning, Matt. Kill the yawn and put the kettle on.' Alan's weathered skin creased like a concertina as he smiled. 'Look lively, now. We've a couple of hours work here and then it's over to Polstead to look at a double garage. The weatherboarding needs replacing.'

Matt inwardly groaned. 'That'll be another outside job, I s'pose?'

'Of course. They're the best. Fresh air, a light breeze…. You OK lad?'

Matt shook his head. 'Not been sleeping too well.'

'Hmm, if you spent more time on the carpentry….'

'That aint fair.' Matt's voice rose. 'Been working late every evening this week on the totem pole and now this raft.'

'What raft?'

Matt pulled the paper from his pocket and silently handed over the crumpled sheet.

Alan frowned as he read it. 'I don't know, Matt. I feel more inclined to sponsor you to build the raft. That's more of a challenge than paddling it.'

'Racin' it. I'd be racin' it.'

'No, you've missed my point. The challenge for you is the hands-on practical stuff. The construction.'

Matt wasn't sure he was following Alan's meaning.

'So can I put you down for a couple of quid?'

'Make the tea, Matt. Then we'll have a chat.'

Matt hadn't expected to be having a soul-searching conversation with Alan. Not that morning, or in fact any morning. Never in his life before had someone listened, a mug of tea in their hand while he faltered through his ambitions and fears. He'd known, almost from the beginning that he wasn't suited to carpentry. For a start, he was clumsy. They'd called it dyspraxia at school. And when the complete ineptitude with his hands was added to his dislike of physical exercise, any careers advisor worth their salt should have steered him clear of carpentry.

'So what do you like doing, Matt?' Alan's tones were calm.

'Computers,' he muttered. He related to them. He felt happy when he sat in front of one. His fingers could work any keyboard and he didn't need a tool in his hand. A mouse didn't count.

'Do they run courses like, I don't know what they'd be called… computer studies?' Alan sipped his tea.

'Don't know,' Matt mumbled. But an idea had taken root.

'Well, you're still an apprentice here, so let's try once more and see if we can get you planing better. Remember to make sure the blade is good and sharp, Matt.'

•••

Matt pushed at the Nags Head door. He knew he was early but he wasn't going to risk Tumble Weed Drive, not until much later, and then only after nightfall. A heavy feeling had descended upon him, deepening his mood. It seemed to have intensified with each mile he rode his scooter nearer to Stowmarket. He imagined Tom, portrayed in comic-strip style as a spider sitting at the centre of a web, each sticky strand extending from him like a spoke from a hub. But the spider had a master. Dard. Who the hell was this Dard, Matt wondered as he pushed harder at the door.

Inside, the early Friday evening drinkers propped up the bar. Matt's pulse quickened as he scanned the room. Thank God, there wasn't any sign of Tom. He let his breath escape in a long sigh. He'd be OK. The jukebox rang out the last few chords of Bohemian Rhapsody as he reached for his mobile, switched it on and checked the time. 18:10. He caught the barman's eye and sauntered over. In true comic-strip manner, he wanted to ask for vodka, something in a shot glass. Instead he settled for a pint of lager.

He pulled up a cushion on a bench seat and sat down heavily. He reckoned he was out of the main view but could still watch the door. Stretching out his legs, Matt rested his head against the wall. He pictured the notice Nick had pinned on the notice board. It invited all students interested in crewing or building the raft to meet in the Nags Head at seven o'clock, Friday evening. Matt hoped some birds might turn up. He couldn't imagine where they'd spring from because there weren't any in the current first year carpentry, but where birds were concerned, he was ever the optimist. His mind started to drift, his eyelids felt heavy and a few moments later he'd slipped into a dreamless sleep.

Matt felt something jolt his foot.

'Hi, Matt. Hate to disturb your beauty sleep, mate, but you're starting to snore.'

Matt opened his eyes and tried to focus. The blur turned into a shape. For a moment he thought it was Tom.

'Shite!' he yelped and half leapt up. His foot caught the leg of a table. His glass tipped. Droplets of lager went into orbit.

'Christ, Matt.' Nick's voice sharpened.

'Sorry, mate. Thought you were Tom.' Matt glanced around, blinking. 'I must've–'

'Dropped off?' Nick finished for him. 'Better drink what's left of that before you knock it over again.' He turned to speak to a tall gangly student. 'Glad you could make it, Seth.'

Seth grinned and then nodded at Matt.

'Huh?' Matt reached for his glass and tipped the last few drops into his mouth.

'Is this the raft group?' A solidly built guy approached, pint in hand. 'Used to row a bit when I was a kid. I'm Andy, by the way. First year.'

'Hi,' Matt mumbled. Two new faces and they seemed to be crowding in on him. He checked his phone. 19:15. Must have crashed for an hour, he thought. 'Where's Chrissie?'

'She'll be here in a minute. You know what she's like. Always late. Come on everyone, pull up a chair. Sit down.' Nick moved the table to make more room and brushed at the droplets of lager with his hand.

While Seth and Andy gulped beer, Nick smoothed out the construction plan for the raft and laid it on the only dry bit of table. 'You OK, Matt?'

'Yeah, sure. Didn't sleep much last night, that's all. Think I might get another before we start.' Glass in hand, he headed for the bar. Last time he'd ordered a drink, the place had seemed half empty. Now he was jostled and buffeted as he tried to get the barman's attention.

Someone tapped him on the back. 'Get me one too, Matt.'

For a moment his stomach lurched. The jukebox burst into full volume. Shite, it's Tom, he thought.

'The usual ginger beer, thanks.' The voice climbed, competing with the music.

Relief washed over him as his stomach untwisted. Matt didn't need to turn around to know it was Chrissie who'd nudged him. He recognised her voice, and anyway, no one else drank ginger beer. Yuck, he thought, but smiled. He'd tasted it once. The ginger caught him like a kick in the throat while the bubbles fizzled into the back of his nose, not the fiery burning of strong alcohol, but a spicy hotness. He remembered belching afterwards. In his book it was a weird irritating brew. Just the punchy sort of thing Chrissie would drink.

Back at the table again he found her with the others, studying the plan. 'This looks really good,' she said as he handed over her glass. 'So it's a four, 55-gallon drum design with a connecting framework? Looks good.' She glanced up and smiled. 'Thanks for the drink, Matt.'

For the next hour they pored over the design, discussed the construction and touched briefly on training. No one else turned up, so there was no argument over who should be the crew members: Seth, Andy, Nick and Matt. Chrissie would take charge of the paperwork and act as a kind of organiser.

'So what are we going to call the raft team?' Chrissie asked as she drained her glass. 'And it's not going to be *North Atlantic Drifters*.' She eyed up Matt's tee-shirt.

'How about: *The Suffolk Clamp & Crampers*, or *Stowmarket Giants & Dovetails*?' Seth grinned.

'Or – *Radial-Arm Bandits*? If we're sticking with a carpentry theme.' Andy's face flushed as they all looked at him.

'*North Atlantic Drifters* gets my vote.' Nick grimaced at Matt. 'Blumfield wouldn't like that.'

'If you really wanted to annoy him, then *Cromwell's Cowboys* would probably do it.' For a moment Chrissie stared into her empty glass.

'Seth! Hi, we nearly didn't see you, sitting there.' A girl's voice rose in a sharp squeak.

Matt couldn't believe his eyes as three birds approached. The tall thin blonde had the same narrow face as Seth. She just smiled, but the one who'd spoken with the squeaky voice shot a glance around the table and then stepped forwards to give Seth a fleeting kiss. Matt hoped it meant the third girl, the square jawed bird with dark plum lipstick, was fair game.

'Hi, Ali,' Seth murmured as he let his hand drift across the squeaker's bottom. 'This is the rafting group.'

Nick inclined his head and smiled.

'We've just about sorted everything we can for today, haven't we?' Seth looked across at Chrissie, raising his eyebrows slightly.

Chrissie smiled at Ali and nodded at the tall thin blonde with a face the spitting image of Seth's. 'Let me guess - and this must be your sister?'

'Yes, sorry, I should have said. My sister Rachael, and Ali here, and....'

'Jo,' the square jawed girl mumbled and then blushed.

'Most people call me Rache,' the blonde added and glanced from Nick to Andy.

'We need to get going, Seth. We said we'd meet up with everyone at…,' Ali checked her mobile. 'In twenty minutes time.' She tugged at his arm.

'OK, OK.' He stood up. 'We'll be at Sapphs later if any of you guys are thinking of going there.'

Matt couldn't believe it. He'd only just seen the girls and now they were being spirited away. It wasn't fair. It was a disaster. 'Hey, you aint goin' are you?' He remembered the sponsorship form and dragged it from his pocket. He kept his eyes fixed on Jo as he spoke. 'Won't anyone sponsor me in the raft? Jo, how about you?'

Red blotches appeared on her neck and spread up to her cheeks. The dark plum lips cracked into a smile.

Matt attempted to curl one side of his mouth. 'Here,' he said, proffering the crumpled, grubby paper. 'Please, Jo.' He hoped he looked sexy.

She took it and a biro still lying on the raft plan. Without a word she scribbled something and then handed it back to Matt. She lowered her gaze.

Matt couldn't believe his luck. 'Thanks, Jo.'

He watched as Seth threaded his way to the door, followed by his girlfriend, his sister and Jo. Disappointment stabbed at Matt. The bird with the dark plum lipstick was leaving. She could have been his lucky date, still might be if he made it to Sapphs. He sat, mesmerised, still holding the paper. 'Hey!' he yelped as Nick plucked the form out of his hand.

Nick grinned as he read her writing. 'Well, mate. She's either sponsored you for an eleven-figure sum, or it's her phone number. Either way, you're in luck.'

For a moment Matt felt elated. 'The Sapphire,' he breathed, but in his mind's eye all he saw was a re-run of the previous evening's CCTV footage. He shivered.

'Isn't that where that student was last seen? You know, the one they found dead in the grounds,' Andy muttered.

Chrissie nodded. 'Anne Blink.'

Matt stared down at the old floorboards. The sight of them helped to blot out the memory of the girl on the CCTV. He knew he couldn't go there. Not to the Sapphire.

The sound of voices talking and laughing in the bar mingled with the jukebox and drifted around him as the mood of the evening changed. Matt hardly noticed when a few moments later Andy got up to leave. Chrissie went soon after, suddenly in a rush because she'd forgotten the time and was meant to be meeting Clive. Then Nick stood up.

Ping! The tone cut through Matt's thoughts. He reached automatically for his mobile and shook his head as he read its screen. 'What you texting me for, Nick?'

'Thought you might like to have Andy and Seth's mobile numbers. Sorry mate, but I can't stay. I'm meant to be picking Kat up after her practice session.'

Matt sat at the table alone, his glass empty and an anxious excitement eating at his insides. It was much too early to go home; Tom might be on the prowl, and apart from anything else, if the CCTV footage was to be believed, Tom might turn up outside Sapphs. No, if he wanted to avoid his brother, then he was safer sitting out the evening in the Nags Head. Pity, because he'd liked the look of Jo and she'd given him a number. That had to mean something.

CHAPTER 11

Across the landing, the shower hissed. Chrissie pulled the pillow over her head and tried to block out the day. What had the digital letters on the bright face of her alarm clock said? 05:59. She groaned. It was far too early to be getting up on a Saturday morning.

She felt warm and mellow as she listened to the heavy footfall of his naked feet. She pictured Clive, with the red tones in his auburn hair temporarily darkened by the torrent of water. It made him look older, she thought. It would be clinging to the sides of his head, hardening the lines of his face. She picked up the sounds as he moved around the bedroom, tip-toeing as he dressed. And then the pillow lifted. Light flooded around her.

'Morning, Chrissie.' He kissed the back of her neck.

She lifted one sleepy arm and coiled it around his head. Her hand rested on his recently towelled hair, still damp.

'Sorry, but I've got to leave to get there as soon as possible. Want a cup of tea?'

She rolled over to face him and opened her eyes.

'Morning. No thanks. Not awake enough.' She tried to remember why he was leaving so early. She puckered her brow. It was easier than finding the words.

'I've had a call. Body found out beyond the railway line, Stowmarket. I'll call and let you know how it's going, but I think lunch in Ipswich will be off. Lucky if it doesn't take most of the weekend.'

Chrissie groaned. 'Sounds terrible.' She stopped fighting the heaviness in her eyelids.

'You weren't joking were you, when you said you weren't an early morning person.' She heard the smile in his voice.

'It's the middle of the night.' She reached out to drag him down for a kiss, but her arms only found air. He'd already turned away to leave. She opened her mouth to speak but his footsteps were now pounding down the old staircase. 'Bye,' she called as moments later, the front door swished and then closed with a solid click. Silence settled in the air. Disappointed, Chrissie pulled the pillow over her head and drifted back into sleep.

When she finally awoke it was 08:45. She had to look twice to be sure. 'God, I've been asleep for....' Chrissie let her breath out slowly and frowned. She remembered Clive taking a call on his mobile. It must have come in with the dawn. What had he said? She'd been half dead to the world at the time. The words, body and railway line seemed to ring in her mind. Firearms? Had he mentioned firearms? The warm mellow feeling evaporated. It was no use. She'd have to get up. Her brain worked better after a cup of tea.

Chrissie pushed back the duvet and sat on the edge of the bed, allowing herself a moment to adjust. She let her feet rest on the pine floorboards, cool and refreshing to her bare skin. She stood up and slipped her nightie on. It was time to get into the day.

Downstairs, with a mug of tea cupped in her hands, Chrissie leaned against the counter and let her mind wander. Her kitchen felt reassuring; its very smallness a bastion against the universe. But sometimes Clive's way of life intruded.

Chrissie expected him to come with a history, an ex-partner or estranged wife. It turned out to be Mary. She'd married and then divorced him. She'd brought her children with her and then she'd taken them away when she left to be with another man. Clive wasn't the kids' father, but the bond had been strong and he still saw them from time to time. Chrissie coped with all that. She expected to. She even managed to handle the guilt she felt about Clive, as if she'd betrayed Bill's memory. And Clive? She felt vulnerable when she admitted it, but she was in love with him. He'd slipped more deeply into her heart than she'd ever imagined possible.

His work was another matter. She hadn't expected it to upset her. She knew it was a cruel world out there; she just didn't want to be reminded. Take this weekend, she thought. It was his turn to be acting on-call DI. They'd met up for a meal after the raft get-together at the Nags Head, and he'd stayed the night. Now, this morning she knew a body had been found. She'd heard it before the newspapers and TV channels, and no doubt she'd hear more grisly details before the day was out. She didn't want to know things like that. Not before she'd had a cup of tea. Not first thing on a Saturday morning.

It hardly took her three steps to cross the kitchen. Chrissie pulled out a chair, set her mug on the pine table and sat down. She rested her head in her hands, as if that would stop her head from bursting with all the thoughts spinning around inside. Clive's words from yesterday evening came back to her. 'Rohypnol and crystal meth. It wasn't just the combination of those two drugs, Chrissie, there were other substances.'

They'd been talking about work over a glass of wine after their meal in the White Hart, a pub serving locally sourced food in Woolpit. He'd just mentioned he'd been assigned the Anne Blink case a couple of days before, and of course she'd wanted to know more. She couldn't help her curiosity. She'd been one of the first to find the poor girl and the image of her dark snaking hair and pink sweatshirt were still as vivid as on that day.

'But isn't Rohypnol suspicious in its own right?' she'd asked.

'Well yes. I'm no expert, Chrissie, but the pathologist also mentioned Tuinal.' Clive sipped his wine. 'And alcohol, of course.'

Chrissie was puzzled. 'I don't remember any mention of Tuinal on the news or in the papers. Anyway, what is Tuinal when it's at home?'

'A barbiturate. We don't release everything to the press, you know, just enough to explain why we're investigating and why we're treating her death as suspicious.' She remembered how Clive had sat back and smiled, the creases around his eyes deepening. 'It's about supply lines. We know crystal meth is easy to get hold of. Rohypnol, less so and Tuinal is rare. That's what rang the alarm bells.'

Chrissie raised her eyebrows and then grinned.

'To be honest I wouldn't have known, but we're working with the Drug Unit on this one.' He laughed softly. 'Rix is a mine of information.'

Chrissie didn't ask who or what Rix was. She didn't want to know. 'So what do you think happened?'

A flicker crossed Clive's face before he spoke. 'Well, either she took a toxic cocktail by mistake, or someone wanted it to look that way. The CCTV footage outside the Sapphire shows her getting into a car willingly.'

Chrissie thought for a moment. 'So, she must have known the person driving the car, if she was happy to get in like that.'

'Or felt safe with the driver.'

'Like a taxi driver? Was it a taxi, then?'

Clive shook his head. 'Doesn't appear so.' There was a silence before he spoke again. 'She was already high on the crystal meth. We think she took some in the club, but we're guessing someone gave her the Rohypnol and Tuinal in the car. The pathologist found no signs of a struggle, so she probably thought they were just offering her another drink and swallowed it. They must have driven her to the Academy and when they opened the car door and let her out... off she goes, into the Academy grounds, as high a kite on the crystal meth but slowing down and compliant because of the Rohypnol... and then the barbiturate cuts in. And remember, she's a student at Utterly, so the place probably felt familiar and safe.'

Chrissie thought for a few moments as she digested what he'd said. 'There must be CCTV footage from the security cameras around the Academy. Does anything show up?'

'Not from around the buildings. The cameras don't cover the car park.' Clive gazed into his wineglass. 'And someone's still got her bag and phone. We haven't found them yet.' He looked at her for a moment. 'Why the frown?'

Chrissie felt stupid. 'Because when Nick found her and we joined him, I didn't notice anything like that. All I can picture now, if I let myself remember, is how pale and still she was. It was as if she was asleep. But I didn't register anything else. It didn't strike me as strange there wasn't a bag with her. I just didn't think about it.'

Clive reached over and squeezed her hand. 'Don't be silly, Chrissie. Why should you? Her phone could have been in her pocket. She could have been lying on her handbag. Unless you were looking to steal from her, as I said, why should you notice?'

'Because....' Chrissie felt something between despondency and failure. She expected more of herself.

Clive shook his head. 'Not an easy one, this one. Not unless we can trace the car or the man outside the Sapphire.'

Chrissie sighed. So it was all down to tracing cars again. The Land Rover in Mrs Hinton's case, and now this car for Anne Blink. It was like reaching a dead end. A full stop at the end of the line.

And that had been yesterday evening. The sound of Clive's voice was still so fresh in her mind she could replay the conversation more easily than a TV drama, but it had unsettled her. Not his voice, she loved that. It was the window he'd opened onto another world. Murky and sleazy. An underworld. How could she have ever predicted she'd be thinking about date rape drugs and barbiturates on a sunny May morning?

And then she had an idea. She opened her laptop and keyed *Tuinal* in the Google search box. It didn't take her long to discover Tuinal was no longer listed as an NHS prescription drug. It had been as good as discontinued and was largely unavailable - unless you ordered it over the internet from somewhere like Ireland or the USA.

'Oh my God,' she whispered. 'Someone must have gone to a hell of a lot of trouble to get hold of the Tuinal.

No wonder the police are suspicious.' A creepy feeling stole over her as she read on and discovered how dangerous it could be. Like all barbiturates, it could knock you out, put you in a coma and stop you breathing. This had been nothing short of murder.

Chrissie rubbed her forehead. Someone had planned this to look like a tragic accident, a student found dead after a bad trip. What could be less suspicious? The Mayday holiday weekend should have ensured Anne wasn't found for days. Time enough for the trail to go cold and no doubt confuse the toxicology and forensic results.

Chrissie shivered despite the sun streaming through her kitchen window. It was time for another mug of tea. She stood up to put the kettle on. But of course, she thought, the murderer couldn't have known about the food fair at the Academy. That's why the body had been discovered so soon. And the killer had made another mistake, as well. He'd used an unusual barbiturate in the mix. What local dealer would supply Tuinal? It was guaranteed to arouse suspicion and point a spotlight on the case. If the killer had made two mistakes, then there'd be more slip-ups and the police would get him. She needed to believe it - had to if she was to move on and get her mind away from it all.

She gazed into her back garden as she waited for the kettle to boil. Small tortoiseshell butterflies sunned themselves on weeds in the flowerbed beneath her window. Chrissie let her eyes rest on them for a moment and a sense of calm washed over her. No, she thought, forget the tea; I'll take a leisurely shower instead.

Five minutes later and she stood with closed eyes as a torrent of water beat down on her head and shoulders. It seemed to purge her of the cruel images and rinse away her troubling thoughts, so that when she finally wrapped herself in a soft towel, she felt refreshed and invigorated. Her new-found peace of mind didn't last long. She'd left her mobile on the dressing table. *Missed call*, the small screen read. *Caller – Clive*. Damn, she thought. He must have rung while I was in the shower.

She sat on the bed and pressed the callback option.

He took a while to pick up. 'Hi.' His voice was brusque, his manner distracted.

'Hi, Clive. Sorry, I missed your call. I was in the shower.' She heard a kind of blowing interference as voices spoke in the background. It was like a bubbling grumble, but too faint to distinguish the words. 'It sounds busy.'

'That's an understatement. I'm still at the scene and it's a mad house here. I wanted to call you because, well sorry, but there's no way I'll make it for lunch. This is going to take most of the weekend.' He paused and she imagined him checking his watch as he continued, 'In the shower? You really are a sleepyhead, Chrissie.'

She ignored the tease in his voice. 'You are OK, aren't you?'

'Yes, of course I'm OK. Stop worrying.' His voice faded out and then cut in again. 'The poor bugger we found isn't OK, though… well it's difficult to know what happened exactly, but it looks as if he'd been attacked by dogs. We thought we might have to shoot them if they were out of control.'

'Oh my God. And did you?'

'No, not as yet. Can't find them. We've got our Dog Unit looking for them, and they've got the armed officers with them.'

For a moment Chrissie imagined dogs with holsters and bulletproof vests. 'So, the man - is he dead?'

'Afraid so. Look, I've got to go. I'll call you this evening. Bye, Chrissie.'

'Bye,' she said as the line went dead.

Oh God, she thought as she sat on the bed. Disappointment was a bitter pill to swallow, but she could hardly pretend she was surprised the lunch date was off. She'd be lucky if she saw him again this weekend.

The attack had sounded horrific. She'd only just managed to empty her head of the drugs overdose killing and here she was, filling it again. This time with images of dog bites. For a moment she pictured savaged arms and legs, torn clothing, puncture wounds and blood. Blinking away the horror, she stared at the mobile, now lifeless in her hand. It seemed to sum up how she felt.

'Now come on,' she breathed. 'You don't know. You're letting your imagination run away with you. Now get a grip. Do something useful.' Her TR7 needed a wash and it was time she phoned her friend Sarah.

CHAPTER 12

Nick slept through his alarm and woke with a start. He felt happy. He supposed there were two main reasons. Firstly, it was the Monday release day and he'd be spending time at the Academy, which he always enjoyed. The second was more elusive and had something to do with Kat. He'd decided to try to stop himself from getting too fixed on her. There were plenty of fish in the sea, he kept telling himself, and he hoped if she sensed he thought along those lines, then maybe she wouldn't mess him about. So far, the strategy seemed to be working and after her rifle practice yesterday, they'd spent what was left of the day exploring the Ipswich waterfront together. 'It feels kind of Mediterranean,' she'd whispered in his ear.

But he didn't have time to dwell on Kate whispering in his ear. Not this morning, not now - he was running late. He dressed on the run and he grabbed a wedge of bread as he hurried through the pale blue and steel designed kitchen.

'Bye, Mum,' he called as he took the back steps in one stride.

'You were very late coming in last night, Nick. Aren't you going to have any breakfast?' His mother's voice, querulous behind him, was lost as the door swung closed.

'Not enough time,' he mumbled to himself. Sometimes living at home could be a real pain, he thought.

It didn't take him long to drive from Barking Tye. The Academy car park was almost full, but he managed to ease the old Fiesta into a space close to the bike stands. He smiled when he saw Matt's scooter amongst the mopeds and motorbikes. There was no mistaking the hound-dog brown Piaggio, but why so early? It was unusual to see him before late morning. Maybe old Blumfield was on his tail.

Nick's stomach rumbled. He could have killed for a mug of tea and a sausage roll. He reckoned if he hurried he might just catch the canteen and not be too embarrassingly late for the next teaching session.

Twenty running strides and Nick had the main entrance in his sights. Hardly pausing for breath, he was through the entrance hall and sprinting up the staircase. The canteen was almost deserted and the smell of bacon butties lingered in the air like a kiss and a promise. Nick caught the faint sound of Radio Suffolk as the presenter's voice drifted from somewhere behind the food counters. A hunched figure slumped at one of the Formica-topped tables. Nick would have recognised him anywhere.

'Hey, Matt. Should've guessed you'd be in here.' Nick smiled at his friend and then scanned the counter for the sausage rolls. 'I thought, for a moment out there, Matt's got to a teaching session before me. That's got to be a first.'

'How'd you know I'd be here?' Matt's voice sounded rough. Desiccated.

'Parked near your scooter.'

'Sheesh! Didn't think of that.' Matt straightened up and opened his eyes wider. Dark shadows stained his skin, making muddy pools out of his eye sockets. For a moment he looked almost wild.

Nick frowned. 'Are you OK? You look kind of....'

'Yeah, yeah, I'm....' Matt glanced at the floor as his voice died.

'You don't sound OK.'

'It's Tom. It aint safe, Nick. He's lookin' for me.'

'Why, for God's sake? What's happened now?'

'It's knotty.'

Nick thought for a moment. 'So you're hiding from him? Here?'

Matt nodded.

'Well, he won't get you while you're in Blumfield's teaching session, Matt. You'll be safe there.'

'But me scooter won't. If you saw it, then Tom will an' he's a spiteful sod.' Matt's voice rose, part whine, part screech.

Nick twisted his mouth into a grimace. He had to agree, Tom was a mean bastard. He'd never met him, but one look at Matt's face told him enough, and whatever was going on between the two brothers, he guessed it wasn't up for discussion. He turned his attention back to the food.

'Hey, please don't take away the last sausage roll. Could I have it and a mug of tea, please?' He spoke to a woman who'd appeared behind the service counter and was clearing the hot shelf. She seemed to hesitate.

'Please. I could starve to death. Please.' He flashed his winning smile.

'Alright then, but just this once and only for you.' She shot a glance at Matt and then smiled at Nick.

'Thanks. You've saved my life.' He rummaged in his pocket for some coins and then turning back to Matt, he continued, 'Look, I don't want to stick my nose in, or any-thing…. Is it still about that dog?'

'You heard it on the news?' A haunted look spread across Matt's face.

'No, listened to Adele's CD on the way in. Since that overdose girl, I try to avoid the news before work. Bad for my nerves.' Nick didn't use Anne Blink's name on purpose.

He felt it helped to distance her, make it less personal, less distressing.

Nick carried his mug of tea and sausage roll to the table and grinned as he sat down next to Matt. He checked his watch. 'Look we haven't much time if we're going to make Blumfield's session without getting a bollocking.'

Matt didn't speak for a moment, but ran a hand over his dark sandy hair. He seemed to struggle with himself as he whispered, 'A man was found dead on Saturday, Nick. He'd been attacked, you know, savaged by dogs, an' the thing is – it's the same bloke Tom thinks took Storm.'

'So? What's that to do with you? Unless…?' Nick watched as Matt sagged into his chair. 'Why'd Tom think this bloke took Storm?' Nick bit into his sausage roll.

''Cause I let 'im think it.'

Nick chewed at the greasy puff pastry and tried to make sense of what Matt was saying. 'I don't think I get it.'

Matt took a slow deep breath. 'See, the thing is… well it turns out the person who's dog it were, a Mr Dard, well-'

'I thought it was a stolen police dog.'

'Yeah, it were. But when Tom got back from holiday an' the dog were missin', he went mental – said a whole lot of stuff. Told me 'e should've been lookin' after it for this Dard bloke. So I reckon Dard must've nicked it from the police in the first place. And in Dard's book, it's still his property. He wants it back. That's what Tom said.' Matt stared at the Formica and traced his finger through some grains of spilled sugar. 'I let 'im think it were the bloke with the ponytail. You know, the pot grower on that walk I told you 'bout. Tom were hittin' me. I had to say summut.'

Nick gulped his tea. 'Why the hell didn't you just say the dog ran off and got handed into the police?'

Matt shook his head. 'Tom were in me face. He'd 've guessed it were me. An' now that bloke's dead, Nick. An' Dard won't have got the dog. They'll be after me next.'

'But....' A dreadful thought struck Nick. It almost caught his breath. 'You think Tom or this Dard bloke had something to do with killing the ponytail guy?' Nick watched Matt's face, trying to read his mind. 'You can't be serious, Matt. Tom's your brother, he's not a murderer. Anyway, are you even sure it's the ponytail guy, this dead man they found?'

Matt nodded silently. 'Sobell. That's the name.' His voice cracked. 'Tom knew of the ponytail guy. Called 'im Sobell, an' that's the name they said on the radio this mornin'.'

A deep sinking ache tightened on Nick's stomach. 'You, we... we can't get dragged into this Matt. You know what happened last time. That business with Tom and the fuel? It spiralled out of control, and the next thing we know, someone's trying to kill me. I nearly got burned to death. Remember? Stop Tom now, for Christ's sake. Go to the police.' Nick watched his friend's face. Fear, defeat, agreement – he couldn't tell which was going to win.

Matt lowered his gaze and went back to tracing patterns through the sugar granules on the table.

'I don't see what I can do to help. You're on your own on this one, Matt.'

'You don't know Tom. It aint that easy.' Matt pushed his hand down on the Formica and stood up. His shoulders drooped; he let his head hang. Misery seemed to ooze from every pore of his body.

'Are you coming to Blumfield's session then?

'No. I've got t'move me Piaggio before Tom gets it, an' then I'm goin' to think.'

Nick frowned. 'See you at Clegg's later, then. Totem pole duties?'

Matt pulled a face. 'Might give it a miss. Don't feel too good. Didn't sleep last night.'

Nick downed the rest of his tea in a couple of gulps and loaded his plate and mug onto the dirty crockery trolley. He caught up with Matt as he pushed through the canteen doors.

'Look mate, Tom's got a hold over you. Time you broke it.' He hurried ahead and down the stairs. 'Go to the police,' he tossed over his shoulder. 'See you.'

Nick broke into a run. If he was going to make it to Blumfield's session, then he knew he had to get a move on. But the old anxieties were starting to take hold. He didn't want to think about it too deeply, but is seemed as if Matt lurched from one drama to the next, and then it became a crisis. It wouldn't be so bad, except he always managed to drag someone else into it as well. Last time that someone had been Nick, and he wasn't going to make the same mistake again. No, he told himself, Matt had to sort this one out himself.

•••

It was the morning after the release day teaching. Nick grasped one end of a manuscript bench unit top and lifted. Two and a half metres away from him, Dave lifted the other end. It had been a mammoth task, joining the boards to make them look like one huge piece, cut from a single giant oak. They were loading the first manuscript bench unit into the van, ready to assemble at Mr Santo's manuscript conservation and restoration business. The roller shutter door was wide open and a cool breeze carried the faint scent of flowering rapeseed into the Willows workshop.

'Achoo!' Dave almost doubled up as he set the wood down for a moment.

'Careful, Dave.' Nick grinned as he watched Dave steady the unit top.

'Less lip, lad or I'll drop it on you, next time.' Dave smiled and rubbed his nose. 'If we get this into the van first and secure it along the side, then we can start loading in the sections of base unit.'

Nick glanced back at the wooden frames and unit sections stacked in the loading area. Everything marked with the number 1 would go first. The pieces labelled 2 and 3 would be transported across to Bucklesham later, after they'd assembled the first manuscript bench. Nick slowly shook his head. The dimensions of each would be two and a half by one meter when fully constructed. Too large to fit through a normal doorway and much too heavy to carry. No wonder Mr Santo wanted wheels fitted to them.

'Why are you shaking your head? Have you got a problem with it, Nick?'

'No, no. Just thinking. Once we've put them together, Mr Santo will never get them out of that repair room again, will he.'

Forty minutes later and they'd loaded the van. It had been heavy work and Nick was pleased to settle into the passenger seat as Dave eased out of the Willows yard. It didn't take long before they joined the slip road onto the A14. While Dave gripped the steering wheel and concentrated on the dual carriageway ahead, Nick started to relax. The steady movement and drone of the engine lulled him into a dreamy state of mind and his thoughts drifted back to the previous evening.

Matt hadn't shown up at the Clegg workshop to help with the totem pole after the release day teaching. To be honest, Nick hadn't been surprised. He just supposed Matt was catching up on his sleep somewhere and had gone to ground. But Chrissie was disappointed. She hadn't seen him at the Academy and assumed he was taking a day out. It was only when Nick repeated the conversation with Matt in the canteen that she'd frowned and nibbled at one of her fingernails. He'd known her long enough to recognise when she was anxious, and chewing at her nails was a sure sign.

'But Tom might have got to him by now,' she'd reasoned. 'How do we know if he's OK?'

Nick didn't have an answer. 'Look, Chrissie. We can't get involved. It didn't help last time. Matt's the one who's got to sort this out with Tom. Not us.'

'But Tom sounds dangerous. And that man was found dead. Dogs had got him.'

Nick remembered shaking his head. 'How or why should Tom have anything to do with that? I can't believe Tom would seriously harm Matt. Knock him about a bit, yes. But not injure him. He's his brother, for God's sake.' When Chrissie hadn't said anything, he'd continued, 'OK, I'll phone him.'

But that had only made things worse, because Matt never answered. And something else had niggled at him. Chrissie hadn't said much, but he couldn't help thinking she knew more about this dog related killing than she was letting on. He had to admit she'd seemed happier since going out with the DI, but much as he liked Clive, he was still a policeman. He reckoned he must have told her something.

That had been yesterday evening and Nick had coped by working on his carving and then listening to the Adele CD on the way home. He'd sung along with it, blocking out his anxieties, controlling his breathing. And now in the van he part-hummed, part-sang as a melody came back to him.

'Hey, isn't that *Rolling in The Deep*?' Dave asked as they crossed the swooping expanse of the Orwell Bridge. 'They've been playing her on the radio. Bird with a big voice. Liked the sound of her.'

'Hmm.' Nick gazed back across the estuary and the song died on his lips. 'You don't really get to see much of the water when you're up on the bridge, do you?'

'Yeah, well that concrete stops the view as well as the wind... and the jumpers.'

The rest of the journey passed with only the occasional comment and it didn't seem long before they were turning off the A14. Nick gripped his seatbelt as they accelerated out of Bucklesham. The small lanes, with their hawthorn hedges and twists and bends, brought Dave's inner rally driver bubbling to the surface. A squeal of brakes and a concealed entrance later, and he swung the van down an old farm track. A cluster of newly constructed, prefabricated buildings nestled where once there had been pigsties and milking sheds. Farm diversification must have been the name of the game, Nick thought as he steadied himself against the armrest. He supposed that just as Dave had chosen to work with Eastern European oak because of the cost, so half the British public had opted for Danish bacon. The profit may have gone out of pigs and dairy, but it looked to Nick as if someone was making good money from manuscript restoration.

'Well, that didn't take long,' Dave said as he parked the van.

Nick closed his eyes for a moment and waited for his stomach to settle. 'Is this the best entrance, do you think, Dave?'

'Don't know. You look a bit green around the gills, lad. Get some air while I go in and ask.'

Nick stepped down from the van and let the cool breeze blow away the nausea of the roller coaster journey. The scent of a flowering lilac bush caught his nose and he followed its trail around the side of the building. He found a rough brick wall joining a chain link fence. It held back overgrown shrubs to form a boundary and appeared to enclose a backyard. 'Hello,' he called as the unmistakable whiff of cigarette smoke blew in his direction.

No one answered and for a moment he thought he must have been mistaken, but then another waft carried on the air. Perhaps the smoker hadn't heard him, he thought as he walked on. A six foot gate made of heavy iron bars stood widely open, almost beckoning him through and into the yard area beyond. The bulky padlock hung unlocked and at an angle from the gate catch, like a broken hand. 'Hello,' he called again.

He moved slowly, unsure of himself. There was definitely someone out of sight and smoking, but why not answer, he wondered. 'Is this the entrance for deliveries?' He used his confident, announcing a song, kind of a voice.

Rapid footsteps echoed from behind the rough wall. They struck the concrete with sharp clicks. Staccato style. The sound got louder. Nick caught his breath. Stilettos and a pencil thin skirt met his eyes. What a pair of legs, he thought. Was it really the same girl? She seemed so much more glamorous than the last time he'd seen her.

'Lia!' He let his breath escape on her name.

She scowled as a kind of surprised disappointment flitted across her face. She took a long drag from her cigarette and then raised her eyebrows as smoke coiled into the air.

'I….' He felt his face burn.

'I know who you are. You're Nick, from Willows & Son.' She looked at him for a moment. 'What are you doing back here?'

'I-I'm…. We wondered if there was a better entrance to bring the sections of bench through, instead of using the front door. And this gate was open, so I thought it was OK to look.'

She nodded slowly. 'The gate was open because we were expecting a delivery.'

'That's OK, then.' He flashed his killer smile, but somewhere in the back of his mind he knew it wasn't so effective when his cheeks were still burning. He felt slightly foolish and he couldn't think why. She wasn't easy to read.

'No. The gates weren't open for your delivery.' She inclined her head slightly. 'You can use the front entrance door.'

He knew he was being dismissed but something made him try again. 'I could drive the van up to here so you could see how large the sections are, if you like. We didn't want to disturb your customers… but it's up to you, obviously.' He let his words linger in the breeze. He smiled again, but this time hardly moving the corners of his mouth. He watched as she took a last drag of her cigarette and then dropped it on the concrete. He tried to read her expression.

She held his gaze while she stepped on the butt and crush-twisted it with the ball of her stiletto.

'Where's the other man… Dave, I think?'

'He went inside to ask, and I came round here.'

She checked her watch. 'If you go back I'll see you inside and we can decide what's best. But I'll be a few minutes. The delivery I was expecting should be here any moment now and I need to sign for the goods.'

Nick nodded. 'See you shortly, then.' He turned slowly, but not before he'd had a chance to scan the yard. Blue plastic drums were stacked in one corner and a wire mesh cage, about one and a half metres cubed stood empty, close to the rough brick wall. Lia must have seen his expression.

'We use chemicals to clean and whiten the old paper,' she explained. 'We get through a lot of calcium hydroxide. It's safer to make sure our chemicals are secure. I can describe the process later for you, if you'd like.' She smiled and then the breeze caught and tousled her hair. She used her fingers to comb it back from her face and smiled again, but this time the smile reached her eyes.

'Thanks, I'd like that.'

Nick took his time as he wandered back to the van. He couldn't make her out. Was she irritated by him? He couldn't tell. Maybe it was the Italian in her, but there was one thing for sure, she presented a challenge.

'You're looking better, lad. Ready for some work?' Dave sat in the driving seat; window wound down and bathed in sunshine.

'I found Mr Santo's assistant, Lia, round the back. She said she'd see us inside in about five minutes. There's a back entrance, but she seemed to want us to use the front.'

Dave shrugged. 'I got the feeling they weren't expecting us so early. I said I'd wait in the van while they cleared the manuscript repair room.'

'Would it speed things up if we helped them?'

'Don't think we'd be trusted to handle the old paper, Nick.' Dave raised one plump hand for inspection. His finger nails were neatly trimmed, his skin clean but callused.

'Well, it won't be much longer,' Nick said as he watched a white Ford transit van drive past and towards the back of the building. He waited while Dave swung the driver's door open and stepped down. The sweet, heady scent of lilac, born from around the side of the building on the gentle easterly, filled the air as they strolled to the front entrance door. A seagull squawked as it flew above. All I need now, Nick thought, is a pint of Adnams and I could be in Southwold on holiday.

Once inside, the air felt cooler. A small table near the lobby was loaded with business cards and pamphlets and Nick idly picked one up as they waited. Nestling beneath the pile was a slim, leather bound book with *Visitors* stamped into the green cover. He opened it, curious to see who would write their name in such a book.

'*Anne Blink*. Shit!' The name leapt off the page. It wasn't the last entry. There were two more below. She'd written in ink, forming her letters in rounded italic so that her name stood out, almost childish in its clarity.

'Jeeze,' Nick breathed as he followed the line with his finger. '*Art & Design student, Utterly Academy*.' And in the comments, '*A fantastic assignment. Thank you, Lia.*'

Nick searched for the date. '*April 21st 2011*. Oh my God,' he whispered. 'That was just about a week before she died.' He looked up to see Dave watching him.

'Are you OK, lad?'

CHAPTER 13

Matt rummaged through his backpack. It hadn't taken him long, the previous day, to bundle everything up as he'd crept around his bedroom. 'Socks, underwear… tees,' he'd muttered as he'd lobbed them in. 'Laptop and phone charger. That should do.' It was only now, as his fingers searched into the depths of the nylon sack that he realised he'd forgotten his wash and shaving kit. 'Hackles!'

There'd been no room for his duvet, but he'd found an old, rolled up sleeping bag. It had once belonged to Tom and he guessed it wouldn't be missed. He'd managed to stuff it into the top of the backpack and then he'd ridden away on the Piaggio. He hadn't wanted to take anything of Tom's. Didn't want to be reminded of him, but he reckoned the sleeping bag would make the night more bearable, and it was years since it'd been used. It didn't even smell of him anymore.

At first he hadn't known where to hide, but inspiration struck when Nick asked if he'd be at Ron Clegg's workshop in the evening to help with the totem pole. He remembered the brick building offset from the main barn. It had once housed a small still and was now used as an additional workshop. When Ron bought the complex of old buildings to set up his business many years previously, he'd chosen to fit a toilet and basin in there. Matt had used it on the Monday evenings when he'd helped out with the carvings. He also knew where the spare key was kept. Under the circumstances, Matt decided it was a good choice. His brother would never think to look for him at the Clegg workshop.

He'd waited until it was late the previous evening and then crept in without being seen. But sleeping rough might not have been such a good idea. By Tuesday morning he felt stiff and his back ached. The old Suffolk brick floor had been cold and unforgiving.

Matt stretched and moved his neck gingerly. It clicked. He ran a hand over his face. His normally smooth skin felt rough. It had been almost twenty-four hours since he'd last shaved, and the hair, still too short to bend, stood out like sharp little bristles. 'Hackles,' he repeated and then for extra effect, 'Bugger!'

He switched on his mobile. No messages from Tom.

'Thank God,' he murmured. If he slipped on a clean tee and left for Hepplewhites now, then he'd be away before Ron arrived and avoid discovery.

Matt glanced around the small workshop. He needed to stash some of his things so they were out of sight. Table legs, pieces of wood and an assortment of broken chairs leaned against a wall. 'That'll do.' He grabbed a corner of the padded khaki fabric and zipped up the sleeping bag. It didn't take long to stuff it behind a mahogany board propped between some ancient shelves and the table legs. Without looking back, he swung the backpack over his shoulder and pushed the old wooden door. It creaked open and the early morning air struck cold through his denim jacket. He shivered. Matt knew he was in danger. Tom had always been unpredictable.

A memory flashed back as he paused in the doorway. His forearm started to burn as he recalled Tom's hands squeezing and twisting at his skin. 'Don't, Tom. Ple-e-ease,' he'd wailed as a nine-year-old. 'I'll find it. I'll put it back, Tom. Honest, I will.' But of course he couldn't. He'd taken the CD with him to school. The shiny silver surface had been irresistible and the fact that it was the latest in Tom's U2 collection had made it all the more desirable. Matt had wanted to show it off. Appear cool, like his big brother. And then he'd lost it.

'You friggin' little bugger.' Tom gripped harder.

'Y-ouch,' he'd screamed, but it hadn't stopped. Fiery pain shot up his arm as Tom applied more pressure. 'I lost it, Tom. A-a-at school.'

The agony eased as Tom let go, but the truth hadn't helped. He lashed out with his fist instead.

Matt howled. 'Don't, Tom. I didn't mean to,' and then as an afterthought he'd added, 'I'll tell Mum about your dirty mags. I know where you hide 'em.' He'd watched Tom straighten up, and for a moment he'd thought he'd be OK.

'Don't threaten me, you little shite, or I'll smash your head in.' Tom's narrowed eyes and clenched jaw had said it all. And Matt believed him. That had been over ten years ago.

He'd always known there was a dark side to Tom, and he doubted recognising him on the CCTV would hold him off for long. And that wasn't the only thing eating at Matt as he stood in the doorway of the small workshop. Somewhere deep down in his conscience, he knew Sobell would still be alive if he'd had the courage to come clean about where Storm was. The fear was bad enough but the guilt was even worse. It gnawed at his stomach, more deeply than hunger.

He took a deep breath and stepped outside. The Piaggio was parked where he'd left it the previous evening. It stood close to the back wall of the small workshop, out of view from the door and barn. Matt wiped the dew from the faux leather seat and swopped his backpack for the helmet in the stowage compartment. A moment later, the engine was running and he rode away, slowly.

•••

'What's the matter with you, Matt? It's only two o'clock and you're burnt out already.' Alan's seasoned face creased into furrows as he frowned.

Matt grunted. It was easier than trying to explain.

They were in the Hepplewhites workshop. Alan sat at a workbench while Matt set up the thickness planer. A sheet of paper lay in front of Alan. He scratched his head and scribbled a number.

'What you workin' on, Alan?'

'You remember the double garage at Polstead? Janet told me at lunchtime they'd phoned. Accepted our quote. I was just checking I'd got the amount of weatherboarding we needed right, before she puts in the order.'

Matt nodded.

'And, let me see the setting you've put on the planer.'

Matt sighed. He felt terrible. He was about to say something but a griping nausea stopped him. Emptiness filled his stomach. He couldn't understand how the stubble on his face was still growing despite having eaten nothing for breakfast. The couple of biscuits from the tin certainly didn't count as lunch.

'It seems to me you've been burning the candle at both ends. You young'uns. I don't know.'

'You've got me wrong, Alan. I-'

Beep-itty-beep! *Beep-itty-beep beep*! The ringtone cut across his voice as he pulled the mobile from his pocket.

'Keep it switched off in the workshop, Matt. You know the rules. You need to concentrate on your work.'

Matt stared at the caller ID. The ringtone stopped abruptly. 'Yeah, yeah,' he muttered as cramps squeezed at his guts.

'Are you OK? You look kind of pasty.'

'I'm… I'm….' *Ping*! Matt caught his breath.

'Oh, for God's sake answer it then. Maybe it's important.'

Matt opened the message. '*Call me*.' The text stabbed at him like a knife. He looked up to see Alan watching, eyebrows raised in faint question. 'It don't matter. It's only me brother,' he mumbled.

'Then tell him not to bother you at work, next time. Emergencies only. Now, back to the job in hand, Matt. Let me have a look before you put that wood through.'

Alan eased himself down from the work stool. He checked the gauge on the planer and then patted Matt on the shoulder. 'Should be OK. Now switch on and pass the board through.'

The ear defenders blocked out more than the droning whine from the rotating blades. They isolated him from the world. All conversation stopped. The faint vibration from the board as he fed it through the planer, seemed to sooth his stomach. He concentrated, and reduced the gauge again before turning the wood over and making another pass.

Time slipped by as Alan checked Matt's work, smiled and nodded. More wood, more planing and soon it was three o'clock. He pushed up his ear defenders and stacked the last piece of planed wood.

'Put the kettle on, Matt, and then go and ask Janet if there's another packet of biscuits cowering, sorry, hiding in the office.'

Matt took his time as he enjoyed the afternoon sun. Warmth seemed to radiate off the old wall as he ambled alongside the converted stables to the office housed in a separate building. Janet looked up from her computer screen as the door swung closed with a bang.

She frowned. 'Yes?'

Matt opened his mouth to speak, but the sound died in his throat as she held a finger in front of her pursed lips. The polished nail flashed in the sun. 'Have you looked at your face in a mirror recently, Matt?'

'No, Janet. Why?' He ran his fingers lightly along his jaw. Felt the stubble.

'Sorry, I thought it was dirt. Now, I see it's a... beard?'

Matt smiled. He reckoned she was being quite nice, so it was probably safe to ask for the biscuits. 'Janet,' he started.

'Matt,' she cut across. 'Somebody came asking for you after lunch.'

'You never said.' Surprise sharpened his voice.

'Well, I am now.'

'But who?' Matt's pulse started to race.

'I didn't ask, and he didn't say.'

'But, Janet?'

'I didn't like his tone and I didn't like the look of him. He reminded me of you, only taller, thinner and without the stain on his face.' She turned her attention back to her computer screen, as if that was the end of the matter.

'No, not Tom. Not here,' he breathed. 'What'd he want?'

'How should I know? I sent him away. Told him he wasn't to disturb you, not on our time.'

Matt stared at Janet. He was looking into the narrowed eyes of a guardian angel. For a moment he imagined her in comic-strip style, with huge breasts, knives for nails and wings neatly folded behind her back. 'Hey thanks, Janet. You aint got any biscuits 'ave you?'

She didn't answer for a moment. Matt watched her face as it mottled pink. 'No I haven't,' she hissed. 'And if you think I've got nothing better to do than take messages for you, then-'

'So Tom left a message?'

'No. I never said that.'

Matt shook his head. What was she trying to say? 'So, no biscuits then?'

'That's right, Matt. Got it in one. No biscuits. No visitors. No more of my time to waste on you. Got it?'

Matt dropped his gaze and nodded. He'd got it, all right. Tom had come looking for him. He closed his eyes for a moment, but it couldn't shut out his next thought. 'My Piaggio,' he whispered. Without waiting for her to say more, he turned to the door.

'He got angry. He called me a bitch. I said I'd call the police if he didn't leave immediately.' The words ricocheted off his back.

Matt stepped out into the sunshine. Thank God he'd left his scooter out of sight when he'd arrived early in the morning. For once he'd ridden past the concrete area outside the office and then parked behind the converted stables. Unless Tom had wandered around the site, he wouldn't have spotted the brown Piaggio nestling beneath the wisteria, the blue flowers hanging down like small waterfalls. Anxiety quickened his pace, but he needn't have worried. It was still there, like a faithful hound, and much the same colour.

CHAPTER 14

Chrissie turned out of Bildeston. She'd arranged to meet Clive at a pub on the road to Monks Eleigh. 'The Plume and Feathers,' he'd said. 'You can't miss it.' With instructions as clear as these Chrissie didn't rate her chances of arriving on time. She followed each bend in the road, expecting at any moment to come upon the old coaching inn. The bright yellow paintwork of the TR7's wedge-shaped nose seemed to blend with each passing field of rapeseed, while buttercups and cow parsley crowded the verges. She drove with the hood down, enjoying the warmth in the evening breeze.

The choice of pub was Clive's suggestion, a meeting place between his home in Lavenham and Chrissie's workplace. He'd phoned sometime after five, and sounded edgy. She knew something was wrong, but she hadn't been able to draw him out over the phone. He spoke as if he was busy and stressed. When she suggested they meet for a quick drink and early supper, he seemed to leap at the idea. She was surprised and guessed if he was driving from Ipswich, then there was no need for her to leave Ron Clegg's until six o'clock. In the event, he arrived before her.

She recognised him immediately. He'd parked where the road broadened out and a flat grassy bank ran down to a small river, slow flowing and shallow. Across the road, and offset, the Plume and Feathers sprawled, part brick, part timber frame. Clive stood, leaning with his back against his car and seemingly gazing across the water. He looked up when he heard the TR7's engine and waved.

Chrissie smiled. It was a scaled down version of a police road block, and just like him to make sure she didn't miss the pub and go sailing on past.

The bar area was friendly and they carried their drinks and a menu away from the crush and to a quiet table in the corner.

'Are you having the Thai spiced lamb?' she asked, guessing he'd choose something piquant or fiery.

'Hmm.' He nodded.

She turned her attention back to the menu. His manner told her something was wrong and it made her feel anxious. She tried to decide between the chicken and the asparagus risotto, but it was no use, she couldn't concentrate. Not until she knew what was troubling him. 'You sounded busy when you phoned. Is everything OK?' she asked.

'It's just this case; you know, the man found dead amongst his polytunnels. It was out beyond the railway line, Stowmarket.'

'The dog mauling?'

'Yes, that's the one.' Clive paused. He seemed to choose his words carefully before continuing, 'The forensic results are starting to come back and the pathologist's report came through late this afternoon. Its building up a picture and it isn't pretty.'

'So what do you think happened?'

He didn't answer for a moment. 'There were colour photographs in with the report and... well I can usually shut off. You know, distance myself. But I haven't managed to yet. Not with this one. Have you chosen what you want?'

'The *asparagus, rocket and parmesan risotto*,' she read out. 'Do we have to order at the bar?'

'I think so.'

She watched Clive as he stood up and made his way across the old flag stones, smoothed by countless feet. He wore his collar loose, no tie, and he'd clipped a pen into the breast pocket of his shirt. It was obvious he'd come straight from work. The tension still showed in the way he held his back rigid as he spoke to the barman. She caught his eye as he returned, almost bumping his head on a low beam as he dodged another drinker. He grinned back at her. Should she change the subject and distract him from this killing, she wondered. She didn't know. It was so unlike him to get phased by his cases.

'They're usually quite fast with the orders,' he said as he sat down next to her again. 'It's not that I don't want to tell you, Chrissie, but you know I can't talk completely openly about a case.' The babble of voices gently played in the background. He picked up his glass, as if to drink and then paused. 'I thought I wasn't squeamish. I thought I knew what a dog bite looked like.'

'Some teeth marks and bruises?'

He nodded. 'Yes, something like that, and some punctured skin. But this was different. Flesh had been ripped away Chrissie. And the edges were jagged, not like a knife wound.' He shook his head. 'Human flesh… it's not like a slab of raw beef that's been cleaned up at the butchers and sanitised. It bleeds. And the fat – well, it looks like bubble wrap, but solid and a kind of insipid yellow colour. On the close-ups, you can make out arteries and nerves as well as muscle'.

Chrissie didn't know what to say. She didn't think she could cope with hearing any more.

'You know how a dog bites at a rope when you're playing with it, and then pulls back, twisting its head and trying to shake you off?' Clive set his glass down on the table. 'That's what must have happened, except it wasn't rope. You could see how skin and muscle had been torn away in strands. It looked as if the poor bloke had been flayed. And bone, Chrissie. It was down to the bone in places.'

'Christ Almighty. What sort of dog can do that? There must have been more than one, surely?'

'At least two, from the tracks and measuring the bite marks. It looks as if the poor bugger tried to fight them off. We think he ran to his pickup to try and escape them. But it was a Jumbuck, more the height of a car than an off-roader, and of course, when he sat down in the driver's seat, it was easy for them to get him. He never managed to close the door. He must have kicked out but they got him by the legs. There was blood on the door lining and car seat. He was either dragged out, or fell, and then when he was on the ground, they got him by the neck and throat.'

'Oh God.' Chrissie started to feel sick.

'You don't live long after your windpipe's been bitten out. The photos were graphic.'

They didn't speak for a few minutes, each absorbed in their own thoughts. Chrissie pictured the scene: angry dogs, their eyes cruel, their pupils dilated. She imagined they'd have snarled, flashing their canines and incisors. She'd watched movies where a pack of wolves howled some-where in the distance and then moved in on their prey. They'd pause, hackles raised, ready to lunge. The camera usually racked up the tension until the victim blinked or twitched and that was enough to trigger the attack. Then the focus panned out, to a soundtrack of snarls and screams. Except what Clive had just described had been real. The post-mortem photos hadn't been tastefully edited. Clive had seen them. This had been brutal. Shocking. 'Oh my God,' she whispered and then shivered. 'Where did the dogs come from? Were they his?'

'No, he didn't keep any. Judging from the savagery, these weren't pets. Our expert thinks they'd been trained to attack and they'd almost certainly been brought along for that purpose.'

Chrissie tried to digest what Clive had just said. The implications made her blood run cold. 'So it was premeditated? But why? I mean, who would do that?'

'That's what we're trying to find out.'

Chrissie's mind went into overdrive. Whoever had brought the dogs must have been able to control them, could have called them off, but chose not to. Why? 'It's gruesome,' she whispered. She felt faintly nauseous.

'I know. It looks as if our food is about to arrive.' He smiled at one of the kitchen staff who walked towards them carrying two dishes. 'I shouldn't have said so much. Let's talk about something else, Chrissie. Otherwise, I'm not going to be able to eat my meal.'

Chrissie nodded. Under the circumstances, she was glad she'd chosen the vegetarian option.

It was later after the meal, when she was getting into her TR7, that a thought struck her. She didn't know if it was just the association of the car that jogged her memory, or whether it had taken time for the connection to bubble up from her subconscious. 'Did you say it was a Jumbuck, a Proton Jumbuck?'

Clive bent down to kiss her. 'What are you talking about, Chrissie?'

'The pickup. Did you say it was a Proton Jumbuck? They're uncommon round here and, well... there was a Jumbuck in the photos Mrs Hinton took of those hare coursers. You remember she broke her leg. I just wondered if it was the same Jumbuck. It might be important. There could be some kind of a connection.'

Clive frowned and shook his head. 'Try to stop thinking about it, Chrissie. It'll give you nightmares. I shouldn't have told you so much.'

She watched his face as his eyes took on a distant look. She guessed he was mentally leafing through the Hinton file, trying to see the photos in his mind's eye.

'I'll look out the file in the morning. Now forget about it, Chrissie and for God's sake drive this thing safely.' He closed the car door for her and stepped back as she turned the key in the ignition. He smiled and waved as she drew away, but when she looked back in her mirror, he was still standing, seemingly lost in thought.

Chrissie left the hood down on the drive home. The evening temperature was starting to drop and the cool air blew into her face and whipped up her short blonde hair. She concentrated on the road ahead. Clive's words had conjured up terrible images and her imagination added full technicolour and soundtrack. She needed to force it out of her head. She accelerated.

The corner came at her fast. She slammed her foot down hard. The tyres squealed. The rear of the car slewed sideways. She released the pressure on the brake, counter steered, then nudged the accelerator. 'Christ!' she hissed. She was round.

Forget about it. Drive this thing safely. That's what he'd said. She played Clive's words over in her mind again.

He must have guessed she'd be affected by hearing about the dog attack. No doubt he'd toned it down to spare her the worst. But why hadn't she stopped him? She could have covered her ears and said 'I can't bear it.' And then she realised, part of her had wanted to hear. Wanted to know what had happened. Did that make her a bad person?

Chrissie drove the rest of the journey home concentrating on the road. It was a relief when she finally locked her front door against the world and threw her keys on the narrow hall table. She made herself a mug of tea and carried it upstairs. 'Focus on the here and now,' she breathed. 'Think about the weekend and make plans to catch up with Sarah. Don't put the TV on. It'll probably show a wildlife programme. Something horrible, like seals catching baby penguins. Lions hunting a zebra.' She closed her eyes for a moment. 'Oh no,' she moaned. 'Just saying that's made me think about the dog mauling again.'

In the end she fell asleep, propped up against her pillow, with a Sudoku puzzle book in her hand.

Chrissie slept fitfully. Without waiting for her alarm, she got up when it was light, showered, dressed and left for work. The clock on the TR7's dashboard read a quarter to eleven in the morning. The watch on her wrist, the Omega Bill gave her to mark their fifth anniversary, read six o'clock. She forced herself to think about the day ahead. Ron hadn't given her any new projects. He'd said she must finish her carvings on the totem pole first. She reckoned old Blumfield was bound to be behind it.

Her tyres scrunched as they spat gravel on the Clegg workshop entrance track. The early morning daylight had brightened with every minute and now shafts of pale sunshine cut over the rough hedge, casting long shadows. She drove carefully, concentrating on the worst of the potholes and then parking in the deserted courtyard. Ron had given her a key to the workshop, but she rarely used it, he was normally there before her. But not this morning.

The lock turned silently. The handle was stiff and she leaned against the old door and pushed. It creaked as it swung open. She stepped into the old barn, breathing in the scents of oils and wood dust. Chrissie smiled. 'This is what I need,' she murmured, inhaling deeply again. The smells conjured up images of tables, veneers, French polish - good things. It made it more difficult to think about snarling dogs and bite marks. 'Kettle - tea first.'

Chrissie slung her soft leather bag onto a workbench and switched the kettle on. She opened a shallow drawer and ran her fingers over the handles of the carving chisels and gouges, neatly arranged by size. In the background, the kettle hissed. For the first time in nearly twelve hours, she was able to control her imagination and suppress the images. She selected the tools for John Constable's head and concentrating her thoughts on the totem pole, made a mug of tea.

'Hmm, that's better,' she murmured. The first taste soothed and the cup in her hand comforted.

A sound cut through the silence. An engine started somewhere outside. It was close by and loud. The notes were unmistakable. Two-stroke, it was definitely a low powered, two-stroke engine, she decided. Then it slowly faded. Chrissie strained to listen. Silence again.

What or who the hell was that? Her pulse quickened. Eight o'clock was her usual time to arrive at the barn, but this was over an hour earlier than normal. So, had she just heard a regular up-with-the-dawn mushroom picker leave after foraging for wild specimens in an adjoining field? Had somebody been snooping around out there? Casing the plot? She didn't know and she wasn't going outside to check. She tried to think logically; she'd heard somebody leave, so it should be OK. Whoever it was had gone. She'd tell Ron when he arrived, but until then, she'd bolt the barn workshop door, just to be on the safe side.

Feeling more secure but still on edge, she pulled a stool close to the totem pole. She focused on the carving. Ron had pointed out earlier in the week, that unless the brim of Constable's hat sloped down, water would collect and rot the wood. She picked up a chisel and applied her mind to the problem. It would be just her luck to split the wood. Perhaps she could thin the rim with sandpaper? A kind of bevelled effect. She started sanding instead.

Thirty minutes later and she'd achieved the slope. If Ron wasn't happy with it, she figured she could always drill a few holes to drain the water. As long as some joker like Matt didn't hang any corks from them, Aussie style, then she'd get away with it.

Chrissie brushed the wood dust from her hands and jeans as the familiar sound of a car approaching on the track filled the air. 'Please God, let it be Ron,' she whispered.

She listened to the engine, recognised the old van's tones. But she wasn't going to pull back the bolts until she was sure. She listed to a van door slam and then slow footsteps. The handle turned. The doorframe creaked as somebody pushed. The bolts held firm.

'You can open the door, Mrs Jax. It's me, Ron.'

She breathed out, long and slow. Relief flooded over her as she tugged at the stiff ironwork. 'Thank God it's you,

Mr Clegg.' She smiled at him as he stepped into the barn. 'I was worried that....'

He held up his hand, the knuckles enlarged and arthritic. 'It's fine. Good idea locking the door if you're here by yourself. Now, unless it's very urgent, may I suggest you tell me over a mug of tea?'

Chrissie glanced up as she switched on the kettle and dropped a tea bag into a mug. She met Ron's eyes as he watched her. Faint lines creased his forehead. 'How did you know I had something to tell you?' she asked.

'Because, Mrs Jax, this is the first time in almost a year you've arrived before me. Something must be wrong.' He paused and smiled. 'And, you've got wood dust on you. You've been working before eight.'

'Mr Clegg, I...,' and then all the pent-up emotion got the better of her. It all came pouring out, words tumbling over each other in the rush: the dog mauling, the restless night's sleep, waking early, her decision to come to work, and the sound of the two-stroke engine.

Ron sat with his customary stillness, mainly listening, occasionally prompting. 'So you think you heard a motor bike?' he asked when she finally fell silent.

'More likely a moped or a-a....'

'A scooter?'

'Yes, could be. It was close outside and then left. That's why I bolted the door.' She watched him frown, a distant look clouding his eyes.

'I think I'll call the police....' He let his voice drift away and then setting his mug down on the workbench, continued, 'Yes, Mrs Jax. That's the best thing to do. I'll phone the police. I'll ask them to come round and check. It's probably nothing to worry about, but after the trouble last year, we should get it checked out. It'll put our minds at rest.'

Chrissie nodded. It was just like him to refer to the terrorist hold-up as the trouble last year. 'Thank you, Mr Clegg. It was probably nothing and they'll think we're fussing, but thank you.'

He smiled. 'Now, I think the best thing for you is to get back to the totem pole. Get your mind fixed on work. Let's have a look at Constable.' He stood up and followed her across the workshop. She waited, watching his face for any sign of disapproval as he scrutinized her carving. 'Not bad. You've done all right, Mrs Jax. And if the worst comes to the worst, you can always drill some holes in the base of the brim.'

Chrissie glowed. She knew it looked like any bloke in a hat, but when she'd added the paintbrush, at least it would narrow the field. It would be an artist, in a hat. And Ron had been nice about it.

'Another block of wavy lines, as a spacer, and then you can tackle the seat of learning, maybe with a university crest, Mrs Jax.'

She grinned. 'I'll sharpen a few gouges, then.'

Time seemed to fly as she worked on her sharpening stone, marked the wavy design on the wood and then picked up the mallet. In the background, Ron's voice drifted through the scents of oilstone and cedar wood. She guessed he was calling the police, but she didn't listen, didn't want to be reminded of the terrorist hold-up. She'd worked hard to lay those memories to rest. It was the more recent ones she was having trouble with. Tap. Tap-tap-tap. She struck the end of her gouge. Tap-tap-tap. The sound drowned out his voice.

It was later, when they stopped for a mid-morning break that Chrissie asked the question brewing in her mind. Despite her best efforts, her thoughts had kept edging back to dogs and break-ins. 'Have you ever thought of keeping a guard dog here, Mr Clegg?'

'Not a guard dog, Mrs Jax. But I agree. Having a dog around might put off an intruder. A pet, but with all bark and no bite. And it'd be company, of course.' He shook his head slowly. 'Nothing bred to attack. Nothing with a jaw designed to inflict such ferocious savagery. That poor man. Sobell, you called him?'

'Yes, Sobell.' Chrissie tried to dismiss the image that flashed into her mind.

Ron sipped his tea. 'It's difficult to believe it could have happened. I mean, dog attacks like that are very unusual around these parts. We're in black Labrador country. The land of soft-mouthed retrievers.'

'So why did it happen, Mr Clegg. Why?' Chrissie tried to keep her voice steady.

'Well, I've been thinking about what you told me, Mrs Jax.' He paused. 'I'm not upsetting you, am I?'

'No, no. Go on, I'm fine now, really.'

'Well, if the dogs were taken along to protect their owner or as a kind of primitive weapon, the obvious question is, why not take a gun with you instead? It doesn't make sense. Not unless the dogs had some significance.'

'What do you mean, Mr Clegg? I don't think I quite follow.'

Ron spoke slowly, as if he was trying to find the right words. 'I was wondering if it could have been a message. Someone making a point. Maybe teaching Sobell a lesson?'

Chrissie frowned. 'You mean like the Mafia?'

'Something like that. The dogs may have had a special meaning. A warning to others.'

A silence hung in the air while Chrissie struggled with Ron's line of thought. 'But aren't warnings meant to be clear to everyone?'

'Yes, Mrs Jax. Or just to those in the know.'

And then something dawned. She remembered Nick telling her about his conversation with Matt in the canteen. This killing could be something to do with Tom. He'd been searching for Storm, and he thought Sobell had stolen the dog. 'Oh God,' she murmured as the implications struck home. Tom could be mixed up in this.

'Are you OK, Mrs Jax? You look….'

'I'm-'

The sound of a car driving into the courtyard cut her words short. She watched Ron glance at the scratched face of his wristwatch.

'That'll be the police,' he said.

CHAPTER 15

Nick tilted his head to catch the full strength of the sun. He closed his eyes and breathed in the heavy scent of lilac. He imagined sea lapping against a stone seawall, yachts moored nearby, Italian voices, and somewhere exotic. Somewhere in Italy.

A coil of cigarette smoke found its way up his nose and he opened his eyes. Dave sat next to him, munching on a sandwich and Lia stood in the doorway, cigarette in her hand. He smiled. 'It's a real suntrap. Thanks for letting us sit out here, Lia.'

'Yes it's nice. Beats the van,' Dave said between mouthfuls.

They were in the yard behind Mr Santo's manuscript restoration workrooms, the area protected from the outside world by a six foot barred gate, a link fence, brick walls and overgrown shrubbery. Nick thought of it as the inner sanctum.

He sighed and shaded his eyes from the sun. It had been a hard week helping Dave construct the bench frames around the units from the Willows workshop. One was complete and the second almost done. They'd tried to keep the disruption to a minimum, but inevitably Nick had to dodge between customers as he made the frequent trips back and forth to the van. He enjoyed doing most of the legwork for Dave and it wasn't long before he was reasonably familiar with the layout inside the building. But not the enclosed yard at the back. He'd sensed it was off limits.

'Why don't you come and sit down, Lia?'

He'd been intrigued from the first moment when he'd wandered around the side of the building, looking for a back entrance and been turned away. And Lia was a challenge, too.

He smiled to himself when he remembered his attempts to charm. It was like a game. Her initial frostiness slowly thawed as she'd talked about the manuscript benches and then more broadly about the business. Nothing personal. She'd given the impression she was independent and unavailable, but he couldn't be sure. After a couple of days he'd felt bold enough to ask if Dave and he could sit out at the back on their lunch break. 'Unless we'd be disturbing you,' he'd said and flashed a smile.

He flashed another smile now.

'It looks better out here now it's been cleared. The deliveries can mount up,' she said, and then glanced at a seagull, raucous and squawking as it flew overhead. 'They're big birds, aren't they?'

He watched her draw on her cigarette as he answered, 'Yes, I'd forgotten how large they are. Don't see so many in Needham Market.'

'Of course, you're inland boys.'

'Doesn't stop them when they want to crap on you,' Dave said, and laughed. He'd finished the sandwich and now looked pointedly at some blue plastic drums stacked in the wire cage by the wall. 'What've you got in those?'

'We fill them with water and then add the calcium hydroxide. We keep adding it until no more will dissolve and there's still some powder left at the bottom. Then we know it's concentrated enough.' She turned to look more directly at Nick. 'Remember, I showed you the large sinks we soak the paper in?'

'Yes and those hydroponic lamps. All part of the bleaching process.' He felt pleased he'd remembered. But he could have sworn the blue drums had been stacked in the corner, and the cage was empty when he'd snatched a glimpse on that first morning, at the beginning of the week.

'Why don't you keep them inside once you've filled them with water? I mean… they must be…,' Dave frowned as he eyed up the drums, 'at least 30 gallons? Easier to move around when they're empty.'

'We do.'

'So…,' Dave dropped his voice. 'I'm thinking raft, Nick.' He smiled and directed his next question to Lia. 'I don't suppose you've got any going spare?'

Nick watched her face. For a moment the only thing that stirred was the smoke as it spiralled up from her dying cigarette. Then she blinked, tossed the butt on the concrete and asked, 'Any what going spare?'

Nick touched Dave's arm. A kind of restraining move, a leave this to me type of touch. 'Let me explain,' he said. 'You've heard of Utterly Academy, haven't you?'

She frowned. 'Yes. We sometimes have students from their Arts and Design course for short assignments with us. Why?'

'Well, the carpentry department is entering a raft at the Needham Lake raft race this year. And we were wondering if… if you had any spare blue drums we could build into the raft?' There, he'd said it. He waited while she watched him, as if expecting him to say more.

Dave broke the silence. 'For buoyancy,' he explained.

Nick took a gulp from his bottle of water. 'I hope you don't think we're being cheeky. It was only if you had some spare, but we'd be ever so grateful, and it's for a good cause.'

Lia frowned. 'I didn't know you were... part of Utterly Academy, Nick. You said you were an apprentice with Willows.'

'I am, but I did the course at Utterly first. Now I'm on my apprenticeship, I still go back for the release days.'

'Oh, I see.' She appeared to think for a moment. 'I'll have to check with Abramo... Mr Santo, but I think we may have some.'

'Oh that would be great. Thank you, Lia.' Nick couldn't help but grin.

'How many did you have in mind?'

'Well, the original plan was four. But that would be using the 55-gallon size, and yours look smaller, so we'll have to work it out.' He turned to Dave. 'What was it? One litre of water displaced, supports...?'

'One kilogram of weight,' Dave finished for him. 'So if you work off some of your lunch, Nick, we can get away with the smaller drums. Maybe six.'

Lia laughed, a muted restrained sound. 'So where are you building this raft?'

Nick was about to answer, but then frowned. 'I'm not sure.'

'I've been thinking about that.' Dave spoke as he put the lid on his sandwich box. 'A friend I went to school with owns a farm out beyond Battisford. Before you get to Hitcham. They've got a huge farm reservoir. It would be ideal. Plenty of space to build and test it. What d'you think?'

Nick felt a surge of relief. 'Great idea. It sounds good. The rafting group meets this evening. I'll ask them. See what they say. Thanks.' He glanced at Lia and smiled. 'I think Dave's just answered your question.'

Dave stood up. 'Come on, Nick. Time to get back to work. Thanks, Lia. Do you want these chairs stacked?'

'Don't worry. Leave them. We're not expecting any deliveries for a few days.'

Nick followed Dave back into the building. They walked through the book binding room with its presses, and into the manuscript restoration workroom. The first bench unit was complete, with wheels and brakes. It stretched across the room. 'It looks magnificent,' Nick murmured.

'It'll look even better when you've varnished it. But the varnishing'll have to wait till we've got the others finished. Too much dust around and we'll probably knock into it.'

'Do you reckon it'll take all of next week, Dave?'

'Expect so. Now, let's check if this drawer unit fits in this one OK before we glue and clamp the frame.'

The rest of the afternoon was taken up with assembling, checking, then adjusting, re-assembling, and finally gluing and clamping the frame. It was hard work.

As Dave drove the van back to Needham Market, Nick thought about the evening ahead. He was meeting up with Kat after the raft get-together in the Nags Head. She wanted to see Johnny Depp; his latest film had just been released. Nick wasn't too fussed, thought he'd probably fall asleep, but if Captain Jack Sparrow was the order of the day, who was he to disagree? He could happily settle for Penelope Cruz.

'As you're not with me on Monday,' Dave said, interrupting Nick's vision of Penelope, 'you can load up the van with the pieces for the third manuscript bench. You've time when we get back to Willows. It'll make it easier for me, come Monday morning.'

'Sure. No problem.' Nick went back to imagining Penelope, but his mind soon wandered down a parallel path – Lia. And then he started thinking about what she'd said. He repeated some of it now, trying to get it straight in his head. 'Restoration, means you restore something to its original appearance, right? But conservation means?'

Dave indicated and changed lanes on the A14. 'You preserve something. Repair it to stop it deteriorating. Why do you ask?'

'I was just thinking about what Lia told me. She said when you conserve something you don't disguise what you've done. You let it show its age, its battle scars, but with restoration you conceal what you've done.' Nick thought for a moment. 'So you could say when you restore something it's a bit like faking.'

'Did Lia say that?'

'Well no, not the bit about the faking it. But that's how it strikes me.'

'Did she say which was the more valuable? Conserved or restored?'

'No. I didn't think to ask her.' Nick let his voice drift away and any misgivings he might have had were forgotten as Dave drove into the Willows yard.

'Right,' Dave said, 'let's get this next lot loaded up then.'

•••

Nick checked his watch as he arrived at the Nags Head. 'A quarter to seven,' he murmured. A quick glance around the bar showed no sign of the rafting team, so he reckoned he had plenty of time for a beer before the meeting at seven o'clock. The barman pulled a generous pint and Nick slopped Land Girl as he edged back through the drinkers. He headed for a small table and chairs, out of the way in the quieter area.

The pub started to fill and he sipped his beer, enjoying the mellow hoppy flavours while he waited for his friends. It wasn't long before Seth and Andy, and then Chrissie arrived, grinning and waving before making their way to buy their drinks at the bar.

'Where's Matt?' Chrissie asked as she set her glass down on the table. 'I've been trying to phone him, but his mobile's been switched off all day.'

Nick shrugged. 'No idea. Haven't raised a peep out of him since Monday morning.'

'So have we finally decided what we're calling ourselves?' Andy cut across, enthusiasm oozing out of every pore. 'I gather from your texts that *Radial-Arm Bandits* is the favourite.'

Seth grinned. 'Radial-arm cutting saw. *Radial-Arm Bandits*. I think it works.' He held out one long arm, bent it at the elbow, rotated it down and then swung it like a robot.

'Good. That's settled then.' Chrissie opened her mouth to say more, but fell silent as she glanced across the bar.

Nick followed her gaze. 'About time too.' He waved but Matt didn't react. He seemed frozen in the pub doorway, his eyes wide, a rabbit caught in the headlights. He cast around the bar as if searching for someone.

'Hi, over here,' Nick called.

Matt kept one hand on the door, and still didn't move. It was as if he was deaf. The door started to move, pulling away from him. He pivoted and leapt backwards. One frenzied movement, as if 12 volts had passed through him.

'Watch out!'

But it was too late. He slammed into a bloke with a full pint in his hand. Someone swung a punch. Matt crumpled to the floor. The babble of talking dwindled to a hush.

'Shit,' Nick hissed as he stood up, chair legs scraping on the wooden boards. He hurried over. 'He's sorry, mate. OK? It was an accident. Here, I'll buy you another pint. What are you drinking?' The words came in a rush.

'What the hell's going on over there?' The barman's tone mellowed as he stared at the heap on the floor. 'Oh, it's you, Matt. Having trouble with the door again, are we?'

'Yeah, stop pissing about,' someone snorted.

'Just watch where you're bloody going, next time. A pint of Greene King, thanks.'

Nick helped Matt up. 'Well, that was a close one. You nearly started a punch-up. Are you OK?'

Matt nodded. 'Tom aint here, is 'e?' The wild look returned to his eyes.

Now he was close, Nick had a chance to study Matt's face. Five days sandy growth sprouted around his jaw line and up onto his cheeks. 'It's ginger! Sorry… it's just the shock of the beard. No, I don't think Tom's here, but as I said, I've not met him before. Now go and sit with us, over there, see? I'll get you a Carlsberg and that Greene King, and don't do anything stupid till I get back. OK?'

When Nick returned Matt seemed calmer. 'I think you're going to be good on the raft, Matt,' he said as he handed over the Carlsberg. 'If you can perfect the pull-back-from-the-door technique, you know, with a paddle instead of the door handle, you're going to be electric.'

'Awesome,' Andy murmured. 'Now where are we going to build the raft?'

'Ah, I think I may have the answer.' Nick sat down and explained what Dave had suggested over their lunch break that day.

'But how do we get the raft back to Needham Lake?' Chrissie asked.

'Easy. The farm is bound to have a trailer we can borrow. Dave'll sort something out. Don't worry.'

'And materials?'

'I think I may have found some plastic drums, Chrissie. I've written down what I reckon we need.' Nick handed the list to Andy and Seth. 'You're first years. You're there all the time. See if the carpentry department can come up with any spare wood.'

'So where did you find the drums?' Chrissie sipped her ginger beer.

'At the manuscript restoration place where we're doing a job. They use lots of chemicals and they've got spare drums.'

'That's kind of them.'

'Well, it turns out they know the academy. They take students for assignments. In fact Anne Blink was there. I saw her name in the visitors' book.' As soon as he'd said the name, Nick wished he hadn't mentioned her. It was as if he'd cast a cold pall over them all. He retreated into his head, waiting for his breathing to quicken and his pulse to race, but it didn't happen. He dragged his mind back from the sadness and the dark snaking hair and hummed quietly.

Andy was the first to break the spell. 'So if we've got the materials, can we start building next weekend?'

'Good idea. Sunday's best for me. I'm singing with the band on Saturday night and there's a practice in the afternoon. So, Seth? Matt? Chrissie? Sunday OK with you?'

They all nodded in turn.

'So that's decided then.' Andy grinned.

Seth stood up, glass empty on the table. 'Well, if that's everything, I've got to go. Meant to be meeting my girlfriend. You'll text me with the address before then, right Nick?'

'Of course.'

'Aint she meetin' you here, like last time?' Matt's voice sounded thin, reedy. 'What about Rache an' Jo?'

'Afraid not, Matt. But they might come to the raft building.'

Andy swallowed the last few drops of his beer in a slow gulp. 'Great. The more the merrier. We don't really need to meet before then, do we?'

Chrissie shook her head. 'Not unless something comes up. See you two, and anyone else who wants to come, next Sunday. Bye.'

Nick looked from Chrissie to Matt. Just the three of them left, he thought. What had happened to Matt? He watched him now, sagging in his chair, even more unkempt than usual and with haunted, hungry eyes. He knew he couldn't stay long but he had to find out. A pang of unease twisted at his insides. 'So what's up?'

Matt didn't answer, just stared at the floorboards.

Nick was about to ask again, but Chrissie shot a warning glance. 'I know where you've been hiding, and you can't stay there,' she said.

Matt groaned.

'Look, I heard your scooter early this morning. You scared me witless. I thought it was all happening again – the holdup and everything. I could have died with fright. Ron called the police. They came to check the place over.'

'What?' Nick couldn't believe his ears.

'Shit, Chrissie. They'll 've found me things. The police'll be lookin' for me as well.' Matt's voice rose to a wail.

'Not quite. When Ron let the police into the small workshop, he recognised one of your tee-shirts with the sleeping bag. The *North Atlantic Drift* one. You hadn't hidden them, must have been getting careless. He worked out it could only be you and told the police it was just a pile of rags he kept for rubbing down and cleaning brushes, etcetera.'

Matt didn't speak. He just bent over, hugging his stomach and moaned.

'And the key Ron keeps in the tin on the shelf? You know the one, in case he ever gets locked in there again? Well, that was missing. You're one of the only four people who know it's there, Matt.' Chrissie looked at Nick and pulled a face. 'You can't stay there, Matt. You can't wash. You obviously haven't shaved. You're running out of clean clothes and... well, look at you. You're a mess.'

'I put on me last tee. Thought the girls might....'

'You can't go on like this, Matt. Are you still going to work?' Nick was having trouble taking it all in.

'I was, but Tom followed me. It aint safe. I waited this evenin' till you were all here. Reckoned 'e wouldn't come for me when I'm with you lot.'

'Oh God,' Nick whispered. 'This is spinning out of control.'

'If I asked Ron, would 'e let me stay?'

'No, but I may have an idea.' Chrissie frowned and then grinned.

CHAPTER 16

Matt waited in the Nags Head car park. He sat on the Piaggio, his position screened by the large waste bins. It felt safer, lingering out of view with the two-stroke engine idling quietly beneath him. A moment later and a throaty grumble ricocheted off the pub walls as Chrissie started her TR7. He slipped his white helmet on as his pulse whooshed fast in his ears. In his comic-strip book he'd be clean-shaven, square jawed, oiled and as taut as a bow string. He took a deep breath and tried not to sag. He was ready.

They'd made a plan, Chrissie, Nick and he, huddled over more beers after the raft meeting. He would ride ahead; Chrissie drive behind. She was to hang back and if Tom was following, Chrissie would see. They'd avoid the A14. The lanes would be quiet and any other car obvious.

'Hmm,' Matt murmured, 'and if 'e's followin', then I just keep ridin' an' come back to the Nags Head.' He hoped the Piaggio Zip's 49cc engine could live up to its frisky name.

Chrissie had said there was no way she'd drive back to Ron's workshop at that hour, and Nick agreed with her. Everything left there would have to stay for now. And any-way, Nick was off to meet Kat.

Matt eased out of the car park with nothing more than the clothes he was wearing. Leaning forwards, he accelerat-ed hard, urging the scooter ever faster. The engine whined and his denim jacket flapped. The air blew cold against his arms, and the speedo read 31 mph. He checked his mirrors. It was clear behind.

When he reached Woolpit, he did a circuit past the church, doubling back on himself into the centre and then back up onto the main road. The only car he met was Chrissie's, coming the other way. He pulled into the side and waited to see if anything was following her. He hoped she would have noticed if anyone was following him. Ten minutes later he parked outside No 3, Albert Cottages. He reckoned he'd made it. The Pale Rider of his comic-strip imagination had outrun the dark forces of Tom.

A few minutes later, Chrissie drew up. 'Why the hell did you double back on me? One moment I'm following you, the next I'm meeting you head on. I drove around for ages afterwards to see if everything was OK.'

Matt pulled off his helmet. 'I saw it in a film.'

'Well, it would've helped if you'd warned me first. Anyway,' and she grinned, 'it looks as if no one's followed you here. Let's get inside.'

Matt hugged his helmet as he hurried into Chrissie's narrow hallway.

'This is only temporary, Matt. You can stay one or two nights, but that's all.' She tossed the words over her shoulder as she disappeared into the kitchen.

'Thanks, Chrissie. Jeeze!' He stopped dead in his tracks.

'Now what's up?' Her disembodied voice glided across the mirror in front of him.

'J-e-eze,' he repeated more softly as he viewed the sandy growth on his face. The Pale Rider had turned into Cut-Throat Jake. He put his helmet on the hall table.

'Before you do anything else, go and take a shower,' she called. 'If you leave your clothes outside the bathroom, I'll put them in the washing machine. You can sleep in the spare room; it's more like a box room, but the bed's made up.'

•••

The evening had passed in a kind of haze. Matt remembered standing under the shower, lathering and rinsing with fancy soaps. He'd probably eaten a pizza heated from the freezer, but he couldn't be sure. Then he'd fallen into a bed with a clean duvet, and died for twelve hours.

Now he lay motionless, as consciousness slowly returned. He listened to the sounds of the house, more muted than Tumble Weed Drive and peaceful. Click!

What's that? 'Tom?!' He opened his eyes. The cold hand of fear gripped him, squeezed his innards and pressed down on his chest. 'Shit,' he whispered and strained to catch every sound as the front door rattled and swished, then clunked shut.

'Great to see you, Sarah.' Chrissie's voice drifted up the stairs.

Matt breathed again. 'Thank Christ....'

He'd met Sarah before, one of Chrissie's friends. She'd been at the firework night celebrations the previous November. Nice bird, he thought.

'Go on through. I'll make some proper coffee.'

'Ooh, wonderful. Can you do the frothy thing with the milk, again?'

The voices moved down the hall and into the living room. Matt's stomach rumbled. He threw back the duvet and swung his legs out of the bed. 'Where are me bloody clothes?' he muttered. And then he remembered. They were in the wash. He was as naked as the day he was born, except now the little rolls of fat weren't cute. He cast around for his towel, but he couldn't see it. 'Shoot.'

Matt wrapped himself in the only thing available. The duvet. He hugged it to him as he thrust each leg forwards, trailing and tripping on it. A wide stepping gait got him to the bedroom door and onto the small landing. 'Oh no,' he mumbled as he swayed at the top of the stairs. He reached for the bannister but he couldn't hold the duvet as well. Something had to give.

He sat down with a thud. 'Ouch.' 4·5 tog quilting tangled his feet. He struggled to free them but started to slide. Bump, bump, bump. Down he went, each step hammering at his bottom and back. 'No-o-o-o-o!' he cried as each thump pounded out his breath.

Chrissie ran from the living room. 'What's going on? Are you all right?'

'Good God, it's Matt, isn't it?' Sarah peered over Chrissie's shoulder. 'What's happened to your face?'

Behind him, the duvet stretched down the stairs. Matt felt winded, stupid and above all, naked. 'I couldn't find me clothes,' he wailed. He sat forwards, letting a roll of fat cover his crotch and avoiding eye contact with the girls. Then he saw his helmet. The mask of the Pale Rider. It seemed to beckon from the hall table. With his face on fire, he struggled to his feet and lunged for it.

Chrissie and Sarah jumped back. They stared, eyes like saucers as Matt stood, facing them, his helmet now clasped to his groin. His bottom burned, his back smarted. He started to sag.

'I've got a better idea,' Chrissie said and turned on her heel. Matt could have sworn she was laughing.

Sarah kept her ground. He thought her face looked kind of pink next to her sleek black hair.

'I wouldn't have missed this for the world,' she said, her voice catching. 'Now, if you don't behave yourself, I'll take a picture with my phone and post it on Facebook.'

'No, don't....'

'Here, your clothes. They're still a bit damp, I'm afraid.' Chrissie had returned and held out the partly dry bundle.

'Hey, that aint fair,' Matt wailed. 'I can't let go me helmet.'

Chrissie dropped the crumpled pile. 'Sarah and I are drinking coffee. Come through when you're decent.'

He watched them go. The tee-shirt cooled his skin and the denim felt wet. Moments later, he padded through to the living room, barefooted but dressed. He collapsed into the armchair and grinned at Chrissie and Sarah as they sat on the sofa. 'Hi.'

'And good morning to you too,' Chrissie said. 'I've explained to Sarah that we found you yesterday, living rough, hiding from your brother. I'll let you fill in the details. Coffee or tea?'

While Chrissie banged and clattered in the kitchen, making tea and toast, Matt mumbled and faltered. He kept his eyes on a knot in the old floorboards as he told Sarah why he was on the run.

'I can see how losing the dog may have upset Tom, but running away and growing a beard to escape him seems a bit extreme, surely?'

Matt's voice almost failed as he tried to explain about the dog mauling. Guilt and horror flowed over him, swirling through his head, rising high and threatening to submerge him.

'But you've no proof Tom was involved with that man's death.' Sarah tucked her hair behind her ear and reached for her coffee mug. 'It doesn't seem enough of a reason to leave your home, live rough, go native.' She sipped at the frothy milk. 'There's more you're not telling, Matt. There has to be.'

Matt stared at her. Could she see into his mind? Could she hear what he was thinking? How had she guessed? His heart crashed.

Chrissie set a tray down on the low coffee table in front of the sofa. It was loaded with hot buttered toast and a pot of damson jam. 'The farmers' market does some interesting preserves,' she said. 'But I drew the line at the elderflower and gooseberry. Now what's this about holding something back, Matt?'

He groaned. 'Tom's on the CCTV footage they showed on telly. Outside Sapphs.'

Sarah frowned. 'What are you talking about?'

Matt gaped at her. He decided she must be playing with him. 'What d'yew mean what am I talkin' about? Yew know. Yew said there wuz more.' The emotion brought the Suffolk out in him, flattening his vowels and rolling off the back of his tongue. His voice faded. He watched as Sarah turned and raised her eyebrows at Chrissie. A pang shot through him. He felt stupid. Tricked.

'Anne Blink, you're talking about Anne Blink, aren't you?' Chrissie spoke slowly, her face ashen. 'I saw that on TV, but I thought the man's face wasn't shown fully. His back was to the camera when he spoke to Anne.' She turned to Sarah. 'Anne was the student we found dead in the Academy grounds on the day of the Food Fair.' Her tone was flat.

Sarah frowned. 'So how can you be so sure it's Tom, Matt?'

'Cuz I've known 'im all m'life. I'd recognise 'im anywhere. It's Tom all right, an' he knows I know.' Matt tried to slow his words, keep his tone even. The Suffolk faded a little.

Chrissie spoke quietly. 'The police want to talk to him. If he's clean he won't mind coming forward. But you think he's involved?'

Matt hardly trusted his voice. 'Yeah,' he muttered.

'It was murder. You do know that, don't you? They found Tuinal in her blood. It's not a drug that's out there on the street.' Chrissie still looked horribly pale.

'Yeah, lethal overdose. Enough to kill an 'orse. But I didn't know which drugs.' Matt concentrated on Chrissie's face. That way Tom seemed more distant. 'It's just... it's just knowin' it was in 'im to kill. See, 'e came round an' told me to keep me mouth shut. Thought 'e'd kill me too.'

'What's Tuinal?' Sarah asked.

Chrissie started to answer. 'It's an unusual barbit-'

Matt cut across. 'I can't get me head round it. 'E's me brother. A killer.' His voice rose to a wail. 'It'll be me next. You see if it aint.'

'I still don't understand. Why should he want to kill you, Matt?' Sarah smiled and helped herself to a slice of toast. 'Thump you, yes, but kill you? No.'

''Cause he aint got the dog and Dard'll be after him. Last time 'e spoke, he thought 'e'd get Storm back. Well 'e didn't. If Dard still wants the dog, it'll be me who cops it next, see?'

'Dard?' Sarah bit into her toast. 'Who's Dard?'

Matt watched her chew. He couldn't answer; he didn't know. He shrugged. It was a hopeless, defeated movement.

Chrissie broke the silence. 'I've been thinking about something Ron Clegg said.'

''Bout me sleepin' in 'is workshop?'

'No, not about that. Well, he said plenty about that, but he also said… the way that man Sobell died smacked of something you'd imagine, well… the Mafia doing. You know, like a retribution killing. A warning to others. Theatrical.'

Matt felt his stomach twist. 'You sayin' Tom's workin' for the Mafia now?'

'Well maybe not the Mafia, but some sort of a gang. What I'm trying to say is I think this is bigger than Tom.'

'You can't be serious.' Sarah coughed as she swallowed the last of her toast. 'Now look, Chrissie, from where I'm sitting, this sounds crazy. First he slides down the stairs on a duvet, and the next moment his brother's a member of the Mafia. I think you've carved too many heads. Get Matt to talk to that nice man of yours and stop worrying about him. It all sounds, well… melodramatic.'

Matt didn't know what to say. He knew how he felt. Tom was dangerous. People had died. He appealed to Chrissie. 'What should I do?'

Chrissie opened her mouth, but it was Sarah who spoke. 'Speak to Clive. Tell him what you know and then get back to your life. Once you've told him, it's for the police to sort out, and if anything happens to you, well, they'll know it was something to do with Tom or this Dard fellow.'

'If anything happens to me?' Matt echoed.

'Nothing'll happen to you. Don't be such a drama queen. Look at you. You're making yourself ill.'

'Sarah's right about that at least, Matt. You're making yourself ill.' Chrissie spoke softly. 'And what's the alternative if you don't tell Clive?'

Matt couldn't answer.

'I'm going out with Clive tonight. I could ask him to come round a bit earlier and… what do you say Matt?'

He let his head flop forwards. He didn't know what to do. He nodded.

'Well, that's decided then.' Sarah stood up and came over to him. 'It'll be OK, Matt. Really it will.' She let her fingers brush over his shoulder. 'Now,' she said turning to Chrissie, 'if you want to do the Ring of Greens, we better get moving.'

Matt frowned. 'Ring of Greens?'

'Yes, it's open-garden season. You know, the villages: Maypole Green, Great Green, Thorpe Green, Cooks Green, Cross Green, Hightown Green and Mill Green?'

'You buy a Green ticket in one of the open-gardens and it'll get you into all the gardens on display. Or you can pay at each,' Chrissie added.

'Come on then, let's get going. Do you want to come as well?'

Matt shook his head. 'No thanks. D'you get a tulip bulb or summut if you get round 'em all?'

Matt listened to the front door slam and wandered into the kitchen. He settled at Chrissie's narrow table and opened her laptop. The screen seemed strangely reassuring as he watched the computer print re-appear and the writing spread. He wasn't being nosey, he just wanted internet access, and after the emotional roller coaster of the past hour he needed something to do. The last time he'd typed *Dard* in the Google search box, he'd drawn a blank. This time he typed in words like *London gangs, organised crime*.

'What the hell's the Clerkenwell Crime Syndicate?' he mumbled, and read on. It was recent history, but stretched back at least a decade. And at its heart there'd been family ties. 'Another pair of brothers,' he muttered. It set him thinking. There were plenty of examples of brothers setting up in crime together, blood bonds much thicker than water. Take the Krays.

Matt shook his head. Is that what Tom wanted? To drag his kid brother into a life of crime? Twisting at his ties of loyalty and family? He imagined a headline such as: *Matt Finch, internet fraud; Tom Finch, the enforcer. Together - the Finches. Yeah, they'll make you sing*. Was his mum to be the matriarch with dyed blonde hair and dark roots?

He held the image for a moment, and then it exploded, shards flying off in all directions, impaling, damaging, destroying. 'No, no,' he wailed holding his head. 'I can't, I can't do it. It aint me. ' But what was the alternative, he wondered. He had to choose a side and live with the decision. He didn't want to die.

Matt agonised through the rest of the morning and into the afternoon. By four o'clock he was exhausted. He closed his eyes and started to drift. Faces appeared: the girl with the dark snaking hair, the man with the ponytail, Tom. Their features swirled into a soup and then re-formed: Tom, with dark snaking hair; the girl, with a thin ratty ponytail; the man, with binoculars and a ruby signet ring.

Rat-at-at-at-at-at! The metallic notes sliced through Matt's dream. In an instant, he was awake, eyes wide-open, heart pounding.

Rat-at-at-at-at-at! There it went again. 'Shit,' he breathed. The sound resonated down the hall, more like a dying rattlesnake than a doorbell.

He crept up the stairs and held his breath as he peeped through the front bedroom window. He'd never looked at the top of Clive's head before, but there was no mistaking his short-cropped hair, slightly bleached by the sun. He watched as the DI stepped back from the door and glanced up at the cottage. Matt knew he'd been spotted. There was no escape, no avoiding it. Clive had seen him.

A few moments later and he'd let Clive in. Matt followed him down the hallway.

'Has Chrissie got any beers in the fridge?' he asked as he headed for the kitchen.

Matt shrugged and trailed behind. It wasn't quite the opener he'd expected.

'Like the beard, by the way. It makes you look older and your face longer.' He opened the fridge. 'We're in luck. Do you want one?'

Matt nodded.

'There's a bottle opener in the drawer behind you, Matt.' He smiled and handed out two bottles. 'See you've been reading up on the Adams brothers,' Clive murmured as he paused near Chrissie's open laptop. 'Come on, let's go and sit down. You know why I'm here, don't you?'

'Yeah, Chrissie phoned you.' His voice cracked.

They walked into the living room with their bottled beers. Matt slumped onto the sofa while Clive sat in the armchair. At first the words came hesitantly, dragged from the depths of Matt's core, but as he spoke, it became easier. Soon it all came pouring out: Storm, Sobell, Tom, Dard, the CCTV footage. He held nothing back.

'Do you have a photo of Tom we can use?'

Matt thought for a moment.

'Well, do you know where we can find him?' Clive asked.

'I always phone 'im. Never been round 'is place. Don't know where 'e lives.' Matt felt his cheeks flush. He felt stupid.

'Hmm. So we know his mobile number, his date of birth, a previous address – that would be Tumble Weed Drive. If you could give us a photo….'

'You'll find 'im on Facebook.' Matt stared at his bare toes and then wiggled them. 'I think he flew from Stansted before Easter 'cause 'e gave me Storm on Good Friday. April 22 is kind of burned on me memory.' Matt watched Clive frown.

'So, at the time the CCTV footage was shot on Friday night, he was out of the country?'

Matt shrugged. He'd thought about this a lot over the last few days. 'I think 'e must've already flown back, or maybe sneaked back secretly on the Harwich ferry. Tom's a sly bastard. May never even've gone away.'

Clive put his beer bottle on the coffee table. 'What you're suggesting, Matt, would take a lot of planning. Forward planning. And several people involved.'

'Yeah, I've been readin' 'bout organised crime. S'pose that's what they mean.'

'Hmm… seems a bit of a leap, a little far-fetched. So who's this Dard character? Any ideas?'

Matt shook his head. 'Tom's scared of 'im. That's all I know.'

'Sounds as if we need to talk to him as well. Dard may be the more difficult to find, of course, but I've got some very keen detective constables. May have to use you as bait to get to him, lay a trap.'

'What? What you sayin'? Bait? Trap?' Matt felt his voice start to rise. He looked up and caught Clive grinning.

'You're joking, yeah?'

'Maybe.'

They sat in silence for a moment. Matt couldn't hold back his next question for long. 'D'you reckon Tom's part of somethin' bigger?'

'I couldn't say. I'd need to speak to him first. So, what are your plans, Matt? You can't stay here for ever, you know that. Are you sure you can't go home?'

'Yeah, I'm too scared.'

They talked for a little longer and then Clive checked his watch. As he stood up to leave, he asked, 'Has your brother ever mentioned Hoxton?'

'No. Why? Who's Hoxton?'

'It's nothing. Just wondered, that's all.'

Matt couldn't get him to say more, but if it was nothing, why had he mentioned it? Time to get back to the computer.

CHAPTER 17

Chrissie looked at the raft sponsorship form again. Clive had written his name on the first line. Below came Sarah, Ron Clegg, a couple of neighbours, the barman from the White Hart, and the man from the garage in Needham Market. She'd got to know him through having her MG serviced at the garage, but now of course it was her TR7. She supposed there were more friends she could collar, but the list seemed short. Did these people make up the sum total of her life? It looked a bit pathetic. A few years ago, she would have enlisted her accountant colleagues and everyone in the firm in Ipswich. But a lot of things had changed since Bill had died.

'You seem very thoughtful, Mrs Jax.' Ron sat on his work stool, sipping his mug of tea.

'Well, I don't seem to have collected many names on this sponsorship form, Mr Clegg.'

'For the raft race? Have you got Oliver Blumfield to sign up?'

'Good idea. I'd forgotten him, Mr Clegg. Let's hope one of the first years hasn't got to him already.' Chrissie glanced over at the pedestal table, now standing in splendid repair. 'Do you think it'd be OK if I asked the Hintons to sign up?' The veneers glowed with the patina born of many hours of layering polish over a water-resistant sealer. The design of flowers and leaves curled and looped across its surface. Even from where Chrissie sat, the green-dyed sycamore veneer stood out, making the leaves come alive.

'It's magnificent, Mr Clegg.'

He nodded slowly. 'I hope Mrs Hinton'll be pleased. Mr Hinton said he'd be over this way today and he'd collect it sometime this morning.' Ron checked his watch. 'It's a difficult one, but I don't think it's a good idea to ask customers to sponsor you, Mrs Jax.'

'Hmm.' She supposed Ron was right, but it was tempting. What she really needed was an excuse to speak to the Hintons. She wanted to know if there'd been any developments in finding the hare coursers. Clive had refused to talk about it over the weekend. He said he'd already spent an hour or so with Matt that afternoon and now it was time to relax. As it was, he currently devoted most of his time to thinking, breathing and talking police business, and sometimes when he wasn't working, he needed a break from it. And then he kissed her, so she'd let the matter rest.

'How about doing some turning, Mrs Jax? You could do Constable's paintbrush for the totem pole, and then some spindles for the Windsor chair we've got to repair.'

Chrissie grinned. She enjoyed using the woodturning lathe. 'Great, I'll measure up the dimensions against the totem pole and draw out the design. Does it matter which piece of wood I use, Mr Clegg?'

'Not for the paintbrush, as long as the grain is running in the right direction. Show me your drawings when you're ready and we can see what we've got lying around.'

It didn't take Chrissie long to work out she'd need the paintbrush to measure at least fifty centimetres. That is if it was to be secured in the wavy waterlines beneath Constable's head. It could then pass upwards at an angle, crossing his face. She wanted it to stick out to one side. Her problem was how to get the angle right so that it passed in front of the slightly wonky eye she'd carved but also miss the brim of his hat. Perhaps she could drill a hole in the brim and pass the paintbrush through? She tried to picture it. Yes, she thought, problem solved. The paintbrush would be fixed at both ends, water could drain through the hole and stop the brim rotting, and she could tick the box for artistic license.

Her thoughts were disturbed by the sound of a car driving slowly up Ron's bone-breaker of a track. 'Mr Hinton?'

'I expect so, Mrs Jax.' He straightened up with a hand to his back. She could see he'd been working on the Windsor chair. He'd previously glued and splinted its broken hoop and now he was making cuts into the wood above and below the glue line. The wood was relatively flimsy but had to take a lot of stress, so the repair was complex and multi-stage. He'd tried to explain, but she'd been too keen to get started on the paintbrush to completely follow the plan.

A car door slammed. A few moments later the barn door opened, hinges creaking as sunlight flooded in.

'Good morning, Mr Hinton.' Chrissie smiled as she spoke.

'Morning.' He stood in the doorway and nodded a greeting. 'It's a lovely spot you've got out here, Ron.' He stepped onto the cool concrete floor and glanced around the barn, as if searching for something. He stopped when he saw the pedestal table standing near a workbench. 'It's…,' he caught his breath and moved towards it. 'It's hardly recognisable. It is my table, isn't it?' He ran his hand over the polished surface. 'Beautiful. Thank you, Ron. It's wonderful workmanship, wonderful. My wife will be thrilled.'

'And how is Mrs Hinton?' Ron asked quietly.

'She's getting about much better now. The plaster came off last week, so she's more comfortable. It's been lovely sitting out in the garden in this hot weather, but not when your leg's in a cast. Hot and itchy.'

'Did the police ever catch those hare coursers?' Chrissie kept her tone even, trying to appear almost disinterested.

Mr Hinton paused and frowned. 'Do you know, we didn't hear a word from the police for almost six weeks, and then yesterday, Monday, they were back all over us like a rash. More questions for us. More "Can you describe the coursers?" They were querying how many people were there and the makes of their cars. They even wanted to download all my wife's photos from her camera. And then they asked her to look at some mug shots.'

'I thought they'd already done all that when you first reported the incident,' Ron murmured.

'I know. It makes you wonder if the police were taking it seriously the first time round.' Mr Hinton ran his hand over the table. 'Six weeks ago they seemed to think an image showing a number plate was sufficient. That's all they wanted.' He laughed quietly, a humourless sound. 'My wife is a typical photographer. She's proud of her work, so originally she only picked the best photos for them. This time they wanted everything, even the blurry rejects.' He shook his head. 'I think they're looking for something specific now.'

'Like what? What sort of thing?' Chrissie couldn't help her voice rising.

'I don't know, they wouldn't say. But my wife recognised one, maybe two of the men in the mug shots.'

'A couple? She identified more than one of the mug shots?' Chrissie bit her tongue. She'd guessed one would be Sobell. 'Sorry, Mr Hinton. It just makes it sound a bit frightening. If the police've got them on their files, they could be hardened criminals.'

'Thank you, Chrissie. That's... very reassuring. Now, Mr Hinton, do you need any help getting the table into your car?'

'No, no, Mr Clegg,' she blurted before Mr Hinton had a chance to speak. 'I meant... what I was trying to say was, they may be getting closer to making an arrest. That's all.' She felt her cheeks burn. 'I didn't mean to be insensitive. I should have said professional. Professional criminals.'

'Don't worry, my wife's called them much worse, I assure you. It's a bit like photography – use a different filter and you change the feel. Use a different word and... it's called spin. No, they're thugs, bullies and bastards, plain and simple.'

Chrissie smiled, her face still on fire. The Hintons were nice people; they didn't deserve to be at the sharp end, like this. 'I'll take one side of the table, Mr Hinton. If you lift the other side, it'll be as light as a feather.'

Chrissie gripped the edge of the table top and stepped backwards. Mr Hinton held the other side and walked facing her, his stride twice as long as hers. They did a kind of two-step-shuffle out through the workshop and to his car parked in the courtyard. 'Did Mrs Hinton find it difficult getting up into your Range Rover when her leg was in plaster?' She gazed at the large tyres as he opened up the back.

'Yes, it was like trying to get the Queen Mary up through a flight of lock gates. A lot of shouting of instructions and waving of arms, but ultimately impossible I'm sorry to say.'

'Oh dear. Poor Mrs Hinton. I was just looking at your tyres.'

'Oh no, have I got a puncture?'

'No, no. It just reminded me of the Land Rover with the false number plates. On the photos your wife gave me, you could see accessorised tyre valve caps. One of my friends noticed. He's a bit of a techy. What sort of person fits those, do you think?'

'Well, as you can see, not someone like me. I didn't even know they made them.'

'Hmm, you could imagine the coursers might change the number plates again, maybe even re-spray, but I bet no one'll think to change the tyre valve caps.' Chrissie spoke as the thoughts sped through her mind. 'Sorry,' she murmured as she realised Mr Hinton was staring at her.

'No, no, not at all. It's just you've said something that... well, if they stay local, we may get them yet. Trouble is, at this time of year the hare coursing should be coming to an end.' He shook his head slowly. 'Of course, that's a good thing, unless we're trying to catch the bastards red-handed. Do you think the police know about the tyre valve caps?'

'God knows. Come on, let's get this table up into your car. You could always ask them of course. The police, I mean.' Chrissie stood and watched as Mr Hinton slammed the rear door shut, reversed into a three-point turn and then slowly swept out of the courtyard. The huge tyres almost growled as they crunched through potholes and spattered stones on the rough entrance track. Ron was right, she thought. It wouldn't have been the moment to tout for sponsorship.

CHAPTER 18

Nick gazed out of the van's side window as acre upon acre of rapeseed flew past. The shock of yellow flowers was starting to fade. It wouldn't be long before millions of tiny seed cases reached out to the sun, ripening into shades of brown and black.

'You're looking a bit green again, lad.' Dave veered into the nearside lane and then swerved off the A14 at the Bucklesham turning. 'I expect you get seasick as well, don't you?' He took the roundabout at speed and accelerated away, swinging Nick against the seat belt and his head into the rest. 'You do realise spewing up'll bugger your raft race? Had you thought about that when you're on this raft?'

Nick swallowed back some bile. 'I expect even you'd feel queasy travelling at sixty nautical miles an hour and then rocketing off a motorway and into a whirlpool.'

Dave frowned as he slowed for a corner. 'The farm reservoir is hardly a whirlpool, Nick. Sixty nautical…?' The words drifted away as open road beckoned ahead. He put his foot to the floor.

Nick closed his eyes and tried to think of something to distract from the increasing nausea. 'Is your farmer friend OK about us coming over on Sunday and making a start on building the raft?' he asked.

'Yes, that's all sorted. Thanks for texting me after your raft meeting, by the way. I think the reservoir's going to work out well. You know, today may be a good day to collect those drums. There's room in the van. By the end of the week we should've finished those manuscript benches and be packing up. The van'll be up to the gunwales, pardon the nautical expression, with the tools and leftover wood, etcetera.'

'Hmm.' Nick closed his mouth as the van swayed to the right. His stomach lurched. He needed to concentrate on something, anything. He ran through the list he'd given Seth and Andy. Twine, cord, rope; he'd forgotten to add them to the list. Hell, how could he be so stupid? His stomach lurched again, and this time he really thought he'd vomit.

'Now you've gone all pasty. Are you sure you're OK, Nick?'

'Forgot about rope,' he muttered through gritted teeth.

'There's a big chandlery, this side of Ipswich. That's if you wanted marine grade. Mind you, I don't think open sea's for you. Stay inland.'

Nick didn't answer. Instead he listened to the engine noise deepen and the revs slow as Dave slipped into a lower gear. Thank God, he thought, as the van turned onto the old farm track. 'Nearly there,' he breathed, thankful the journey would soon be over.

Dave drew up slowly, almost drifting to a stop in front of Mr Santo's long low building. 'There, never let it be said I don't consider my passengers.'

They were early, just before nine in the morning. Nick opened the van door and jumped down onto the concrete. It was still cool, almost grey with a hazy sky.

'The forecast said it'd be a scorcher, later today.' Dave's voice followed him from the driver's seat.

Nick raised his hand in answer as he started to walk. He wasn't going to make the mistake of wandering into the back courtyard uninvited again. Instead he headed across the front of the building and towards the entrance track. It was hardly a track, he thought as he gazed at the gravelled tarmac meandering into the distance. There were two other prefabricated business units nearby, part of the cluster of new buildings, but far enough away to give a feeling of privacy. He could just about see the corrugated metal of some distant warehouse-sized barns, their outline softened by the haze in the air. Farm machinery, fields, agriculture – they all seemed to be on such a huge scale. He sighed. At least the queasiness was starting to settle. He turned and began to walk back to the van.

At first he hardly noticed the throaty rumble behind. The sound was distant, barely audible, but as it neared, a swishing crunching of tyres added more tones. He couldn't help himself, he had to look.

'Wow.' All traces of nausea evaporated as he watched a sleek black Audi R8 glide up the track and head to one of the two other buildings in the complex. He tried not to stare, but it wasn't every day he saw a mid-engine supercar. The air vents were part way along its body. They looked like gills, as if for a living breathing creature. The smoked glass windscreen obscured the driver and Nick waited for a moment as it slowed to a halt. If it had parked outside Mr Santo's building he'd have had an excuse to look at it more closely. 'Pity,' he murmured.

He started to amble back, imagining how it would feel to drive something like that. Behind him footsteps clipped on the concrete. He decided not to turn around; he'd done enough gaping. After all, he had some pride. And then he heard the familiar voice.

'Morning, Nick.'

He spun around. 'Lia! Where did you come from?' The ink-black shape of the Audi rested fifty yards away.

Dormant. 'Is that… is that your car?' He felt the rush of blood to his face as he realised how rude he must sound.

'Sorry, I mean….'

Lia followed the direction of his gaze. 'The Audi? You must be joking.' They both watched it slowly draw away and glide back up the track.

'Beautiful,' Nick breathed. 'So how did you get here, then?'

'The Audi.' The words were soft, hardly audible.

Nick frowned. 'So why not drive up to Mr Santo's building? Why drop you off over there and make you walk?'

Lia smiled. She seemed amused by his reaction. 'My friend hasn't been here before. He didn't know which unit I work in. And then I thought – why not walk? It'll do me good.'

He, Nick wondered? They walked on in silence. So was *he* her boyfriend? A boyfriend who drove a supercar? Was she glamorous enough? And then he smiled. There was nothing like a politically incorrect thought to make you feel better.

'The manuscript benches are coming along well. Mr Santo's very pleased with your work.' She glanced up at Nick, her heels tapping a beat with each stride. 'Very pleased.'

'That's nice. Thank you. Is he still happy for us to take some of those plastic drums?'

'Of course, but I'm not sure exactly how many we'll have until the end of the week. There should be enough for you though.' They'd almost got back to the van and Lia let her voice trail away as Dave stepped down from the driver's seat. 'Morning, Dave,' she called.

Dave raised his hand in a kind of salute.

'So can we take some today, Lia?' Nick asked. 'We may not have room in the van by Friday.'

'Of course, Nick. Now, if you'll excuse me, I'll go and unlock and open up.'

He watched as she left him. Her black trousers seemed to both hug at the hips and flap around her legs as she walked. Nick started counting. 'One, two, th-'

'Did you see that Audi R8?' Dave hissed as he opened up the back of the van.

'Th-three. Yes.'

'Three? What are you talking about, Nick?'

'It took you less than three seconds to mention the Audi. You're slowing up, Dave.'

'Cheeky bugger! I s'pose that means you're feeling better. Come on, get the tool boxes out.'

There was still a lot of work to do, and they both knew they had to keep the pace up. Nick hoped it would get easier. This was after all the third and last manuscript bench, but when Dave was in a jovial mood, he talked. And today it was about the Audi and then Lamborghini. Between a critique on the subtleties of the Audi's all-wheel drive and a lecture on the advantages of frame-and-panel versus solid wood construction, Nick found his mind wandering. He was intrigued, not so much by the car but by Lia herself. He ran through her qualities. She seemed: quiet, peaceful, knowledgeable, and yes that was the word, generous. She was also unfathomable and attractive.

By mid-afternoon they had reassembled the frame, with the side panels for the second time. They'd shaved a few more millimetres off one of the tenons on the bottom rail. 'That's a better fit,' Dave muttered. 'Now let's see if we can get it glued up.'

Nick used the wooden mallet to help ease the sections of the frame apart. He placed them in some kind of order while Dave squeezed trails of white PVA glue into mortise cavities and onto tenon surfaces. At least no glue was required for the side panels. The grooves would hold them and allow for movement in the wood. Then it was a race against time as they reassembled the frame, clamping it and wiping away the excess glue with handfuls of soft, blue paper towel.

'We'll leave that overnight. Not much more we can do with it till tomorrow, Nick. You might as well start doing a final sanding down on those two other benches so they'll be ready for the varnish.'

Nick had already used the orbital sander on the bench tops when they were still in the Willows workshop, so now it was time for fine grade sandpaper over a wooden block and some good old-fashioned elbow grease. It was tiring work and the time flew. He looked up as Lia walked into the manuscript repair room.

'There are a couple of drums out in the courtyard, Nick. Blue. They're stacked by the wall. You can take them now if you like.' Lia moved to one of the completed benches and leaned against it, her face serious as she watched him.

'Oh thanks, Lia. That's really kind.' Nick glanced at her long legs. 'I think we got the height OK for you, yes?' He checked his watch. It was time to start tidying up.

She nodded. 'There'll be more drums as the week goes on.' She smiled. 'Do you think you'll win?'

'Win? The race? That would be nice.'

'You bet,' Dave added.

She followed Nick out into the rear courtyard and lit a cigarette. The drums hadn't appeared overly large when stacked, but one look at Lia and Nick decided it would take him two journeys. 'Do you visit Italy, at all?' Nick asked as he grasped the first drum.

'Mr Santo goes back to buy manuscripts, sell at auctions, that sort of thing. Sometimes I accompany him. Why? Have you been?'

'The nearest I've got to Italy is the Ipswich waterfront.'

'Then you should definitely go one day. It's beautiful. If you like the water, then you should go to Venice or Lake Como. And if you like cities, then Florence or Rome.' She looked beyond him as she spoke, a kind of wistful quality to her voice.

Nick didn't waste any time getting the first drum into the van. He hoped to catch her before she'd finished her cigarette, but he needn't have worried. He found her exactly where he'd left her, the only movement being a wisp of smoke coiling into the air. 'Last one,' he said lifting the second drum. 'Are you Italian? I mean. Lia is an Italian name, isn't it?'

'Yes, it's short for Amalia.' She stood up and dropped her cigarette. It smouldered on the ground. 'Better get that loaded.' She watched him as he carried the drum away.

It only took a few minutes to tidy up the manuscript room and pack the tool boxes in the van. Nick closed the passenger door, and reached for his seat belt as Dave pressed the ignition. He tried to relax. He thought it might make the roller coaster ride back to Needham Market a little easier.

Nick smiled at Kat. 'I'm really pleased you've come with me, thanks.' It hadn't taken them long to reach the first of the Ipswich turnings off the A14.

'Yes, for once it's worked out quite well for us. You've got your band practice this afternoon while I've got a session with my shooting coach. So, this morning we're both free.' She brushed his arm lightly with her fingers. 'Now, where did Dave say this place was?'

'Badgers Mariner? Not this exit. We take the first one after the A12 junction.' Nick had been looking forward to the trip. He knew how much Kat enjoyed walking along the Ipswich waterfront, and it was an excuse to take her somewhere similar. 'If it's too pricey, we can buy the rope somewhere else,' he said as the old Ford Fiesta's engine droned in the background. He remembered how disappointed he'd felt when Lia told him the last two drums wouldn't be available until Saturday. Then he'd thought, why not combine the trips? And *hey presto*, it had the makings of a great morning out with Kat.

'I'm looking forward to this,' Kat said as they sped under the A12 roundabout junction.

A couple of miles later they turned off the dual carriageway and headed for Ipswich. The road swooped down a hill towards Ostrich Creek and the River Orwell. As they got closer, Nick saw bare masts pointing high above tall wooden paling. 'That has to be the marina.' He followed a road skirting the Orwell, and sure enough, within a few hundred yards he read, *Badgers Marina and Chandlery*. It was written in bold lettering on a large notice and the entrance was bounded by chain link fencing. He drove in slowly, suddenly awed by the sight of a sailing boat standing out of the water, supported on a frame and with its keel and rudder exposed.

Once inside the chandlery, it was easy to find the rope section. Every type, thickness and colour imaginable was racked on huge reels along one wall.

'Well, you should be able to find something here,' Kat murmured. 'I rather like that one with the red fleck in it… or maybe the blue?'

'Can I help?' An assistant approached. He smiled while they explained what they needed. 'A raft? So the rope is to hold the drums to the body of the raft?'

Nick described the design.

'So you think five, maybe six drums? And they're each about a thirty gallon size. You'll need a fair length of rope.'

Nick listened as the man talked him through thickness and length. 'And the price per metre?' It didn't sound too bad until he multiplied it by the number of metres.

'I don't suppose you could do a better price for us?' Kat pulled a sponsorship form out of her handbag. 'It is for charity, the Needham Lake raft race. You'd be supporting a good cause. I hope you don't think I'm being cheeky, but,' she smiled and unfolded the paper, 'we've only got a few weeks left before the race and we need to get building it.'

Nick couldn't believe her boldness. She looked amazing; her long toffee coloured hair, normally a riot of curls, was held back in a loose plait. Her pale hazel eyes exuded a kind of honest hopefulness, as if from a rating to an old seadog. He braced himself for the embarrassment of the rebuff.

'Well,' the man said, 'I'm sure we can do something.'

'Really?' Nick tried to hide the surprise in his voice, but it must have been obvious. The man laughed.

'Come on, let's work out exactly how much you need... and I think we can stretch to a 30% discount. You don't want fancy rope with a red fleck. This will do the job for you just as well.' He unrolled some of the white nylon they'd been looking at.

Ten minutes later, Kat stood next to the Fiesta and waited as Nick unlocked the car. He glanced over his shoulder and upwards in the direction of her gaze. 'The Orwell Bridge is awesome from here,' he said. 'We have to go back up the hill and onto the A14 if we want to cross.' And then he realised something. This was a well-kept secret; you could only sense the true power and elegance of the bridge from almost water level, and close to.

'Can you remember all he said?' Kat kept her eyes on the bridge as she spoke.

Nick settled into the driver's seat and leaned across to open her door. 'Kind of. It was quite useful, those tips about tying the drums on. He lost me on the knots, I'm afraid.'

'Nice place,' Kat said as she did up her seat belt and pushed an empty bottle of water from under her foot.

The drive to Bucklesham didn't take them long and for once Nick didn't feel carsick as he turned up the entrance track to the small complex of business units. 'It's in the middle of nowhere,' he sighed. 'You must come in, Kat. It's a really amazing place. Lia might show you around if she isn't busy.'

Kat followed him into the main entrance lobby. The air felt cool and the faint sound of Puccini's *Nessun Dorma* drifted from somewhere deeper in the building. 'She's probably working on something. Come on, Kat. I'll show you the manuscript benches, and then we'll go and find her.' He led the way into the manuscript repair room. The three benches straddled the space like an ancient refectory. The tight grain of their oak tops almost glowed with a deep sheen. 'It's incredible how good they look after just one coat of varnish.'

Nick walked around the benches, pointing out the various features. 'The bench tops stick out a little so it's easier to sit at them on a work stool.' He bent to point out the units in the bases. 'And see, we made the drawers especially wide and shallow to take manuscript paper. And shelves, look.' He flapped his hand. 'The manuscript benches are on wheels so they can be moved. You can even push them together, side-by-side or end-on. You can create any shape you want, depending on what's being worked on.'

'They're wonderful. We're very pleased with them.'

Nick spun around. He hadn't expected to hear Lia's voice 'Hi. I've popped in to collect the last two drums and… I hope you don't mind but I couldn't resist showing Kat what I've been working on for the last few weeks.'

'Of course, that's fine.' She smiled at Kat. 'Are you from Utterly Academy as well?'

'No, I only met Nick once he'd started his apprenticeship. He often talks about the Academy so I almost feel as if I went there as well. Does that count?'

Lia smiled. 'If you come this way….' She led them out of the manuscript repair room and though to a small kitchenette off to the side of the wet room. 'We wash and dry the manuscripts in there, Kat, but if you don't mind I was working on something in here and I can't leave it. It needs constant stirring.'

Nick noticed a small plastic tub. Its lid was on the counter, and close by, there were traces of white powder. Some liquid in a pan boiled on a small electric ring. 'What are you doing, Lia?'

'Making glue. Why, what did you think I was doing?'

'I-I don't know.'

Kat peered into the pan. 'It looks gloopy, like porridge.'

'You're almost right. We use purified wheat starch to make the glue, but hopefully not lumpy, like porridge. It has to be boiled first and then it turns into a kind of paste. I do this every week because it tends to go mouldy so quickly. I'd just put that pan on when I heard you arrive, and I need to watch this and stir. So, if you....'

'Collect the drums from the rear courtyard,' Nick finished for her. He didn't wait to hear more, his cheeks were still burning and he needed to get away for a moment. He hurried out through the back of the building. He stared at a single blue plastic drum standing against the wall. There wasn't anything else. Even the wire cage was empty. How could she? She'd promised two and he needed them for tomorrow.

He seethed as he picked up the drum. *Nessun Dorma* had run its course and a different operatic character sang in the background. He walked back slowly, forcing himself to try and quash his irritation.

'I should think the art and design students love coming here.' Kat's voice drifted out, above Princess Turandot. 'Of course, you must've heard about that poor student who died. What was her name? Anne Blink?'

Nick felt his guts twist at the familiar name. He stopped dead in his tracks and hugged the drum.

'We have so many. I find it hard to remember them all. Anne Blink? Yes, I read about her in the paper.' Lia's tone sounded cold, matter-of-fact even. 'Tragic,' she added, as if a comment was expected from her.

Nick was surprised. He knew they each had to handle her death in their own way, but hadn't the visitors' book suggested more of a bond between student and teacher? Still holding the drum he stepped into the kitchenette.

'Good, you've found it, Nick.' Lia looked up as she lifted the pan off the electric ring. 'Let me just do this and then I can check you've got the right drum.' She poured the viscid mixture into a small glass Kilner jar and clipped the airtight lid down.

'There was only one out there,' he said. 'Looks like jam making, Lia.'

She smiled. 'Doesn't taste so good, in fact it doesn't taste of anything.' She held out the pan. 'Try it if you like. There's some left on the side.'

'I think I'll pass, if you don't mind.' He watched Kat dip her finger in and then touch her tongue gingerly.

'You're right. Bland nothingness.'

'I said so. Now let me see the drum.' She moved towards Nick and looked more closely at its screw top.

'Fine, you can load it into your car.'

The tone was like a dismissal and Nick didn't argue. He had noticed how she could change, sometimes with the speed of an electrical switch. He'd wait until he'd packed the drum into the Fiesta before asking about the second one.

When he returned a few minutes later, something had changed. He felt the tension. Lia stood facing the wall, her mobile pressed to her ear. Kat stood watching, her normally open expression changed to a frown.

'*Dio, Dio*,' Lia breathed into the phone. She bowed her head, as if the floor might help.

Nick caught Kat's glance. He mouthed, 'What's happened?'

'*Cristo*!'

Kat shrugged and shook her head, a kind of hopelessness to her gesture.

Lia slowly turned around, still listening to her mobile. Her gaze fell on Nick. '*Momento*,' she said to the voice on the other end of the call. She lowered her hand. 'You'd best go. Something's come up.'

'But what about the second drum?' He was about to say more, but Kat grasped his arm.

'Not now.' She started to guide him out of the kitchenette.

Lia's voice drifted behind. 'Dave can collect it on Monday when he puts on the last coat of varnish. But now you must leave.'

CHAPTER 19

Chrissie dropped three packs of sausages into the basket.

'That'll be enough for Nick and Kat, Matt, me and… Clive.' Her hand hovered over a fourth pack. How much would Matt eat, she wondered. Not a whole pack, she decided. 'Bread next.'

Chrissie moved around the food store picking out salad, tomatoes, onions and some barbecue dressings. Then she went back and chucked in the fourth pack of sausages. The boys were in charge of the beer but they'd never think of anything else. 'Bottled water,' she murmured and headed for the soft drinks aisle.

'Good, now that's done I can get on with the rest of Saturday.' Outside again, she loaded everything into the TR7. Tomorrow was to be the raft building day and it promised to be another scorcher. Dave was bringing his portable barbecue and Seth the burgers. 'Camera,' Chrissie added to her imagined list as she turned the key in the ignition. 'Mustn't forget my camera.'

Driving home, Chrissie thought back over the past week. Matt had been her house guest for seven days, fourteen hours, and still counting. She'd shared a home with Bill for more than eight years, but nothing could have prepared her for sharing a fridge with Matt. She'd come to think of him as the bearded yeti. There were no sightings of him actually in the fridge, but he left his footprint, or rather his paw print in the spread of cheese fragments, empty cold meat wrappers, spilt milk and cracked eggs. He was the world's clumsiest grazer with a voracious appetite. Thank God he shied away from her low fat yogurts and vegetables.

Brrring brrring! *Brrring brrring*! Chrissie pulled into the side of the road. She grabbed her mobile from her bag.

'Hi, Clive,' she said, one eye on the rear view mirror. It wasn't the most sensible place to stop.

'Chrissie, glad I've caught you. Is it OK to talk?'

'I was driving, but I've pulled off the road now. Why, what's up?'

'Well... I've some news. Matt's not with you is he?'

'No, I was just buying some food for tomorrow, you know, for the raft building shindig. Is everything OK, Clive?' She strained to listen for the telltale sounds that placed him in his car, the station or out on some active case.

'Yes, of course. I just...,' Clive's tone sharpened. 'I wanted to let you know, Matt can go back to his own home now.'

'Why? Has-'

'We've picked up his brother.'

'Tom? Good. That's good news, but you sound rather stern. What's happened?'

'It's complicated.'

'Well, I'm not going anywhere. As I said, I've switched the engine off now.' She glanced through the sparse hedge. The Woolpit cricket ground waited on the other side, tranquil and surprisingly green. 'You've got to tell me, Clive. You can't just leave it like that.'

He must have sensed her irritation. His voice softened.

'It's a long story.'

'I'm listening.'

'The police helicopter spotted some illegal hare coursing and-'

'A police helicopter?' Chrissie interrupted. 'You sent a helicopter out to look for hare coursers?'

'I thought you said you were listening. No, the helicopter was already out on a call for something else. It was on its way back to Wattisham. The crew always keep an eye out for things like fly-tipping, hare coursing... anything unusual while they fly back to base.'

'And Tom was fly-tipping?'

'If you'd just let me finish, Chrissie.' She heard his frown. 'The helicopter spotted the hare coursers red-handed, driving through some beet fields. They alerted police control. It was relatively easy after that to track them from the air, and the patrol cars rounded them up as they tried to get away on the roads. We got most of the coursers and all their cars.' He paused for a moment, as if changing to another gear. 'You don't stand much of a chance when you're being pursued by a helicopter in broad daylight.'

'Wow, good for the helicopter. And Tom, was he coursing?'

'It seems so. We've got quite a few to interview. I expect it'll be a nightmare of phony names and addresses, and half the cars will turn out to be stolen or have false number plates. So there's a lot of checking to do. We'll hold them for as long as we can. And Tom, well we'll be talking to him for much longer.'

'Matt will be stunned,' Chrissie said as she pictured a helicopter and a pack of patrol cars. They'd turned the tables on the coursers; the hunters had become the hunted.

'Don't tell Matt any of this.' Clive's voice cut through her thoughts.

'Why ever not?'

'Because I don't know how much Matt may be involved.'

'But you can't think Matt's any part of this, surely?'

'I hope not. But I'm not prepared to chance it at this stage. I'm going to phone him now and tell him we've found Tom and he doesn't need to stay with you any longer. He can go home. That's all I'm going to say to him. And I'd like you to take the same line.'

A whirlwind of emotions and images ripped through Chrissie's mind. Relief was tinged with irritation. She'd never responded well to high-handed directives and Clive's tone was perilously close to one. Tom in custody was good. Reclaiming her fridge was good. But hadn't he just questioned Matt's integrity?

'Chrissie, are you still there?'

'Yes, I was just thinking about what you'd said.'

Clive let the silence hang in the air.

Chrissie finally spoke. 'So have you told me all this because you don't trust Matt to tell me about it. You know, in case he doesn't want to go home yet?'

'Well, I wouldn't put it past him. I expect it's much more comfortable at your place than back on the Flower Estate. I know which I'd choose.'

She bit her tongue. Clive had already as good as said he didn't trust him. Now he was adding liar to the list. A spark of indignation surfaced. Her cheeks burned. 'Matt's not like his brother.'

'I know, Chrissie. But Tom still has a hold over him and I can't let that compromise our investigation. You do understand, don't you?'

Chrissie struggled with herself. 'Yes, of course,' she said in a tight voice. 'And thanks for phoning me. Where are you, by the way?'

'Heading for Bury.'

'Sounds like you're going to be pretty busy.' She glanced beyond the scrubby hedge as she spoke, her mind already moving on. Cricketers were taking up their positions on the pitch, ready to start a summer league match. Seeing them reminded her. 'It's not really the hare coursing season at the moment, is it, Clive?'

'No and I bet this lot are wishing they hadn't come out today. Look, I'll call you later, Chrissie. Sorry I can't talk for longer. Bye now.'

The line went dead, leaving Chrissie to follow her own thread. She sat for a moment and watched the smattering of cricket spectators settle themselves on rugs and deckchairs beyond the boundary. She sighed and started the car, her pulse now restored to a more normal pace. She eased the wedge-shaped bonnet in the direction of home. There was no hurry. Clive needed time to phone Matt before she arrived.

CHAPTER 20

The wind buffeted Matt's chest and arms as he accelerated hard. For the first time in over two weeks he felt free. Totally free. Now he could ride the Piaggio without fear. No more pulling off the road and waiting to see if the car behind would follow. No more burning petrol as he kept his eyes glued to the wing mirror. For the moment the police had Tom. Clive's call changed everything.

Matt grinned behind his Perspex visor as he hit 30 mph. The engine whined and buzzed as he zipped down the hill, gaining a further 2 mph by the time he reached the corner leading into Coombs. He leaned with the scooter and eased round the bend. He pictured the route. In all, it was another six miles or so. He must remember to turn right at the Bowl & Pitcher, and then follow a series of rights and lefts to the raft building site.

He hadn't thought how he might feel when he returned to Tumble Weed Drive the previous afternoon. The kitchen sink still overflowed with greasy pans and plates. His bedroom walls hadn't got any bluer since he'd left. His duvet was still in a heap on the floor where he'd left it. The only change was the piece of paper stuck to his door. His name had been scrawled in bold letters, and underneath, *if you're not back in a month I'm getting a lodger*. It wasn't signed, but he recognised his mother's hand.

Matt sighed. The nights living rough had been grim. He'd spent every waking moment consumed with terror. He'd hardly eaten and he hadn't washed. Anxiety squeezing at his insides had become the norm. When Chrissie said he could stay with her, he dreaded she might change her mind and chuck him out. His nerves were in such a state of high tension he feared everything and everyone. He hardly noticed she was serving up salad. He had no appetite. But as the days went by and the security blanket of No 3, Albert Cottages slowly enveloped him, he'd started to relax. That's when the hunger returned and he realised the misery of rocket leaves and watercress. Clive's call came as a lifesaver. To be honest, he couldn't have taken a further week of healthy eating.

So Tom was behind bars, he thought as the road surface vibrated up through the front wheel to the handle grips. He imagined the picture. Pure comic-strip style prison bars crossed Tom's face in profile. A speech bubble ballooned from his mouth. F••k you, it said. But Clive had told him they couldn't keep Tom for ever, maybe only 48 hours. Matt's innards did a flip. What would happen?

Matt knew he wasn't good at answering those sorts of questions and neither, so it seemed, was Clive. He'd said very little when pressed. Matt was to go home, he'd be safe and not to worry. They'd picked Tom up for questioning and that's all he'd say. Nothing about where they'd found him, if he'd talked or what would happen next. So that was it. 'Let's keep it simple,' Clive had said, and if Clive was happy with that, then Matt would have to be as well.

Knowing Tom had been contained was like being freed from toothache. Matt needed to bite into something sweet. He craved some fun. The raft building shindig, as Chrissie had called it, was about to start and he didn't want to be late. Matt kept the revs high, gritted his teeth and headed on. The road narrowed as he zipped alongside hedgerows and wheat fields. Corners sharpened, and after a hard left, he knew he was getting close. The farm entrance was well maintained and he swung the scooter off the road and down the wide track, spitting a shower of gravel as he went. The courtyard, when he reached it, was huge.

He rode on past, the whole feel of the track changing. At first it was tree lined, and then rough hedges and ditches bordered on either side. Gravel became packed earth. Grass struggled to survive between the well-worn tyre tracks. He took a right fork and the fields were left behind. A young wood closed in on the track. It felt wild and remote. He slowed. Old shotgun cartridges lay scattered amongst the thin undergrowth, the bright plastic casings catching his attention. The reds, oranges and greens were almost luminescent. He pressed on and the track opened into a large rough grassy area with blue, upstanding pheasant feeders. He recognised Chrissie's TR7 immediately. She'd parked close to a huddle of cars on the edge of the grass.

'Hi,' Seth shouted and then waved both arms in the air as if flagging down a plane.

The Piaggio bounced and juddered over the ruts. Matt slowed and stopped before the uneven ground threw him. He pulled off his helmet and sat for a moment, the sweat in his short hair drying as he took in the scene. 'Where's the reservoir?'

Chrissie walked over and grinned. 'Hi, Matt. Through there.' She pointed to a large gap in the line of a rough coppice-like hedge where blackthorn fought with hazel, and young alder and field maple reached for the sky.

'Come and meet Dave. Everything OK at home?'

'Yeah,' he said but his eyes were on the girls. 'Wow.' They were heading in the direction of the water, shorts no longer than the crotch and skinny tee-shirts skirting belly buttons.

'Come on, over this way,' Chrissie said, grabbing his arm and guiding him. 'Dave, this is Matt.'

A tubby middle-aged man turned and shook Matt's hand. 'Morning. You're just in time. You can help me unload this lot.' He opened the back of an old Land Rover and passed out lengths of wood, tools and then four large blue plastic drums. 'Take it over there.' He indicated some ground close to where the track led down to the edge of the reservoir. 'We'll build it there. It's closer to the water and good an' flat.'

Matt hadn't expected to actually do anything. He'd reckoned that with Dave, Seth, Andy and Nick being there, he'd concentrate on the girls and let the others do most of the building. He started to lift and carry, working up heat and sweat as he added each load to the growing pile. This wasn't part of his plan. He paused to catch breath. 'So how big's this reservoir? I aint seen it yet?'

'It's down there.' Dave indicated with a nod. 'Go and have a look, and while you're about it, send the others back. It's time to get building.'

Matt followed the rutted track through the wide gap in the hedge, then down a short steep bank to one corner of the reservoir. 'Shikes,' he gasped. This wasn't your average farm reservoir. This was huge. It stretched out, larger than a football pitch. It was bounded by the rough hedge along one bank and the young wood joined it at the corner. From the other two sides, fields spread into the distance.

'How deep, d'you reckon?' he asked.

Andy stood and gazed out over the water. 'Deep enough. It's more what's under the surface that's important. Don't want to get tangled in weed. I reckon we've got at least four feet at the edges and six foot or more towards the centre. Best wear the life jackets.' He turned and smiled at Matt. 'Are you a good swimmer?'

'Why'd you ask?' Matt watched as Andy seemed to size up his chest.

'One of the jackets is from when I used to row as a kid. Might be a bit small on you, that's all.'

Matt shrugged. He glanced down as he smoothed his tee-shirt, an old find in a charity shop. *Reservoir Dogs* was printed above a picture of five men with slicked-back hair, dark glasses and dark suits. It made him feel like a cool dude, one of the pack.

'Like the tee-shirt, by the way. Reservoir Dogs? You might not need a buoyancy aid. Throw you a stick instead.'

'Hi, Matt.' Nick strode along the bank. 'Isn't it fantastic here? You're looking the part, by the way.' He was followed by the three girls, Ali, Rachael and Jo.

'Aint Kat with you today?' Matt asked. He frowned. He didn't want any competition.

'Kat's busy shooting. She'll join us later if she can. Come on, better get to work.' Nick tossed the words over his shoulder as he led the way.

Jo, with her square jaw and dark-plum lipstick smiled at Matt as she caught up.

'Hi Jo,' Matt said. He touched his face, a nervous habit he'd grown with the beard. She didn't answer, just dropped her gaze. He felt stupid.

He fell into step beside her, stealing glances at her as they climbed back up to the grassy area. Was her skin for real? Milky pale, he thought. Partway down her neck it seemed to pink up and match the rest of her body. A small black star was tattooed on her shoulder.

'What you looking at, Matt?' Her tone was sharp.

'Nothin'.' His face flamed beneath his beard.

'If anyone should be doing the staring, it's me. You've changed.'

'I-I've been ill.'

Her tone softened. 'Is that why you didn't call me?'

'Yeah,' he muttered on a cough.

'Well, it suits you.' Her words were barely audible.

'What, bein' ill?'

'No, stupid. I like beards and you look... kind of thinner.'

Matt touched his face again. Was she being nice? He couldn't tell. Birds, why did they talk in such riddles?

'Come on, Matt; time to get on with some work. Less of the chatting up,' Seth shouted and then laughed.

Ali squeaked a giggle.

While Dave directed the rafting team, Matt tried to keep an eye on Jo without it being noticed. He helped to measure the lengths of wood, but left any sawing to the others. When they laid out the frame on the grass he managed to edge closer to Jo, but just as he was about to talk to her, Dave had him carrying a blue drum. He heaved it to the corner of the frame, then shifted it nearer to another, and finally helped position the fifth one from Nick's car in the centre. He waited, catching his breath.

Dave stood with his hands on his hips as charcoal smoke wafted through the air. 'The central drum will destabilise the raft. Let's try it with two along each side, first. If that doesn't make it float enough, well... we'll need three drums at the sides.'

Chrissie prodded at the barbeque. 'It'll be a while yet,' she muttered.

They nailed the wood together and tied four of the drums on with the nylon cord. Matt staggered as he took the weight of one corner and lifted. He could almost taste the excitement in the air.

'Let's just try it in the water before we eat.' Nick's face was flushed, sweat glistened on his forehead.

Matt hadn't expected it would be so awkward to carry a raft down a slope. As he slipped and slithered, his corner went down and Seth was forced forwards. The pace quickened. Nick and Andy tried to save the raft from falling. Suddenly they were all running. The raft hit the water with a smash.

The cold reservoir shocked. Matt gasped for breath. His feet searched for the bottom and then kicked out and pushed. There was little resistance in the soft cloying mud.

'Shit,' he yelped and clung onto the raft.

'Don't push it out any further,' Seth yelled.

'I can't stand up. It's like quicksand.' He imagined it pulling him deeper and his pulse raced.

'Someone grab that rope.' Dave's voice rang out above the splashing and yelping. 'Pull the raft in. You're OK, Matt. Push your weight onto your chest. Try to float or swim. Keep your legs up. Hold onto the raft.'

Matt held on with one hand and splashed around with the other. He felt the raft move, saw the bank getting closer. He lifted his legs and made swimming movements. He could float. He breathed. The dark hands pulling down on his feet disappeared.

'Bloody idiot. Why didn't you let go? You didn't have to go in with the raft,' Nick muttered as he pulled on the rope.

'Careful, Matt. When you get to the edge, come in as close as you can and then walk fast and light. Don't push your feet down into the mud. Three steps and you're out.' Dave held out a hand and grasped him. 'Right, everyone... ruddy well wear the life jackets when you're on the raft.'

While his mobile phone dried in the sun, Matt ate his barbequed sausages and bread roll. Mud caked his feet. Reservoir water distorted his tee. He reckoned he had less than a dog's chance now of impressing Jo. Everyone else looked tanned, sexy and dry. It's not fair, he thought. This wasn't part of the plan.

He didn't fare much better in the after-lunch trial either. Dave said the heaviest should paddle at the rear and put Matt astride a drum behind Nick, and Andy behind Seth. When they were all aboard, the wooden frame floated an inch or so below the water. Matt held his breath as his weight pushed the drum low. His feet and calves dangled in the reservoir, acting as drag as they paddled. It was nigh impossible to move forwards. Instead of going straight, the raft tended to pivot around him.

Matt didn't want to say much in the post-practice debrief. Wet again, he sat on the grass and felt bad. After all, he was the heaviest. Andy suggested fixing the frame so it was higher on each drum. Everyone agreed they'd need six.

'It's a shame you couldn't pick up more than one drum on Saturday, Nick.' Dave shook his head as he gazed at the raft.

'I know, but at least Lia promised me another one would be ready for you to collect on Monday, when you're over there.'

'Hmm, oh well,' Dave sighed. 'I think we'll modify the frame so there's a wider length of wood on both sides of the row of drums. Then you'll be able to rest your feet on the wood. Keep them from dragging in the water.' He glanced at Matt. 'The frame will be stronger as well.'

'And you'll get a better paddling stroke if your feet are anchored,' Andy added.

Matt noticed Jo looking in his direction. He stopped listening as the discussion played back and forth and tried his sexy half smile, the one where he only raised one corner of his mouth. He hadn't attempted it with a beard before.

'Are you OK, Matt?' Dave asked, interrupting the debate about the frame. 'You've been in the water a lot today. Is your eye all right?'

'Yeah, you old Reservoir Dog, we couldn't keep you out the water,' echoed Nick's voice in the background.

Matt rubbed his chin. Fine silt detached and sprinkled onto his chest. The five men printed on the damp cotton had already lost definition. Now they blended with some mud. Only the writing stood out. 'Yeah, I'm OK. Why?'

'Just wondered….' Dave turned his attention back to the raft.

'Are you at the Academy tomorrow?' Jo's sharp tones had softened and Matt looked up to see her standing next to him.

'D'you want t'sit down? Why you askin'?' He dropped his gaze and noticed a tiny black star tattooed on her ankle. 'How many of those've you got?'

'None of your business. Will you be at the Academy?' She remained where she was, looking down at him.

'Yeah, it's the release day.' He wanted to ask why, but she'd snapped at his last question, so he bit his tongue and waited.

'I'm looking at the computing and IT courses there. Might take it up in September, but I'm still deciding. Do you know much about it?'

Matt knew there were business, computing, and information technology courses. He'd heard you could even design computer games, but merely knowing of their existence was the sum of his knowledge. How to keep her talking? 'Yeah,' he muttered, 'I know 'bout those.'

'Really?'

'Yeah, if you're over there, text me.' Then he remembered shaking the water out of his phone. 'I'm usually in the library, if me mobile's not workin'.' He watched as she nodded.

She lingered a few moments, then seemed to notice Ali talking to Rachael and drifted off to join them. Matt frowned. Mixed messages. Why was it always mixed messages with birds?

Later, after they'd covered the raft in a tarpaulin and placed it safely out of the way to one side of the track, Matt started the Piaggio. He rode at a slow speed, bumping and rocking on the uneven ground. Chrissie tooted her horn and passed him as they joined the road. 'Bye,' she yelled and accelerated away.

It was only as the bright yellow paintwork disappeared into the distance that he realised he'd hardly spoken to her all day. And he hadn't seen Clive either. He'd been too busy with the raft and watching Jo.

•••

Monday morning dawned dull and overcast. Matt groped under his pillow. He was still somewhere between dozy comfort and awareness as his hand closed on the familiar shape of his mobile. The unfamiliar feel of soft plastic film and hard grains of rice slid under his fingers. He forced his eyes open. 'Oh no.' He'd forgotten about the water.

He'd spent the previous evening, once he'd got home, with the back cover off, the battery and SIM card out, and more sheets of paper towel. The breezy warmth of the day had done its job, and there'd been no obvious moisture left in the phone. Just to be sure, he'd popped it in a plastic bag with a handful of dried rice overnight. Trouble was, he couldn't see the time read-out through the rice. He tore at the plastic and grains pelted down on his face and bedding.

'Argh!'

He threw back the duvet and his triceps smarted. He curled around and burning agony gripped his ribs. He straightened his legs. No pain. He tried to sit up. 'Ouch!' Muscles he didn't even know he possessed complained as he moved. And why did his neck hurt, he wondered. What had he been doing with it?

Of course, the swimming and paddling. And then he remembered Jo. He squinted at his mobile again. Dead. He needed it to work. Perhaps the battery was flat? With one Herculean effort he swung his legs out of bed and stood. Pain shot through his muscles as rice rat-a-tat-tatted onto the shabby flooring. He wobbled and then he was on all fours. In a flash he was Swamp Man dropped into a comic-strip pit of crocodiles. His backpack shrieked to him, begging to be saved from a heap of discarded clothes. He started the painful journey across his bedroom to retrieve the phone-charger from its depths.

Forty minutes later the Swamp Man of Matt's imagination had mastered the upright position. He had dressed and there was life in the phone. He could even move his arms. He mounted his scooter awkwardly. As he rode, the wind buffeted his denim jacket, and for a moment he forgot his pains. He only had one aim as he headed for the Academy: to reach the library before Jo. 'Ouch,' he yelped as he stepped off the scooter in the parking area.

'Mornin', Rosie,' he murmured as five minutes later he crumpled onto a chair at the nearest computer station, the one close to the door.

'Did I just see you limping again?' Rosie's whisper travelled softly from the librarian's station.

He smiled and touched his sore ribs. 'Been raftin'.'

'Ah, and how was New York?'

Matt frowned. What was she on about? His *North Atlantic Drift* tee-shirt had ridden high and he pulled at the cotton fabric. He hoped it was lucky. He'd worn it to the original meeting of the rafting group, the first time he'd met Jo in the Nag's Head.

He logged onto the computer and quickly found the Academy site. He wanted to read up on the computing and IT courses. At least working the mouse was painless and by the time he'd combed the website for every nugget of information, he'd made up his mind. Jo or no Jo, he was interested in the modules on his own account. He was going to change courses. After all, he was wearing the lucky tee.

Jo still hadn't shown up and Matt glanced at the time on his computer screen, 13:16. Almost from habit he keyed Hoxton into the search box. Without a first name, previous trawls of the internet had told him it was a district in East London. 'Hot bed of crime,' he mumbled as he reread the familiar crime statistics. 'Big council estates, gangs, drugs....' He clicked on a history site and read about the *hothouse of painters and cutting edge artisans in the Sixties*. No wonder galleries had sprung up. 'Like bloody field mushrooms,' he mumbled as he pictured the Google map from an earlier search. There were still loads of galleries around Hoxton Square. So, art and chemicals, Matt mused. Strange mix? More likely to be two sides of the same coin, he decided. But who was the Hoxton Clive had mentioned?

'Hi.' The voice was soft, the perfume strong.

Matt looked up, disturbed from his thoughts. 'Hi, Jo. You came!' He grinned and then felt foolish. He decided to play it cool.

'Yeah, just had a look at the computing and IT departments.'

'And?'

'Not sure. It's kind of... well I'll look at some other places before I decide.' Strands of pink hair fell across her cheek as she bent to look at his computer screen. 'I don't have to decide yet. Hey, what you staring at?'

Her skin was the same lime-wash pale as on Sunday, but Matt was sure the bubblegum-pink streak was new.

'Nothin',' he lied and turned his eyes back to the screen. 'It's nice, your hair,' and then he felt his cheeks burn under the beard.

'Shell,' she murmured. 'Shell pink.'

Matt thought candyfloss. He hadn't eaten for hours.

'So where else you lookin'?'

'Maybe London. That would be great, hey?'

'But how'd you afford it?'

'Don't know, but there's bursaries and things. Don't have to pay if you're still under eighteen.'

'An' where'd you live? You'd spend all your time travellin'?'

'It doesn't have to be London. There's courses other places too, you know. Closer. Ipswich or Bury.' She frowned. 'Your mobile working now?'

Matt nodded. 'Think so. Charged it this mornin'.' He thrust his hand into his pocket, wincing as stiff muscles protested.

'Bye,' she whispered.

'You goin' already?' Matt watched as she walked away, skin-tight jeans hugging her thighs. It was only after the library doors swung closed that he looked at the lifeless mobile in his hand. 'Shit,' he hissed as he shook it.

Had she texted him? Matt didn't know. There was no point in running after her, it wouldn't look cool. Perhaps he could find something to impress her? He had an idea. He typed *bursaries* into the Google search box. Then he narrowed the field to London. It was a painstaking business and the information was difficult to find on the college websites. He was about to stop for a break when a name leapt off the screen. *Hoxton, Hoxton Community College.* He drilled down further. There were some bursaries, but not for computing and IT.

The Dard Bursary, he read. Excitement prickled his fingertips as he clicked the mouse. *A bursary to support disadvantaged students living in the district of Hoxton, specifically to pursue a career in Art & Design.* He let his breath escape in a low whistle and browsed on. So who was this benefactor? Could there be any connection to the Dard who'd stolen Storm? It seemed unlikely. He clicked on a tab labelled *Alumni* wondering if Dard might have once been a student or lecturer at the college. And then he found *A. Dard, 2002 – 2004. Art & Design.* It was too much of a coincidence. The Dard of the bursary and the alumnus Dard had to be related in some way, but that still didn't tell him anything about Tom's Dard.

Dead ends, Matt thought. All roads lead to dead ends. Perhaps it was time to go and make an appointment with Blumfield and see if he could change courses. After all, he was still wearing his lucky tee.

CHAPTER 21

'Morning, Dave. Did the last coats of varnish go on OK? You know, over at the manuscript place?' It was Tuesday morning and Nick really wanted to know if Dave had picked up the last drum for the raft. But good manners dictated at least going through the niceties of appearing more interested in the firm's work than the raft.

'Morning, Nick. Yes, those benches looked a million dollars. Mr Santo's very pleased.' He smiled and ran his hand over his thinning hair.

'And Lia, was she pleased as well?'

'I think so. She was on the phone most of the time. I thought I'd catch her at lunch, but she left and didn't come back before I'd finished there.'

Dave and Nick stood in the Willows office, the tired chairs and filing cabinets still dull in the eight o'clock light. Alfred Walsh studied the work sheets.

'So did you get a chance to ask her for-'

'It's turned out well, you two being free, today.' Alfred's voice cut across Nick. 'We're behind with that loft conversion over at Stowmarket, so it'd be useful if you gave Tim a hand for the next couple of days. You're not due in Somersham till Thursday.' The foreman scribbled something on the work sheet. 'Yes, that's worked out well. He'll be pleased to see you.'

'Like the cavalry.'

'What you saying, lad?' The furrows deepened in Alfred's brow as he strained to catch Nick's words.

'He said he'd get the van ready,' Dave answered loudly. 'There's a load of brushes and varnish pots still in there from Mr Santo's job.' He grinned at Nick. 'Come on, lad. What you waiting for?'

'Did you get the drum?' he mouthed, but Dave didn't seem to notice and turned back to the foreman. Nick flicked the van keys off the rack by the door and headed outside. The air felt cool as a light breeze gently feathered his skin. Dave can't have forgotten, he reasoned. It'll be his idea of a joke.

The link-fence gate to the van parking area stood wide open. The other carpenters were already loading up their vans and leaving. Doors slammed and engines revved.

'Bloody pedestrians,' Kenneth, one of the carpenters shouted and tooted his horn.

'Bloody van drivers,' Nick called, stepping out of the way at the last moment and laughing. He watched the van pass, the fancy lettering on its side transforming the name from Willows into *Widows*.

Only a couple of vans were still parked up, and Nick aimed the key fob at the one with fine cracks coursing the near-side tail light, the result of a recent encounter with a bollard. It was Dave's signature. He knew it without having to check the number plate. He flung open the rear doors, eager to find the drum. Containers holding tools and materials were stacked and locked into a rack along the side of the van. Dave's tool box, wood off-cuts and a pile of dust-sheets filled the central space. The empty varnish pots were piled neatly, close to the door. Something blue caught Nick's eye. 'Bloody joker,' he muttered and then smiled. The drum was wedged to one side and partially hidden by the portable saw bench.

Nick gathered up the varnish pots and brushes. It didn't take him long. He used the shutter-door entrance into the workshop loading bay, and threw the empty pots into the bins. But how to turn the joke back on Dave? He wrapped the drum in a dustsheet and carried it to his Fiesta where he stowed it out of sight. Now he had to find something of similar size or colour to put in its place, but there was little time, and even less choice. The blue biscuit tin in the office was barrel shaped, but Dave was still in the office talking to Alfred Walsh. He needed something easy and to hand.

'Are you done, yet?' Dave called as he stepped out of the side entrance and strolled through the open link-fence gate.

Nick stood waiting, one hand on the van's open rear door. He shook his head.

'What's up, lad?'

'It won't work, Dave. We'll never float the raft with these.' Nick let his voice break.

'What d'you mean? It's the same size as the others.'

'The same size as the others? You're joking. It'll never work, Dave.'

Dave pushed past him and looked into the back of the van. He opened his mouth, then seemed to change his mind and closed it.

Nick sucked in his cheeks, fighting back the laugh erupting in his throat.

'Y-y-you cheeky beggar,' Dave whispered, his voice barely audible.

Nick waited, tears now threatening to film across his eyes.

'Evian,' Dave muttered as he launched the first missile at Nick. 'Co-Op's own brand carbonated... Shropshire Spring....' He raised his voice as each empty quarter-litre plastic bottle flew from the back of the van. 'Lincolnshire Natural,' he continued. 'Scottish Spring....' They bounced and rolled across the concrete. Dave paused, a second empty Co-Op's own brand in his hand.

'No, Dave. Not the Co-Op's.' He ducked, his laugh exploding as the last 250 mls of air, contained in lightweight plastic, spun past.

It had been worth it, Nick thought as he chased the empty bottles. The wind drove them onwards, catching and turning them, the plastic grumbling and chattering over the uneven surface.

'I'll be waiting in the van,' Dave shouted. 'And stop mucking about. We need to get over to Stowmarket.'

Nick zigzagged across the secured parking area, scooping up each one in turn. He was pleased he'd found a use for the empties he'd tossed in the footwell of his car. Now he hurried with his arms full and lobbed them into the bin. Dave might have had the last word - but to see his reaction had been brilliant.

Back in the van, Nick grinned as he caught his breath.

'Why didn't you say you'd got the drum? I wouldn't have played you around if you'd just said.'

'You don't know how close we came to not having the drum. Lia and Santo were having a bit of a barney. I don't know what about, because it was all going on in Italian. I couldn't get a word in edgeways... so I just took it.'

'Thanks, Dave.'

Nick didn't give the drum episode another thought as the rest of the day sped by. He was too busy lifting and carrying tongue and groove chipboard panels for Tim and Dave to have time to think of anything else. While they measured and sawed, the air in the loft space turned hot and sweaty. Nick hauled the last panel across the reinforced flooring joists and into its interlocking position.

'Thank God the floor's down. Can't put a foot through the ceiling now,' Tim said as he stood up, arching his back as if to loosen his aching muscles.

'Are we doing something to the roof?' Nick asked. He'd noticed scaffolding on the back of the house.

'A skylight roof window. But that's for tomorrow. Now, tidy up and we're done for today.'

•••

Nick knew there was something wrong as soon as he drove into the Willows site the following morning. A police car had drawn up near the entrance into the secure parking area. Alfred Walsh stood with Mr Willows and a uniformed constable. They scowled and frowned, body language shrieking outrage as they pointed at the gate and vans. Heads were shaking, notes were being taken. The second police constable leaned into the open squad car and then straightened up, radio in his hand.

'Bloody hell, what's going on?' Nick murmured as he turned the Fiesta and parked on the rough concrete at the front of the workshop.

He hurried out of his car, curiosity pulling him past the side entrance door and along the wide unevenly gravelled space to the chain-linked fencing at the rear. 'What's…?' The words died as he took in the scene.

The gate stood ajar, the chain and padlock still partly attached and hanging like a broken promise. Bolt cutters had been at work. 'Not the diesel again? Have they siphoned off the tanks?' No one answered. It was obvious the thieves had been after more than just diesel. Rear doors had been forced open and the contents of five Willows vans strewn onto the concrete.

Nick stamped on a Twix wrapper as a sudden gust caught it, whisking it a few inches above the ground and through the open gate. It would have escaped if it could.

Alfred turned, as if he'd just noticed Nick. 'We've had a break-in.' His shoulders hunched, his body drooped, he'd as good as taken a mortal blow to the solar plexus.

'Don't go in there, Nick. The police want us to wait until they've dusted the vans for prints and taken photos. You know the kind of thing.' Mr Willows spoke evenly.

'Then you can check them over, see what's missing.' Alfred's voice cracked.

'Oh God, I s'pose this means they'll want our prints as well.' Nick tried to block the memory of a previous interrogation. 'This'll take forever. Nothing'll happen till the SOC team arrive.'

'Better make a mug of tea, lad. What's a sock team?'

'Scene Of Crime team, Mr Walsh. D'you want a mug of tea as well, Mr Willows?'

Back in the office-cum-restroom, Nick filled the kettle. As he waited for it to boil he let his mind drift over the scene. Had someone stood in each van and systematically thrown out: tool boxes, lengths of wood, stepladders, rechargeable drills, dustsheets, and anything that came to hand? What had they wanted and who were they? He wondered if they'd been kids out to trash the place for a laugh, or maybe a dissatisfied customer, or even a rival firm wanting to set Willows back a day or two. Except Willows wasn't the sort of business to excite strong feelings. Why bother to target it? Nothing made sense.

'What a bloody mess,' Dave grumbled as he opened the door and walked in.

Tim automatically ducked his head as he followed Dave through the doorway. 'This'll put us even further behind.' He was tall and wiry, and middle-age had been kind to him so far. Unlike Dave, he'd failed to gain the extra pounds around his midriff. 'If you're making tea, I'll have one, Nick.'

The rest of the workforce, consisting of Kenneth and two more carpenters, arrived a few moments later and the room began to feel full and bad tempered. When Alfred and Mr Willows came in with one of the police constables, full changed to claustrophobic. Nick edged between the chairs handing out mugs of tea. 'Sorry,' he muttered as steaming hot liquid slopped onto an outstretched work boot.

'They'll be selling our tools at car boot sales in Lincolnshire, by now.' Tim stared into his tea.

'Or scrap....'

'Yeah, melting them down more like,' Tim finished for Dave.

'We need better security, Mr Willows.' Alfred's voice sounded old, broken.

'I know, Alfred.' He turned to speak to the constable, 'Pat, the firm's secretary, can give you a list of all our carpenters.' He checked his watch. 'She should be here in a few minutes.'

Nick sank to the floor, his back against the wall. There weren't enough chairs and somehow it felt less crowded at ground level. He hardly listened to the conversations playing back and forth. Only fragments penetrated his thoughts.

He felt a light tap on his shoulder and Dave's words drifted down from the stratosphere above. 'You can wait outside, lad. You don't need to stay in here.'

Nick took Dave at his word and hurried out. He immediately spotted a police van parked close to the open chain-link gate. A technician wearing plastic overshoes, disposable overalls and latex gloves, dusted for fingerprints on and around the van door handles, while another in similar garb moved between the vans taking photos. 'The SOC team at last,' Nick murmured and headed in the opposite direction.

He walked briskly. He wanted to clear his head and the fast pace helped. I'll go once round the block, he thought as he strode out of the Willows entrance. Cars were parked along the roadside. He guessed some of them must belong to workers, temporally unable to park on the site. He glanced into each one as he passed. 'Empty, empty, emp....' He looked away quickly. He'd registered a pair of brown eyes, heavily lidded. The man raised his hand. It was as if to screen himself from Nick's sudden intrusion. And then he was gone as the momentum of Nick's stride carried him on. 'Occupied,' he muttered. Three steps further and he stole a glance back at the Audi saloon. He heard the gentle purr as the smoked glass electric window closed.

Nick felt as if he'd disturbed something: nose picking, ear de-waxing, wanking, something personal, something distasteful. He lengthened his stride, almost breaking into a run. He kept his eyes dead ahead, intent only on the movement of his legs and the thudding from his feet. Ten minutes later and he was back at the Willows entrance, but this time panting for breath.

'Come on, Nick,' Dave called. 'We've had the OK to check what's missing. Try and look lively.'

Nick followed Dave to the secure parking area. His heart was already pounding from his circuit, but now anxiety fluttered in his stomach. His tool box, his favourite chisels, the Japanese saw - would they all be gone? He picked his way to their van, stepping over dustsheets strewn in heaps. Dave's tool box lay on its side, sprung half open from its impact with the concrete. The contents had spilled out. He caught his foot on a screwdriver. It rolled and clunked against the portable saw table, one set of legs still folded, the other set extended like some broken animal. He let his breath escape. 'Sh-i-t.'

It took the best part of an hour for everyone at Willows to sort through the mess and put things back into their vans.

'That's bloody strange,' Dave muttered. 'I can't see anything big that's missing. It's as if they just threw things around.'

'Bloody vandals.'

The diesel had been left in the tanks, so by midday they were finally able to start their vans and leave the site.

Nick felt frustrated and drained. All the hanging around made the hours stretch, and then when he finally got to do some work, there wasn't enough time to begin the roof window. Instead he carried lengths of wood which they laid out on the chipboard flooring. When screwed in place, they would form the base for the upright timbers of the new inner walls.

Dave made a start at closing off the roof lagging and rafters on the side not taking the window. Nick looked up as the sloping ceiling started to take form. 'Ouch,' he muttered and rubbed dust from his eye.

'Come on, lad. Is the next piece ready for me?'

'Sure.' Nick lifted the next sheet up and held it while Dave screwed in the plasterboard screws.

When Nick eventually sat in his Fiesta at the end of that day, he could hardly summon the energy to start the engine. Mr Walsh had told everyone to store all their tools inside the workshop for added security. 'Bloody hooligans,' Mr Walsh had grumbled to Nick. 'S'pose they thought it was funny. At least they didn't take anything.'

A new and heavy chain held the gate, and Mr Willows had ordered CCTV cameras for the outside areas. They would complement the alarmed security for the lockup and workshop.

Nick eased his car forwards. He waved as Dave drove past, revving hard and accelerating ahead of him, hardly pausing at the Willows entrance. Nick smiled as he caught the faint smell of rubber left behind in the air. It was so like Dave, he thought as he listened to the engine grumbling in low gear from somewhere ahead up the road.

Nick waited to turn out of the entrance as a sleek black Audi saloon coasted past, almost silent on the tarmac. He watched as it followed Dave. There was something familiar about its smoked glass windows. Nick frowned.

CHAPTER 22

Chrissie was looking forward to seeing Clive again. She'd hoped he might have made it to the raft building shindig, but he'd been working. In fact, from a police point of view, the whole weekend had turned out to be busy. She'd barely even spoken to him on the phone since then and now it was already Wednesday. The week was slipping by.

'If you're off this evening, why don't you drop over for a bite to eat? We don't have to go out anywhere special. I could cook something, if you like.' She kept her tone light, the invitation low key. To be honest, she only had a few onions and tomatoes in her fridge, so any meal was likely to be frugal.

'That would be nice, Chrissie. God, it's been mad here. I'm dead on my feet.' He paused and she heard him stifle a yawn. 'I may not be the best company but... yes, it would be nice.'

And so the conversation had ended. That had been less than half an hour ago, and now she stood in her kitchen, holding the fridge door open and hoping for inspiration. She shoved the tub of low fat spread to one side and frowned. She'd forgotten about the slim box of ready-made filo pastry, nestling behind. She'd bought it while Matt was staying. A moment of madness had made her think she could broaden his palate a little.

Chrissie rummaged through the cheese. 'Suffolk Gold,' she murmured as she picked up the remnants, still in the waxed paper wrapper. 'Port Salut, Gruyere.' She lifted them out. The Cheshire was crumbly and acidic. 'That might work... and of course Parmesan.' She looked at the motley collection she'd laid on her kitchen table and then put the Port Salut back in the fridge. 'Fresh herbs, that'll lift it.' A pot of basil still survived on her kitchen windowsill. She checked her watch. Six o'clock. There was just about time to have a quick shower and change before starting on the cooking.

Rat-at-at-at-at-at! Chrissie heard the doorbell's low metallic notes as she towelled her hair dry. Damn, that was quick she thought and pulled on a pair of figure-hugging stretch jeans. She hurried out of her bedroom, shoving her feet into some pumps and dragging a soft cotton top over her head. She reached the front door as the *Rat-at-at-at-at-at* repeated itself, like the death throes of a dying rattlesnake. 'Hi,' she said as she tugged at the door. 'Bloody doorbell sounds like something out of a Hammer Horror. You got here quickly.'

'Hi.' Clive smiled and kissed her lightly as he stepped in through the doorway.

'I'm afraid there wasn't much in the fridge when I had a look, so I'm concentrating on style rather than contents.'

'Hence the wet hair.'

'I meant the meal. It's a good thing you like tomatoes.' She led the way to the kitchen. 'Not very promising at this stage.' She waved vaguely at the ingredients still on the kitchen table.

'It looks a bit like the start of one of my cases. Not obvious how you're going to pull it all together.'

'With some pesto, olive oil and basil. Now, what would you like to drink? Coffee? Beer? Wine?'

'A beer and a coffee, if that's OK?'

Chrissie opened the fridge. 'It's Belgian lager.' She handed him a bottle. 'Let's go and sit down. You must tell me what's happening with Matt's brother, and then I'll start the cooking.' She flicked the switch on the kettle as she followed him out of the kitchen.

Exhaustion showed on his face as he sank onto the sofa. He stretched out his legs, his feet under the coffee table and then let his head flop back against the cushions.

'Ahhh....' His breath escaped in a long sigh.

'So, tell me. Are we safe from Tom?' Chrissie sat down next to him, hoping he'd say they'd locked Tom up and thrown away the key.

'Well, we've charged him under the Hunting Act, so theoretically he could be released on bail until he's due in court.'

'Bail? So he's free to terrorise....'

'Conditional bail, and I said *could* be released - but let me finish. It turns out Mrs Hinton, our human hare coursing victim, identified him from his mug shot. So, that's more than one count of hare coursing, and also perhaps grievous bodily harm.'

Steam whistled from the kettle in the kitchen. 'Still want that coffee?'

'Thanks, it might wake me up.'

Back in the kitchen, Chrissie thought about the dogs as she prepared the coffee. So why had Tom, and hence Matt, been looking after a Labrador? From the sound of it, a lurcher or greyhound would have been more in keeping with Tom's interests.

'Looks as if the coffee's just in time,' she said as she set the cafetière and a couple of mugs on the coffee table. She had already added an extra measure of ground coffee, but now she figured she'd let it steep for even longer. The stronger the better, if they were to get through the evening.

'Do you want milk in yours?'

Clive opened his eyes. 'Better have it black.' He smiled sleepily when she handed him his drink.

'And what about Anne Blink? Did Tom admit to being outside the Sapphire? I assume you've asked him.'

'Yes, he can't deny it, because he's caught on camera, but he says he can't remember it. He was walking to meet up with some friends. There were people on the pavement....'

'But he opened a car door for her. Surely he can remember?'

'He says he's a polite guy.'

'Oh, come on. He's lying.'

'I know, Chrissie. But short of beating it out of him, we can't get him to say any more.' Clive sipped his coffee and then screwed up his face. 'Christ, you make a strong brew. Better put some milk in it.'

'Sorry, thought it'd stop you falling asleep. I suppose these friends can confirm he was with them?'

Clive nodded. 'And it seems he never left the country.'

'The bastard. So that was just a wheeze to get Matt to look after Storm for him. What a lazy, devious, slimy snake. I suppose it's just another dead end for poor Anne Blink.' Chrissie sipped her coffee. 'Yuk, it is a bit strong, isn't it.'

'We've rattled him with something else though.' Clive paused and watched Chrissie, a half smile playing on his lips. 'We found his fingerprints at Sobell's place. He's sweating a bit now that we're linking him to Sobell's murder. At first he denied having ever met the chap, but we know he must've known him because Mrs Hinton recognised Sobell on the mug shots.'

'So both Sobell and Tom were at the fateful hare coursing? Good old Mrs Hinton.'

'Hmm… let's just hope she's a good witness in court.'

Chrissie made a decision. 'Come on. This is making me hungry.' She stood up. 'Time to get some food in the oven. Do you really think Tom killed Sobell?' She tossed the question back at Clive as she headed to the kitchen.

She didn't hear Clive's answer. She was too busy picturing the dog attack. Could Matt's brother really have presided over something like that, she wondered. It was too horrible to imagine. She opened the fridge.

'So how are you going to turn those scraps of cheese into a meal, Chrissie?'

She turned to find Clive behind her. He leaned against the white porcelain sink and raised his eyebrows.

'You followed me!'

'Well, yes.' He rubbed his hand over his forehead and then ran his fingers through his short hair. Chrissie thought it somewhere between *I can't believe you just said that* and a waking himself up gesture.

'Then make yourself useful and wash and slice these. Thanks,' she said grinning and handed him the punnet of tomatoes. She switched on the oven, laid a silicon mat on the table and opened out the filo pastry. It didn't take a moment to wrap portions of cheese and sliced tomato laced with pesto and olive oil, in the sheets of filo pastry. 'Oh no, nearly forgot the basil,' she cried as she lunged past him to reach the plant on the windowsill. She broke free from his rugby tackle of an embrace and added the fragrant green leaves to the parcels. A moment later, seasoned and brushed with oil, she slipped them onto a baking tray and into the oven. 'Done!' she said triumphantly.

While the little parcels cooked, Chrissie washed some watercress that she found hiding in the crisper compartment at the bottom of the fridge, sliced some onion and mixed a balsamic vinegar dressing. 'Tell me about the helicopter chase,' she said as she worked.

'Ah, now that was fruitful. Two patrol cars and a police motorbike, and then a couple more police cars right at the end. Of course it was all videoed from the air. Brilliant. We've got some good drivers, you know.'

'So how many were you chasing?'

'Well, not me personally, you understand, but... Tom's car, a Land Rover, an Audi and a Mitsubishi.'

Chrissie pricked up her ears. 'A Land Rover?'

'Yes.'

'The same Land Rover Discovery that ran down Mrs Hinton?'

'We didn't think so at first, but once the forensic techs started looking at it, the colour under the re-spray matches. It has a rear access ladder. And, you know what? Accessorised tyre valve caps.'

Chrissie closed her mouth. She bit back the words on the tip of her tongue.

'You know, I wish we had more witnesses like Mrs Hinton. Her husband phoned and mentioned the tyre valve caps. Might have just missed them otherwise. But it's difficult without the same number plate. Could all just be a co-incidence.' He stifled a yawn. 'Might not hold up in court but it's enough to allow our boys to take the vehicle apart. We're still waiting on the forensics.'

Chrissie smothered a smile.

'Are you OK, Chrissie?'

'Hmm… the onion, it just got to me.' She rubbed her eye with the back of her hand. Mascara smeared onto her skin and she rinsed it under the tap. 'I don't imagine the chassis number matched the registration. Bet it was stolen.' She addressed her words to the running water.

'Yes, you're right. It was stolen.' The scent of cooked cheese and the bouquet of herbs filled the kitchen. 'Smells delicious. Good enough to eat, Chrissie.'

'Cheeky bugger,' she muttered and caught him with the flick of her tea towel. 'Come on, let's eat in the sitting room. Can you take some plates and the salad through? I'll bring the burnt offerings from the oven.'

They perched on the edge of the sofa and balanced their plates on their knees. It might have been easier to eat at the kitchen table, but somehow it felt right. For a moment she imagined a life of easy domesticity with Clive.

'I think that was a Gruyere one,' he murmured.

'This one tastes like Suffolk Gold and Parmesan. So,' Chrissie continued between mouthfuls, 'if the Land Rover was the same, what about the driver?'

'Yes, even without Mrs Hinton, we can match the man's face with the photo, and of course there's the gold ring with what looks like a red jewel. So we've definitely got him on two counts of contravening the Hunting Act, and as he was the driver, one of grievous bodily harm.'

'Great! She'll be pleased. What about the others?'

'The usual lowlifes. But one of them was interesting. Dutch. He'd come over on the ferry for the hare coursing. Said he had no idea it was illegal, and before we know it, some big name city lawyer turns up and demands he's released. As good as threw the book at us. In the end we released him with a caution. He may have to return as a witness when the others go to court.'

'But the others are locked up, yes?'

'No. Conditional bail for the man with the ruby ring, but we've still got Tom. We've been allowed to hold him a few days longer.'

'Why?'

'Because we suspect him of murder, but if we don't find anything more to link him with Anne Blink or Sobell, then we have to let him go.'

'Oh God,' Chrissie moaned. 'Let's hope Matt doesn't go on the run again and end up here. Does he know any of this? I mean, can I tell him?' She watched as weariness etched deeper lines on Clive's face. She could have sworn he looked heavenwards before answering.

'Matt's already involved. He's a witness, Chrissie, and he could feed information back to his brother. I can't even be sure he hasn't got a foot in both camps.' He kept his tone even. 'So, none of this goes further.'

Chrissie thought for a moment. 'You could use that. Feed him information you want to get back to Tom. You know, false information, as if you've got more evidence than you have. Keep Tom rattled.'

Clive nodded slowly. 'He'll be at the next raft practice, won't he?'

'Should be. It's on Sunday. Are you free then?' Chrissie smiled. 'Please come, it'll be fun. I kind of missed you last time.' She felt a little self-conscious and stood up, but Clive seemed miles away and deep in thought. She gathered the plates.

'I'll need to speak to him before then. The way things are going, we can only hold Tom another 36 hours,' he sighed.

'Well, if you tell me what to say, I can feed Matt whatever line you have in mind. I'll be seeing him on Friday. We're all meeting up at the Nags Head for a quick drink after work. Hopefully he'll have sorted his phone out by then.' She almost laughed at the memory. 'It took a bit of a dousing at the rafting practice and he's not easy to get hold of at the moment.'

'That sounds like Matt,' Clive murmured and then added, 'You know, I think your suggestion might just work, Chrissie. I've had an idea about what you can tell Matt. I'm guessing it might just break Tom's nerve. He's bound to believe we plant false evidence when it suits us.' He closed his eyes. 'If he knows more than he's saying, then I reckon this'll unnerve him.'

'Good. I'll just clear these away and then you can tell me what I'm to say.'

By the time she came back from the kitchen, Clive's head had lolled back on the cushions. His eyes were closed. She heard him breathing slowly and deeply, the gentle sound threatening to develop into a fully-fledged snore.

'Are you awake, Clive?' Stupid question, she thought. He was dead to the world.

CHAPTER 23

Matt dressed with care; he hoped he might see Jo that evening, after all. Wasn't it Friday, the night for dates?

He'd felt pretty pleased with himself. He'd upgraded his phone without letting on it was damaged, and when by some miracle the SIM card worked in the new one, he considered he was doubly blessed. He said a silent prayer to Saint Sam, the un-sung patron saint of mobiles, and sent the first text of his new machine to Jo. To be honest, he hadn't heard from her since Monday when she'd dropped into the library, but he'd put that down to his phone's water damage.

'*C u at the Nags Head this evening?* That should do it,' he muttered.

He hadn't heard from Tom, either. Whether it was because his phone had been on the blink, or Tom wasn't allowed to make calls while in custody, he wasn't too sure. Either way, it was a relief. 'Tom could be a murderer,' he reminded himself and shuddered.

Keep focused, he thought and smoothed the dark blue cotton tee-shirt over his chest. It was time to practise his sexy half smile for Jo. He raised one corner of his mouth a little and then frowned. He adjusted the mirror and tried again. It wasn't working. The beard, or rather the hair on his upper lip hid the movement. It was no good. 'Scissors,' he murmured.

He trimmed and snipped. 'Ouch!' His lip stung. He tasted blood. Matt stepped back from the mirror and inspected his handiwork. He'd only attacked one side and now the effect gave him a permanent half smile. Sexy was looking weird, and the bleeding didn't help.

'Shit.' It wasn't going to be easy to even up the other side. He checked the time. 18:21; the numbers looked sharp through the glassy face of his new mobile. Better get moving if he was going to be at the Nags Head for Jo. He'd sit with Chrissie and Nick till she arrived. 'Should've said a time,' he mumbled and snipped a bit more.

Matt parked the Piaggio near the large waste bins in the Nags Head car park. He reckoned it wouldn't be visible from the road, and although Tom had been safely shut away for the past week, hiding it from him had become a habit. He glanced around. Only a few cars, he thought, and ambled towards an old blue Fiesta. He didn't need to see the number plate to know who owned it. Apart from anything else, the fine scratches along the passenger side gave it away. 'Close encounters with a hedge,' Nick had once told him.

Matt couldn't help but look as he passed. 'Why's 'e got dustsheets heaped in the back?' Matt shook his head and sauntered on. A kernel of excitement grew in his chest. Jo might be inside.

Strains of *Hotel California* met him as he pushed at the pub's heavy wooden door. The jukebox pounded out the bass and music filled the air as he stepped onto the old floorboards. He scanned the room, but there was no sign of a bird with a bubblegum-pink stripe in her hair. A couple of drinkers stood at the bar. One of them was Nick, his hand resting on its surface and tapping to the beat of the music. Matt swallowed his disappointment and wandered over.

'They've got a craft lager on tap,' Nick shouted. 'Local brewery. Do you want to try it?'

'Yeah,' the barman added. 'It's a German- or Czech-style lager. They've even used the same hops and fermentation process. It's been quite popular. One of this week's specials. I think the brewery's out Coddenham Green way.'

'OK, but only an 'alf.'

They carried their drinks over to a table. 'You aint seen Jo, 'ave you?' Anxiety spilled into his accent, lengthening and sharpening the long Suffolk vowels.

Nick held his pint partway to his mouth and raised an eyebrow. 'Not since the rafting. Why, were you expecting to see her?'

'Kind of.'

'You old sea dog!' Nick sipped his beer before adding, 'See you're supporting the Lifeboats.'

'Yeah, R.N.L.I.' Matt read out the letters printed across his blue tee-shirt and touched the smart flag design, its golden crown and anchor emblazoned on the sleeve. He was pleased with the look.

'God, I'm glad it's Friday. It's been one hell of a week.'

'Oh yeah?'

Nick nodded. 'It started with some bloody hooligans breaking into the Willows van lock-up. That was on Tuesday night. Took us half the next day to clear it all up. And since then Dave's been in a foul temper 'cause he got burgled on Wednesday night. It's been bloody miserable at work. Hope he's in a better mood by Sunday.'

'Dave? What'd they take?'

'Not much, but he said they turned the place over a bit. They even went through his garage and garden shed. They took some credit cards and a set of keys, I think. How about you? Good week?'

'Got an upgrade.' Matt fished his mobile out of his jeans. He passed it to Nick and then shifted closer to show off its settings and programmes. The room reverberated with sound as the jukebox belted out a medley of rock anthems.

'Hi.' Chrissie's voice was almost drowned by AC/DC's *Highway to Hell*. She pulled up a chair and set her ginger beer down on the table. 'Is that an upgrade?'

'I didn't see you arrive, Chrissie. Yeah, it's Matt's.'

Matt nodded. 'Got it today.' He'd been too engrossed in showing Nick to notice her ordering her drink at the bar.

She held out her hand for his new mobile. 'Thanks. Have you got another dog, Matt?'

'What you talkin' about?'

'You've got hair all over your tee.'

Matt pulled a face and frowned.

'Ah, I see it now. You've attacked your beard. So, it's not dog's hair. Wrong animal.' She sipped her ginger beer and examined his phone. 'Nice,' she said and handed it back.

Matt brushed at his chest and glanced around the bar. He still couldn't see any sign of Jo. He turned his attention back to Chrissie as his mild anxiety grew. 'Has Clive said anythin' 'bout Tom?' He watched as Chrissie opened her mouth to speak, seemed to change her mind and then frowned.

'Is it something you're not meant to tell us, Chrissie?' Nick asked.

She nodded. 'Yes, but it's all wrong, so I'm going to tell you anyway.'

'What d'you mean?'

'The police, they shouldn't do things like this. It's immoral. Clive said they couldn't pin anything on Tom, apart from the hare coursing. The CCTV footage outside the Sapphire isn't enough on its own, so they're going to fabricate something.'

'What?' Matt whispered.

'When they searched his flat, they found some weed, but nothing of any consequence... so they're going to say they found some Tuinal as well. They'll maybe use that to try and pin Anne Blink's murder on him.'

'Shit, that aint right, Chrissie.' For a moment Matt forgot about Jo as the injustice of it sank in. Tom had never had a sense of fair play. That had been obvious the first time he'd loosened the links on Matt's bicycle chain as a kid, but that didn't mean the police could throw away the rule book. 'So they've still got 'im?'

'Don't know. Last time I spoke to Clive he said they'd have to let him go unless they came up with some new evidence. I don't know if he meant the planted Tuinal. So yes, I suppose Tom could be out there somewhere. Has he contacted you?'

The sudden spectre of Tom somewhere out there on the loose made Matt's guts twist. He checked his new mobile: no missed calls, no new texts - nothing from Tom, nothing from Jo.

'Look if they haven't got anything on him, he's hardly going to come after you to keep you quiet. As far as he's concerned he'll think he's in the clear. It'll be OK.' Chrissie sipped her ginger beer as the jukebox leapt into life again and the first few notes of Whitesnake's *Here I Go Again* drifted across. 'If he does contact you, you'd better warn him about the Tuinal, that's if he doesn't already know. You're looking very smart, by the way.'

'Yes, Matt's either hoping to be the first one rescued if the pub sinks, or it's to impress Jo.'

Matt felt the blood rush to his face. 'Just 'cause I've prinked m'self up, don't mean nothin'.' The Suffolk threatened to take over as a roller coaster of emotion swept through; first Tom, then Jo, and finally his misery with carpentry.

'Are you OK, Matt?' Chrissie watched him and frowned.

'Well, I've….' It wasn't a secret. Everyone knew he was clumsy. They'd all seen his ineptitude with tools. It was obvious. They must've already guessed. 'I'm goin' to see Blumfield. Goin' to change… to computin' an' IT.'

'But why now, after sticking it for so long? Where will you go?'

'Tools aint my thing, Chrissie. They don't work for me. Carpentry aint for me. But I'm good with computers. An' if I stay here, at the Academy, it won't cost me. I've looked up stuff on the internet an', well I think I can swop.'

'You've been thinking about this for some time, haven't you?'

Matt nodded.

'And if you can't, will you drop out… or carry on?' Nick spoke quietly, the beat from the jukebox almost swamping his words.

'Don't know, mate.'

'Well, you're not dropping out till the totem pole's done.'

'And the raft race,' Nick added.

Matt frowned. 'I thought the totem pole was done, Chrissie.'

'Yes, but we might add some more carvings, make it taller.'

'You must be bloody joking.' Nick stood up. 'I think you'll be OK with computing and IT, Matt. Anyone want another?'

Matt checked the time. Eight o'clock, the pub was starting to fill and there was still no sign of Jo.

•••

Outside in the car park, the night air felt cool. Matt looked up. Tiny, far away stars spattered the inky-blue. He searched the sky, trying to see patterns in the dots, hoping to recognise a constellation. Jo hadn't shown up, and it was well after eleven o'clock. It would be nice to spot something, he thought. The Pole Star. That would be a good omen.

A sudden peal of chimes rang from his pocket. For a moment he wondered what it was. Then he remembered.

'Bloody joker's gone an' changed me ringtone.' He dragged his mobile out, all the while cursing Nick for having set his phone to such a ridiculous jingle. He fumbled in the dark trying to find the answer function.

'Hi. Jo?' His heart pounded.

'Matt?'

The familiar rough tones grated on his ear. His stomach flipped. 'Shit.'

'Shit? That aint no way to greet your brother.'

Matt felt his throat go dry. His pulse quickened. He swallowed hard and waited.

'Where are you? Been lookin' for you. You weren't at Mum's. S'pose you heard the police got me? The bastards.'

'Yeah, Tom. Word gets round. Heard you'd been hare coursin'.'

'Well, they couldn't keep me long. I'm out now, on some kind of bail, but that'll be OK. You'll see. They thought they'd try an' stick somethin' else on me while I was in, but they forgot….'

'What? What they forgot, Tom?'

'They forgot what you used to call me.' He sniggered and then whispered, 'Mr Teflon Man.'

Matt closed his eyes and tried to shut out the image. It was as if he was eight years old again. Beads of sweat broke out on his forehead.

'Are you still there, Matt?'

'Yeah, I'm still here. Look, I've heard somethin' you ought to know, Tom.'

'What? You've found Storm?'

Matt shivered. 'No, it's just I heard the police are plannin' somethin'. A trick to stitch you up.'

'Well, the bastards had me and didn't manage it, so what you talkin' about, Matt? Is this another of your scare-mongerin' tales?'

'No, Tom. I heard they're goin' to plant drugs on you. Honest.'

'What? Don't be daft. All they found were a couple of spliffs. Weed aint a big deal.'

'I heard Tuinal.'

'What?' Tom's voice sounded sharper. 'Where'd you hear that?'

'One of me mates knows a copper.' Matt held his breath but all he caught was silence on the phone. As the seconds ticked by he felt his insides wrenching. He knew

Tom's rage. It could be violent, terrible, but the slow burn of his silence was even worse. 'A-are you still there?'

'Yeah. Tuinal, you say?' His words melted into the night.

'That's what I heard. So what'll you do, Tom?'

'Disappear.'

'But Tuinal aint class A.'

'You're a bloody thicko, Matt. What d'you think? When they come calling, I won't be hangin' around while they pin a murder on me. I'm goin' to vanish, evaporate, fade away before then. Got it? The bastards'll never find me. I'll have long since gone.'

'But-'

'But what, Matt?'

'Nothin'.'

'That's right, Matt. You don't remember nothin'. Right?'

'Right.'

'Bye.' Tom cut the call.

Matt let his hand drop to his side. He gripped his mobile but his muscles felt limp. Relief and shock flowed through his body in equal measure. There was only one word he could find. 'Shite.'

So why had Tom phoned? Just to let him know he was out? The messages were oblique, the threats tangible. What would Chrissie say? He could almost hear her voice as he remembered a previous conversation. 'It's to keep the pressure on you. Tom's a bully. He likes to taunt you when his mood is low or he's been bullied himself. He just passes it down the line. It makes him feel bigger.' And tonight? Matt knew the answer to that. Who wouldn't feel low after several days in police custody?

'Stand up for yourself,' Chrissie had said. 'Tell Tom to piss off. Remember it's Tom who needs you, not the other way round.'

'He don't need me, just someone to bully, more like,' he'd reasoned.

'Yes exactly, but that's his weakness. Needing to bully. You're not like him. Stand back from it and you'll see what he's trying to do. That makes you the stronger one. If he can't bully you he'll leave you alone.'

It sounded very logical when Chrissie had explained it to him, but alone in the Nags Head car park just before midnight, was a very different matter to lounging on a comfy sofa in Chrissie's sitting room. Easy to sound brave then, he reckoned. Did Chrissie realise that just the sound of Tom's voice made him sweat? Misery weighed down on his shoulders.

There was no point in hanging around. Nick had left hours earlier to meet Kat, and Chrissie soon after.

And Jo? Well he still hadn't spotted the Pole Star. He put on his helmet. It was time to ride back to Tumble Weed Drive.

CHAPTER 24

Nick was on a mission. This was something he knew he had to do. Chrissie was either with him or not on this one. Either way, he'd made up his mind. He'd just dropped Kat off at the rifle club in Hadleigh and now he had a few hours to kill. He drummed his fingers on the steering wheel while he listened to the ringing tone and waited for Chrissie to answer.

'Hi, Nick.' Her voice sounded tinny on his mobile.

'Morning, Chrissie. Not too early for you?' He listened to her yawn.

'No. I'm wide awake now. Why?'

'Did you mean what you said last night in the Nags Head, you know about adding some more carvings to the totem pole?'

'Yes, of course. It looks brilliant at the moment but an extra few feet of, I don't know... someone else's head, and it'll be amazing. With the extra height, well... spectacular comes to mind.'

It wasn't what came to Nick's mind. 'If you're really set on this, I thought I'd go over to Clegg's and work on it. Will he be there this morning?'

'He's always there. Look, I wasn't expecting to go in today. I'm meeting Sarah in Lavenham at eleven. I might just about have time to get there later this afternoon, but I'm not sure. Is that OK?'

'Of course, but don't mess up your day over it. See you at the rafting tomorrow. Bye.'

Nick slipped his mobile into his pocket and Adele back into the CD player. He started the Fiesta. The road from Hadleigh to Bildeston had a couple of hills and he drove fast as Adele's voice filled the car. He swooped downwards between rough hedgerows and trees, *Rolling in The Deep* following the groundswell under his tyres. The beat gave him courage and urged him on. He swept up out of Bildeston and headed for Wattisham and the perimeter road. He almost missed the Clegg workshop turning and breaking hard, rattled onto the rough track. Even Adele's voice couldn't cope with the potholes and he flicked the player off as he steered between the ruts.

When Nick stepped into the old barn workshop, the feeling of nostalgia for a past age hit him as it always did when he visited Ron. Scents of wood dust and linseed oil carried on the cool air. He scanned along the bench tops, past the band saw and thickness planer and to the far end where Ron sat at the lathe, the motor humming. He held a roughing-out gouge to a spinning block of wood. The shavings dropped and scattered at his feet. Nick waited as Ron stopped the motor, straightened his back and reached for a sizing tool.

'Hello, Mr Clegg,' he called.

Ron looked up slowly and smiled, pushing his safety glasses up onto his forehead. 'Hello, Nick. I didn't hear you above the lathe. Come on in.'

Nick walked the length of the barn, past the totem pole stretched out on blocks, and up to Ron. 'I hope I'm not bothering you.' He glanced at the lathe. 'What're you turning, Mr Clegg?'

'I need some wooden knobs, you know, as handles for some drawers. It's easier to make them all identical if I turn them from one length of wood. They'll start as a series of knobs joined together in sequence. A bit like a fancy banister. Then I'll use a fine saw. Yes, I think my Japanese saw, to part them. So what brings you here this morning? I'm sure you didn't come all this way just to watch me turning wooden knobs.'

Nick shook his head. 'No, I....' He didn't know where to begin. He knew what he planned to do, but with Ron sitting there watching, his courage evaporated and his momentum stalled.

'I was about to stop for a mug of tea. How about you put the kettle on?' Ron stood up, pushing the stool back and scraping its legs on the concrete. He paused to glance at Nick, the beginning of a frown playing on his forehead. He moved stiffly. 'At one time I thought you'd never get that finished.' He looked towards the totem pole.

'I've still got some neatening up to do at the top, but I'm pleased with the way the Spitfire's angled. The plane looks a bit like an eagle launching into flight.' They stood and gazed at it for a moment. 'It doesn't need any more carvings does it Mr Clegg? The totem pole doesn't have to be any taller, does it?'

'What ever made you say that?' Ron sounded surprised. 'The Spitfire, our modern-day eagle, should top the totem pole and that's exactly what it's doing. It's fitting. You've all done enough. A little tidying up and some painting, but then it's finished.'

'Chrissie seems to think we should....' Nick let his words drift away. He couldn't bring himself to give voice to her suggestion.

'Mrs Jax does a lot of thinking.'

'I know,' Nick murmured. He took a deep breath and summoned his nerve. 'Do you have a chain saw, Mr Clegg?'

Ron nodded slowly. 'Are you happy to use one?'

'Very,' Nick replied and grinned.

'And what do you plan to do with it, might I ask?'

'I'm going to lop the top off, Mr Clegg. Before Chrissie's thinking firms up into anything material.'

'Good. And Mrs Jax…?'

Nick cleared his throat. 'I didn't reckon I needed to involve her at this particular moment.'

'That's probably wise.'

'She'll find out soon enough. At least this way it won't spoil her weekend, Mr Clegg.'

'A saw cut now is a kindness. Is that the sort of thing?'

Nick shrugged. What could he say? If they were all to keep their sanity, the top had to come off. 'The sooner the better.'

Ron sighed. 'Well I reckon tea can wait. Better get on with it then. You'll need something to support both sides where you're making the cut. You don't want the end of the trunk falling away, splitting off and damaging what you've already carved. And give yourself an inch or so margin.'

'So if things go wrong I've got the option of adding a gunner turret on the top and making the Spitfire look like a bomber?'

'No. In case your saw cuts too close or you don't' cut straight. Allow a margin for error, Nick. A margin for error.'

Nick was impatient to get started. He just wanted to hold the chain saw and hear the snarling motor whine as the cutting chain bit into the wood and sank through the trunk, like a knife into butter. But Ron insisted he plan and prepare before even starting the motor. He had to wear the right gear, sharpen the teeth and oil the chain. In the end Nick wished he'd just picked up a large-toothed handsaw and used his own shoulder power and elbow grease to cut through the trunk. He had a sneaking feeling that was precisely Ron's intention.

'Thank God,' he muttered as he straightened up and switched the motor back into idle mode. The deed was done, the cut was made. 'Thank God,' he repeated, relief brightening his horizon.

Later, as he drove back to Hadleigh to pick up Kat, the enormity of his action struck home. A year ago he'd never have had the guts to do something like this, but now, almost a metre of cedar trunk lay across his back seat. It balanced on dustsheets with the blue drum hidden beneath. He felt pumped up and heroic. Kat would no doubt call him decisive, but he guessed Chrissie would find other words. He'd deal with that tomorrow at the rafting practice. For now, it could wait. He slipped Adele into the CD player and grinned.

CHAPTER 25

Chrissie glanced at Clive as the tyres of her car crunched on the rough track. She was pleased he'd wanted to come to the raft building on his weekend off, but unease crept like a cancer at the back of her mind. It had grown from the moment he'd first told her about the developments in the Sobell killing. The implications horrified her.

She thought back to their conversation only a few hours earlier. She'd stayed over at his house in Lavenham, and they'd been shuffling around his kitchen, sleepily throwing together a simple breakfast.

'I told Matt,' she remembered saying, as she warmed some croissants. 'All that stuff you said I should let slip. You know, about the police wanting to plant some Tuinal on Tom, or rather in Tom's flat. It shocked him. I know he'll tell Tom.'

Her mind had only been half on what she'd been saying. At the time she'd been more intent on trying to remember where Clive kept his marmalades and jams.

'Well that might explain why he's disappeared,' he'd said, as he opened a fresh pack of coffee.

'What? Tom's disappeared? You never mentioned it.'

'No, I hadn't got round to telling you yet.'

Even now it made her feel anxious.

'We wanted him back for more questioning but I'm afraid he's broken bail and scarpered.'

She'd watched as he filled the coffee pot from the kettle and then reached for the pot's lid with its plunger.

'Christ, I knew you wanted to rattle him a bit, but out there on the loose, well that wasn't the idea, was it?'

'No, and Len Carter's gone missing as well.'

'Len who? You've never mentioned a Len before.'

'No. He was the man driving the Land Rover. I think you called him Ruby Ring.'

'Oh my God.' A terrible thought struck. 'It's not because of what I told Matt on Friday, is it?'

'Well I don't know exactly what you said, but I doubt it, Chrissie. I reckon Carter's got bigger worries on his mind. We've finally got the forensics back from stripping down the Land Rover.'

'And?'

'We found dog's hair.'

'And? Is that it? He's already been charged for the hare coursing, so why break bail over that?' All thoughts of breakfast vanished as she'd waited for him to say more.

'It's the type of blood they found on the dog's hair that's interesting, Chrissie. It's human.'

'Oh God. Do we know whose blood?'

'Yes. It matches the samples we've got from Sobell.' His words punched through the aromas of freshly brewed coffee and warm croissants filling his kitchen.

'Sobell's blood? That means....' She'd put her hand to her mouth, the implications were horrific.

'Carter's our main suspect,' he finished for her.

Chrissie's brain spun into overdrive. 'D'you think this Carter bloke could have done something to Tom as well? And Tom's not just bolted but he's dead?' She tried to brush the image away.

'Steady, Chrissie. Now you're leaping to–'

'Sorry. It's just that my mind....' She'd read the frown on his face.

To Chrissie's eyes, Clive's kitchen was a reminder of his past failed marriage, with its beige tiles, tired wooden cupboards and his ex's kids' photos stuck to the fridge door. It wasn't the place to vent her worst fears.

He hadn't volunteered any further information and she sensed not to ask more. She'd been determined not to ruin what was left of the weekend and bit her tongue. It had been Clive who'd suggested they drive to the rafting session in her TR7 and she'd leapt at the idea, keen to put down the hood and blow away their breakfast conversation along with her growing unease.

And so the wind had caught her hair on the journey, whipping it into chaos, massaging her scalp and easing the tension. She'd turned onto the track, the tyres spattering gravel as she glanced at Clive.

Flashes of bright sunlight cut between the trees and straight into her face. She screwed up her eyes. 'Don't you just love it with the hood down? You know we could be in the middle of nowhere out here. It's not very easy to find.'

'Well, certainly not with your sense of direction, Chrissie.' Clive sat in the passenger seat and grinned. 'I'm amazed you ever found it last time.'

'So am I. Now was it right or left here?' Chrissie slowed to a halt and looked at the fork in the track. The sight of young alder mixed with silver birch and oak failed to jog her memory. A light breeze carried the scent of their foliage as she looked at the trail. She made a decision and took the left fork.

•••

Nick checked his rear view mirror. It looked clear, just as it had for the last few miles. There were rarely many cars around on a Sunday, and he'd glanced at the mirror more from habit than expectancy. His thoughts were on the raft. He hardly noticed the patterns in the barley fields; the greens already ripening through a palate of shades towards brown, creating patches and streaks of colour-wash. He watched as a black Audi saloon cruised towards him. It slowed as it approached and he waited for it to pass before he turned off the road and onto the gravel driveway.

Not far now, he thought as he slipped the Fiesta into second gear. Ahead, he caught a glimpse of Dave's old Land Rover. It rocked and tilted as it veered out of the main courtyard and then disappeared from sight. Nick grinned. He pictured Dave at the wheel, careering along the tree lined track, with its tall overhanging branches casting shade between the rough hedges and ditches. The 1975 series III was Dave's weekend toy. A chance to off-road in retro style. To feel the drive. Taste the grit. Relive his youth.

The first raft building effort the previous Sunday had been more of a party than anything else, and the result they'd produced, a half floating disaster. Nick knew they only had a week left. 'It's getting serious now,' he'd muttered to Kat and she'd seemed happy to pass it up and go to her shooting practice that morning. Secretly he hoped Seth's girlfriend and sister weren't coming either. They distracted everyone and Matt would play to the gallery if Jo was there. He tried to concentrate on the task ahead as he followed the track, the gravel giving way to packed earth and the Fiesta pitching into the ruts. The cedar trunk threatened to roll forwards from the back seat as he took the right fork.

•••

Matt dressed without enthusiasm. He hadn't heard from Jo and she'd never turned up at the Nags Head. He'd been counting on her coming to the raft building that morning, but now he didn't hold out much hope, not after going onto Facebook and looking up her time line. He hadn't known what to think after he'd read it. He knew he wasn't good at riddles and satire, but poems? He hadn't needed to cope with rhyme before. There wasn't much demand for poetry on Tumble Weed Drive.

He pictured the words as he dressed. He could see them, exactly as they'd appeared on the screen. The title: *For all the Matts out there.* He guessed that meant him. And the poem?

Go float a rope.
This Jo don't show without more warning.
Shan't give up hope
But won't make aqua trap Sunday morning.

What did she mean, he wondered for the hundredth time. Did she fancy him? Was she playing hard to get? He didn't know. He supposed the aqua trap meant the reservoir, and shook his head as he reached for an old grey tee-shirt. It matched his mood and was much the same colour as the water in the reservoir. He wished he could come up with something smart to post on his Facebook page, but all he could think of that rhymed was aggro, mojo and elbow. How to make a poem out of that?

It didn't take him long before he was perched on the Piaggio and zipping along the familiar route, the engine whining and droning with each bend. His helmet seemed to disconnect him from the world. Beyond the visor were the people who caused pain: Tom, Jo and maybe Blumfield. On his side of the Perspex, with the wind against his chest and arms, he could forget his emotions. Separate and protect were the words that sprang to mind. It would make a catchy phrase for a tee-shirt, he decided. His spirits were riding high by the time he slowed to turn onto the gravel driveway. Nick had said there'd be six drums for the raft, and that meant he might keep his bum out of the water.

The front wheel hammered down into a pothole and jarred him forwards. He yelped and lowered his gaze to the track. He focused a metre ahead and wove a path along the ruts made by larger tyres. He tried to keep the Piaggio's narrower tread in line. Sunlight flashed across his eyes. Leafy branches swept by, fleetingly blocking the rays. For a moment he was a dispatch rider, a tin helmet on his head, an army jacket on his chest and urgent papers burning a hole in his backpack. The reedy engine played the soundtrack.

He pressed on. Beneath him, the surface changed. Grooves criss-crossed the packed earth and he slowed to a halt. The engine idled as he scanned ahead, searching for the quickest route. What had the General said? He imagined the comic-strip book with a bubble to the General's mouth. *Whatever you do, don't leave the path. Watch out for landmines.*

Matt smiled the tough, no-nonsense smile of a superhero. In front the track split. To the right, the way led to the reservoir and to the left, well, he didn't know. He sat with the scooter slightly tilted, one foot on the ground, the other on the footrest. Something caught his attention.

Twigs cracked somewhere ahead. The soft throaty purr of an engine cut through the foliage. He strained to see. A black metallic form moved ahead along the left fork. 'An Audi,' he breathed as he recognised the shape. The car drew away.

Matt frowned. Who drove an Audi, he wondered. Not Seth or Andy. It had to be something to do with the raft building, he reckoned. And then he remembered Jo. Could it be anything to do with her? It was a long shot, but then he hadn't quite understood her Facebook message. 'Bloody poems,' he muttered and engaged the two-stroke engine. He headed his scooter along the left fork.

•••

Nick followed the track through the wooded area. He remembered the way the young trees and shrubs encroached, as if trying to reclaim the ground. He imagined if a car didn't pass that way for a few months, saplings would spring up and soon it would become single track. A path for walkers only, and then no path at all. He drove on, soon breaking cover from the trees and swaying against his seatbelt as the Fiesta lurched onto the open grass. He parked next to Dave's Land Rover.

'Morning, Dave,' he shouted as he slammed the driver's door.

Dave didn't answer. He stood in front of a tarpaulin, hands on hips, head bowed.

Nick strode over to where they'd stowed the raft the week before and stared at the rucked up sheeting thrown into a heap. 'See you've started already.'

'That's not me. I haven't touched it. I found it like this.'

'What? You mean some joker's done this? Christ, they've pulled it apart. Look.' Nick caught his breath as he took in the scene. The drums had been cut free and scattered. Lengths of cord hung from the frame like drying spaghetti. 'Sh-o-oot. D'you think it's a rival team?'

'God knows,' Dave moaned as he bent to examine a drum. 'The caps have gone. Someone's unscrewed them. If we don't find them, we'll never get the raft to float.'

'But can't we hammer in some bungs, or something?'

Dave shook his head. 'It won't be good enough, Nick.'

'Well, at least the one in my car's still got its screw cap, and I've brought a huge lump of cedar wood. Cedar's meant to float well. Better than pine.' Nick crouched down and ran his hands over the rough grass near the raft. 'Found one!' He held the blue plastic screw cap up for inspection.

'Well done. Now screw it on, for God's sake, before we lose it. Only four more.' Dave knelt down and moved forwards, feeling his way, patting the grass.

'You look as if you're at a religious meeting for the visually impaired,' Nick muttered. He tightened the cap on the first drum as the faint sound of an engine seeped along the track and into the grassy space. He checked his watch. 'This should be the others.'

His words had hardly left his mouth before the garish green of Andy's Citroen shattered the harmony of nature's shades and pitched out of the trees. 'Blimey, what a gross colour.' But then as Andy had once told him, beggars can't be choosers when you're a first-time driver and you're looking for a cheap second-hand deal. Nick grinned and waved, his spirits starting to rise.

'Hey, what's going on?' Seth called as he got out of Andy's car. 'You could've just untied the drums, you know. No need to hack at the rope like madmen.' He walked across. 'Morning, Dave. Have you lost something?'

'It's a disaster,' Nick butted in. 'Someone's trashed the raft. The drums are useless.'

'But that's sick. Have they punctured them?' Andy's voice rose.

'I can't see any holes, but....' Dave shook his head.

'And who's *they*? Could it have been... foxes or something?' Seth stared at Dave, still on all fours.

'Foxes don't unscrew drum caps.' Dave held up another screw cap he'd just found in the grass. 'This is bloody weird, though. Why leave the caps lying around and the drums intact if you wanted to disable the raft permanently?'

'It doesn't make sense.' Nick turned and stared into the wood. It looked peaceful enough but it didn't feel right. Had someone stumbled across the raft and simply felt the urge to pull it apart? Destruction on impulse? Nick reckoned it must have taken real determination to cut the drums off the frame, and whoever it was had been carrying a knife. He shivered. This wasn't the work of impulse. An icy hand gripped at his guts. He tried to shake off the feeling, but the prickles at the back of his neck told him something was very wrong. With each breezy gust rustling the leaves, each branch dipping and swaying and each pigeon abruptly taking flight, the sense of malevolence amongst the trees deepened.

'What've you seen?' Seth asked.

'Nothing. I just....' He forced himself to turn his back to the wood. 'Well done, Dave. Come on, you two. We've more screw caps to find.'

'Ouch!' Andy knelt on something sharp.

•••

Matt drove slowly. The track was potholed, and the Audi wasn't far ahead. One moment the black paintwork reflected the sunlight, and then the next, it blended with the dappled shade. He hung back, staying out of sight, keeping his throttle low, his engine quiet. He was stalking prey. He hadn't decided what he was going to do if he got up close.

After he'd followed for less than a quarter of a mile Matt inched around a bend, just holding back before he was seen. He guessed the Audi was stopping. He pulled back and killed his engine. He listened as a car door opened and footsteps crunched on stones. He held his breath and merged with the hawthorn and alder, but no one walked back along the track. He breathed out.

'This is a fucking farce.' A man spoke, the tone grated. 'It's like they've got every shit bag in the world turning up.' He almost spat the words.

Matt tried to place the accent, Essex or Cockney? He'd have to hear more to be certain.

'Just put a sock in it, for once, Highland.'

The sound of the familiar voice punched Matt. 'Tom?' he whispered to the inside of his helmet. He'd hoped for Jo and instead his worst nightmare stood less than 30 yards away. What the hell was going on? Panic squeezed his throat. A pulse hammered in his ears. He only had one thought; to get away. He began to push his scooter around.

'Did you hear something just then?'

Matt froze.

A pigeon took off high above, cracking its wings, the leaves rustling and trembling as a branch swayed.

'It's a pigeon, Highland. Wood's bloody full of 'em. D'you reckon we leave the car, then take the shortcut, like you said? You checked it out earlier this week, remember?'

'Yeah, it's an easy walk from 'ere. We'll get up close and see if they've brought that friggin' drum.'

'Better get the guns out the boot then. An' if anyone asks, it's squirrels an' pigeons we're after, not pheasant.

Aint the season.' Tom's rough tones cut through the stillness.

'Yeah right, wise arse. Since when did you start givin' orders? Now turn the bloody car round. It'll make it easier for afterwards.'

If he wanted to get away he had to move now, Matt thought as a car door slammed and an engine purred into life. He pushed the Piaggio back onto the track. He knew he couldn't risk starting the scooter. The sudden metallic guffaw and chortle of the two-stroke would give him away in seconds, so he crept and pushed and sweated.

By the time he reached the place where the track split, he was panting. Off to one side, the track led to raft building, his friends and possibly Jo. He knew if he carried straight on and rode out along the main track, then he could escape onto the road and Stowmarket. The urge was strong. It tugged.

'Tom aint got nothin' on me,' he muttered between gasps. 'I'm the one tippin' him off. He's the one owin' favours and it's me he owes. Why should I be scared?' He stood, catching his breath, trying to think all those positive thoughts Chrissie had told him to think. But fear and Tom went hand in hand. It was a learnt reaction. It was like Pavlov's dog and the ringing bell. He'd seen it on a science programme once.

And what had Tom been talking about to Highland, the man with a Scottish name and a cockney accent? Probably out to nick pheasant feeders, those smaller blue plastic drums he'd noticed with cone bases. He'd seen them last week standing high on legs in the grass at the edge of the wood. 'Reckon he's got a deal going down.'

Matt made a decision. He sank onto the Piaggio's seat and started the engine. The pounding in his ears slowed, his breathing eased. The grey cotton tee-shirt clung to his skin where patches of sweat stained darker shades. The wind caught at the material, flapping and chaffing as he followed the ruts and rode the right fork. He glanced at the coloured cartridge cases. They still lay, as on the previous Sunday, discarded amongst the dead leaves and sparse undergrowth. And all the while his tyres cracked twigs and popped stones.

The end of the trees came abruptly and then he was out in the open. He grinned as he spotted Nick's old Fiesta. It was lined up between Andy's Citroen and Dave's marine-blue Series III, the rear door widely open. Lengths of rope, tools and drums littered the grass. For a moment it remind-ed him of the car boot sales at Needham Market, with all the hustle as punters moved between the goods, and every now and again a voice breaking through the background ripple of talking.

'It's Matt,' Seth yelled. 'The Grey Rider.'

Matt liked that. He smoothed his damp tee and waved.

'Have you been in for a dip already?' Nick asked, eye-ing up the sweaty patches. He walked over to the Piaggio and tapped Matt's helmet. 'Better take that off. You're starting to look like a nervous rafter.'

'I took the wrong fork. I could sink a pint, though. Where're the birds?'

Andy stood up. 'Don't think they're going to show, Matt. 'Fraid you'll have to concentrate on the rafting. That's if we can find the last bloody screw cap. Hey, come and help look for it. Drinks later.'

'What you talkin' about, Andy?'

'Some troll trashed the raft. Probably thought it was funny to cut the ropes and take the screw caps off the drums.'

'Bloody joker,' Dave added.

'What? But Chrissie? She's comin'? I mean she'll be bringin' the food, right?'

'Hope so Matt. Can you help me unload my car before you join the screw cap hunt?'

Matt watched as Nick opened the Fiesta's side doors and hatchback.

'I stowed it on the back seat under these dustsheets, but we'll need to move this first.'

Matt couldn't believe his eyes. 'That's... that's the top of the totem pole, Nick.'

'Damn right, it is. I'm not carving any more heads. Are you?'

'Shite, no. But won't Chrissie...?'

'I'll just say it was your idea, mate. Now come on and give me a hand.'

Matt heaved and pulled while Nick lifted. They flipped the cedar trunk over the back of the rear seat, into the boot and then rolled it out to fall on the grass.

'Right, the float-drum next.' Nick pulled the dust-sheets away and folded the front passenger seat forwards. Between them they manhandled the blue drum out through the side door. 'This one's screw cap looks different to the others,' he murmured.

CHAPTER 26

Chrissie frowned. She didn't want to say anything to Clive, but she wasn't at all sure if she was going the right way. If I just keep driving for long enough, she thought, then I'll pass something I recognize and I'll know I'm on the right track. The young silver birch and oak all looked familiar, she'd seen thousands before. The shapes of the branches and the patterns they made failed to trigger a specific memory. She drove slowly, hoping to identify the next turn in the track or some combination of rut and pothole. *We should be breaking out of the tree-cover by now*, her inner voice wailed, but all she saw were more silver birch and oak. She drew to a halt. She needed to think.

'I agree; it's much too beautiful,' Clive said, as they sat in the open top TR7. He looked up through the over-hanging branches. 'If you insist, we could skip the raft building and just sit here and enjoy the wood instead.'

'No way. We can't miss it. And anyway, I've got all the food in the boot.'

'Ah, and there was me thinking we were taking the long scenic route just for the joy of it.' He turned and smiled. She noticed the way the skin creased near his eyes. It usually meant he was about to laugh. 'For a moment there I thought you might be lost,' he murmured.

'No way. It can't be far now.' The words popped out, a knee-jerk reaction.

'You'd think, wouldn't you, that as we're so near… we'd hear the others.'

'I know, Clive. It's amazing how trees seem to absorb the sound.'

'Quite remarkable.'

Chrissie struggled to keep her face straight. OK, she knew he'd guessed they were lost but she wasn't going to admit it. At least not in so many words. The charade could run a little longer, she decided. The track must lead somewhere and if she drove on further, then they were bound to find the reservoir. It was too large to miss, she told herself.

She slipped the engine into gear and moved forwards. She'd felt a little self-conscious, almost nervous when she'd realized she'd missed a turning on the way, but now Clive was on board with it, and clearly amused, she allowed herself to relax and enjoy the adventure. She breathed in the air, mildly damp and cool in the shade, but warm where shafts of sunlight cut onto the track. She concentrated on the scents of the living foliage and ignored the undercurrents of leaves in their various stages of decay.

'You don't hear much bird song, either.' She'd calmed down enough to talk and drive.

'That's because someone's probably shot most of them. I noticed a fair number of old shotgun cartridge cases lying around when you stopped the car back there. Probably aren't too many foxes or rabbits either.'

'I expect they hold shoots here in the winter. Did you see that wire-mesh fenced area where they rear the young pheasants? I don't remember noticing it last time.'

'You may not've come this way last time, Chrissie.'

She kept driving. 'If you want to get out and walk, Clive, you've only got to say.'

'No, I have every confidence in your sense of direction. So what time did you say you'd be there?'

Chrissie grinned. 'Today.'

She eased around a bend and ahead the wood gave way to fields. 'Wow! I don't remember this,' she murmured as she gazed across acres of rapeseed.

'Is that the reservoir?' Clive pointed to one side.

Chrissie followed the direction of his hand and nodded. 'I see what I've done. We've come through the wood and we're out on the other side of the reservoir. Of course. I remember now. The wood borders the water along one side.' She turned and smiled at him. Relief made the sun feel brighter, the volume of glassy water inviting. 'If we'd taken the other track, way back at that right fork, then it would have brought us out on the other side.'

'You must be getting better, Chrissie. Only ninety degrees off course. It's impressive.'

She dug him in the ribs with her elbow.

'Ouch! I meant the reservoir, not your natural compass. It's a fair size for a farm. Now you know where we are, what d'you want to do? Drive back and round to the other side?'

'It looks as if I can get the car closer to the bank, just up there. I'll park, and then we could walk along the water's edge to the other side and join everyone. It'll probably be quicker than driving and it'll give them a surprise. What do you say?'

'Sounds OK to me, Chrissie. You know I'm always happy to walk. Is there a lot to carry?'

'Bread rolls, cheese, ham, salad - that kind of thing. The boys were bringing the beer. I've a couple of big bottles of water, but that's about it.'

Chrissie followed the track another fifty yards and parked close to the bank. She'd already stowed the food in a couple of small backpacks before they'd left Lavenham.

If Clive didn't know me better, she thought as she reached into the boot, he might have assumed I'd planned the whole thing, just so I could take a hike into the woods with him.

Clive grabbed the heavier pack and the bottles of water she'd wedged behind the seats. She watched him sling the carrier bag from his backpack.

'Were the three-litre bottles a mistake, Clive?'

'If it gets too bad you can always carry them for me.' He laughed and strode up the bank.

'Not if I can't catch up with you.'

They followed a narrow path, in some places only a few inches wide. It looked as if it had been made by animals, tracking along the edge of the water. On one side: trees, shrub-sized hazel and alder crowded. On the other, a rough grassy slope tumbled into the reservoir. From a distance the water took on the colour of the sky, but when Chrissie gazed down at the edge, it looked slightly brackish. Coarse grass gave way to heavy clay earth and she noticed how in some places the ground had been trampled, as if used for a hide, perhaps to shoot wild duck.

'Hey, look at those Canada geese.' She pointed across the water to the furthermost corner.

'I wish I'd brought my camera,' Clive said over his shoulder. 'It's so peaceful. I'm glad you suggested this stroll.'

They walked at a brisk pace and it didn't take long before they were half way. Soon Chrissie began to pick up muffled sounds of the raft building team at work. She guessed they weren't far away.

•••

'Here, Matt. Give me a hand. This one seems heavier than the others.' Nick dragged the blue drum. He hadn't noticed its weight when he'd loaded it into his car at the beginning of the week. He'd been too busy thinking about where to hide it from Dave.

'Probably still half full of stuff,' Matt muttered as he took one end.

'Better empty it then.'

They set the drum down on the rough grass.

Nick tried to unscrew the cap. Nothing moved. He bent to examine it more closely. 'It seems kind of..., well you'd hardly notice, but it's a deeper cap than on the others.' He struggled again.

'Cross threaded, d'you think?'

'Hope not, Matt. But if it's jammed on, as long as it's watertight....'

'Yeah, but it won't float so well. Not if it's full of stuff. Don't want me bum wet again if I can help it.'

Nick summoned his strength for one last effort, held his breath, locked his grip and turned. He felt something give. The cap shifted a fraction. 'Yes,' he hissed and strained again. 'I think it's because I'm pushing down. You know, like those child-proof tops?' A few moments later he held the cap in his hand. 'Well that's bloody strange.'

Matt peered over his shoulder. 'What d'you mean?'

'There's something blocking the hole. Like a second cap.'

'Oh yeah, so there is. And there's two little slots, like you need a key. Like with a manhole cover.'

'I wonder if we've got something we can open it with. Go and see if Dave's got anything in his tool box, will you?' Nick scratched his head. He knew he'd seen something that might fit the job. He tried to picture it. Of course,

Andy. He'd nearly cut his knee when he knelt on something earlier. Nick remembered him yelling in pain.

Matt wandered back, smiling. 'Dave gave me this.' He held out something resembling a large flat key, but with two prongs at one end.

'That's what Andy knelt on. It looks bloody vicious.' Nick remembered Dave saying it was a bit like a golfer's pitch repairer. 'Go on then, Matt. See if it'll fit.'

Nick watched as Matt lined up the prongs with the slots.

'So, does it fit?'

'Yeah, seems to, mate.' Matt pushed, twisted and then pulled.

Nick stared as Matt lifted out the locking mechanism with the key. A long cellophane tube, a bit like a hose and filled with white powder was attached to it base. 'Bloody hell.' The snake-like structure just kept on coming as Matt pulled.

'What've you found?' Seth yelled.

'I don't know. It looks like….' The words died in Nick's throat as he tried to remember what Lia had said. 'Calcium hydroxide? Purified wheat starch? I don't know. Something they use at the manuscript restoration place?'

'It's all coiled up in there,' Matt muttered as he took the weight of the cellophane with both hands and pulled some more. The transparent hosing kept appearing.

Andy, Dave, and Seth walked over to them. 'What's going on?' Seth asked.

'Oh God,' Dave murmured. 'That looks… well it's been hidden, hasn't it? This is the last drum, isn't it? It's the one I just took on Monday. Now it makes sense.'

'What makes sense, Dave?'

'I've been getting weird phone calls. No name, just a voice saying, *you've got somethin' that don't belong to you. We want it back....*'

Nick frowned. 'You collected this drum on Monday, didn't you? Why not just ask for the calcium hydroxide or the wheat starch, or whatever it is? Why the weird calls? D'you think they were looking for this when they ransacked the Willows vans?' Nick pictured the Audi saloon outside Willows. A connection slotted into place. 'Your break in?'

'Shoot. So is this the calcium hydo stuff you're talking about, or... something else like drugs?' Andy whispered.

'I don't know.'

'So it wasn't animals or rivals ransacking the raft, was it? That's why someone took the screw caps off. I reckon they were looking for this.' Seth's face turned ashen.

'Oh God, what should we do?' Nick breathed. He turned his back on the drum and faced the wood. Was someone lurking in there? Anxiety twisted his stomach.

'Well, we don't know for certain if it's drugs, do we?' Dave kept his tone even.

'No, we don't.' Nick's words sounded hollow, even to his own ears.

'We can call the police now and abandon the raft, give up on the race, call it a day, or... leave the white powder out, screw the cap on, build the raft and contact the police after the practice. It could just be a big fuss over some calcium hydroxide. We need this drum to float the raft. So....'

'Five drums and call the police now,' Andy finished for him, 'or six and call them later. Is that what you're saying, Dave?'

'Yes, we've only a week left. The race is next Sunday.'

'And our phones are back in the cars. An hour or two won't matter.' Seth pulled up the zip on his wet suit. He caught Nick's eye. 'Yeah, well after last week, I thought I'd wear this.'

'Come on. Let's get this barrel tied onto the frame. No one's going to come snooping around again. And anyway there's loads of us here, we'll be OK.' Andy bent down and picked up the outer screw cap.

•••

'Nearly there, now.' Chrissie directed her words at Clive's back as he strode ahead.

She didn't know why she'd felt the need to state the obvious. Perhaps she was picking up the excitement in the air. Voices carried across the water, clearer now they'd almost reached the gap in the hedge. It separated one side of the open grass area from the reservoir.

'Lift your end, Matt.'

She recognized Nick's voice, felt the frustration in his tones.

'Steady now. Just walk nice and easy down to the water. No breaking into a run, this time.'

'That's Dave. He's one of the carpenters at Willows,' she explained. 'Slow down a moment, Clive. They should be appearing through that gap. See, where the ground slopes into the reservoir. If we time it right, we can give them a bit of a surprise.'

They hung back, waiting for the first glimpse of a grubby trainer or the leading edge of the raft. Chrissie tensed, all her senses focused on the gap. A twig cracked and leaves rustled. She touched Clive's arm and frowned.

'Something's, just ahead,' she mouthed. 'It's too close to be the rafters.'

'Grizzly bears aren't indigenous to Suffolk,' he whispered back to her.

She tried not to giggle and clasped his hand. She was about to ask if you were meant to lie down and play dead, or leg it as fast as possible, but she caught sight of the raft emerging through the gap. Nick and Seth led the way. Matt and Andy followed; each took a corner of the frame. Three blue drums were roped the length of each long side.

Chrissie saw their eagerness, felt the thrill, and stepped forwards ready to shout and wave. Her arm was still linked with Clive's. He didn't move. He seemed to anchor her. She spun back, as in a flash rustles broke into movement ahead. Clive pulled her into the undergrowth. She read the warning in his eyes.

'What the…?' she mouthed and then followed the direction of his gaze. Two men hurried half crouching, out from the cover of the trees. They wore lightweight walking trousers and jackets in autumn hunting colours. They headed towards the slope.

'I don't think they noticed us,' he said in an undertone. 'Are they part of the group?'

Chrissie caught her breath. She'd seen the shotguns. She wasn't an expert, but from where she was hiding, it didn't look as if the barrels were broken. They were ready to fire.

'No way. Not unless Kat's playing games with her mates from the shooting club.'

'It doesn't look like a game to me, Chrissie.'

Splash! The raft hit the water. 'Come on, onto your drums!' Andy's voice rang out loud and clear.

'Hold it. Stop right there,' a Cockney voice shouted.

Bang! A shot rang out, echoing off the trees behind.

•••

Matt's stomach flipped. He'd recognized Tom immediately. He watched as his brother's mouth contorted, like the face of a runner striving to reach the finish line. Someone shouted but he couldn't make out the words. His pulse drummed too loud. He only had one thought – to get away from Tom.

He hurled himself at the raft. The water hit him like an icy hand. He remembered the chill from last time. It was so intense it hurt. He gasped, hardly feeling the whack as his arm struck the raft frame. He saw the blueness of a plastic drum and reached for it. His fingers slipped. The raft floated further into the reservoir.

'Must keep me legs up, swim with 'em,' he muttered, kicking back and launching into something between breaststroke and doggy paddle. Buoyed up by his life jacket, Matt kept the raft in sight and concentrated on his breathing. The effort seemed to help and with each stroke he headed further from the bank. He didn't dare look back. Enough sound floated across the water for him to guess what he'd see.

•••

Nick twisted around and froze. He stood looking into the barrel of a shotgun. He fought to control his breathing as his heart thumped against his ribs. He hardly heard the sound of Matt splashing in the water behind him.

'Bring back the raft,' a harsh Cockney voice yelled.

Andy started to move.

'No not you.' The gun jerked aggressively in Andy's direction. 'You, in the water, bring back the fucking raft, or I start shooting your bloody friends.'

'He can't, he hasn't got a paddle.' Dave's voice cut though the turmoil spiralling in Nick's brain.

'Stay where you are. Nobody move,' the second man shouted. The tones were Suffolk, harsh but familiar.

Nick struggled to focus. He forced himself to breathe slowly and take in the scene. The men were dressed as if for a day's shoot, except the guns weren't pointing at pigeons or the ground. He knew their faces, but from where?

'H-he'll,' Nick's voice failed. He tried again. 'He'll need help to get the raft back.'

'Stay where you are.' The nozzle of a gun swung closer.

'Matt's a useless swimmer and an even worse rafter. He'll need help.' The words came easier. Nick felt steadier.

'Maybe, but not your help. I don't trust you, you lippy bastard.' The Cockney jabbed his head at the other man. 'You! You go. And take a couple of paddles with you.'

'What, me?' The man with the Suffolk accent scowled.

'Yeah, and you.' The Cockney pointed his gun at Andy. 'You look as if you know how to paddle. Now get the fuck after that raft. Fetch it back.'

Oh God, Nick thought. *I know why the Suffolk one's familiar. A bit taller and slimmer, but he's definitely a Finch. Give him a beard and fatten him up and he's….* 'Tom,' he breathed. 'That man is Tom.'

'You go first. I'll be right behind you,' Tom snarled.

Andy paled.

'Move, you bastard.'

Andy hesitated, then walked into the water, a paddle in each hand.

Nick watched as Tom handed his shotgun to the Cockney and grabbed another paddle. He held it like a weapon. 'If there's any funny business, me mate here'll

271

shoot you. Understand?' He picked his way into the reservoir.

'Why? Why d'you want the raft?' The words came out fast before Nick had time to think. He cringed as the Cockney swung around and narrowed his eyes.

'Shut it.'

'Oh God, you're....' Nick made the connection. He'd seen the man's face exactly as Mrs Hinton had captured it on camera. His world spun.

'It's a reasonable question,' Dave said quietly. 'What's so special about the raft, or are you after the drums?'

'You bastard.' The Cockney's mouth twitched as he glared at Dave. 'You took that drum on purpose, didn't you? I've been following you most of the bloody week.'

'Call your man out of the water. It's not in the drum anymore.'

'So, what've you done with it? Come on, tell me or I'll smash your miserable face in.'

'Call your man out of the water.'

Nick felt the tension as the Cockney stilled. When he spoke, each word seeped malice. 'I'm the one giving orders round here. You've nicked something that ain't yours and you're going to return it.'

'Just give it to him, Dave.' Seth spoke for the first time.

Nick held his breath. The Cockney raised his shotgun and pointed it at Seth's head. 'Seems one of you bastards is getting the right idea.'

CHAPTER 27

Chrissie instinctively ducked as the shot rang out. She crouched amongst the shrubby bushes on the treeline bordering the reservoir.

'Those men just fired at our rafting group. Did you see that Clive? That wasn't an accident.' She turned and looked at him, her pulse racing so fast she could hardly breathe.

His face seemed tight. She'd seen that look before. It was like a mask. He was slipping into police mode. 'It's a hold-up or something.' He grasped her shoulder. 'No, don't stand up, Chrissie. Stay out of sight.' He pulled his phone from a pocket and squatted next to her.

'But….'

'I'm phoning for help. Keep your voice down.'

The orders made her feel safer, as if he'd taken charge, had a plan. She turned her attention back to the reservoir.

'Oh my God,' she moaned under her breath. She strained to hear their voices, but only caught occasional phrases and single words. She tried to read their body language. The pigeon shooters waved their shotguns, made sudden movements, leaned forwards and shouted. Nick and his friends stood, heads lowered, backs straight, hands still and voices hardly audible. Clive muttered into his phone beside her. Chrissie felt sick.

The grouping started to shift. Her heart pounded faster. 'What's going on? Is any help coming?' she whispered.

'Yes, they're sending an armed unit and also scrambling the police helicopter. We've got to hang on till then and just hope nothing really bad starts happening.'

'But it could take forever. We're in the middle of bloody nowhere. Shouldn't we try and do something, now?'

'Just stay still. The helicopter'll be here soon. Wattisham isn't far away. And keep your head down.'

'Look.' She started to point. 'They're making Andy go into the water. We've got to do something, Clive.'

'Shush.' He took her arm. 'I think I recognise those two men. They're dangerous. They may start firing if we rush in and surprise them.'

'You never said? When did you recognise them?'

'Since we've got closer. I think the one with dark sandy hair is Tom Finch.'

'Matt's brother?'

'Yes, and the ugly bastard's Len Carter.'

'Ruby Ring? Oh my God.' Her innards lurched.

•••

Matt pulled his arms through the water, forcing himself forwards with each stroke. He spat out the brackish liquid. It slapped and splashed his face. He screwed up his eyes, opened them and blinked away blurry images. The life jacket warmed his chest, made him weightless. He concentrated on the raft ahead.

•••

Nick let his breath out in a low hum. 'Seth's right. Just give it to them, Dave.' He kept his voice steady as he caught Seth's eye. He read the distress behind the clenched jaw. 'Please, Dave.'

'Where is it, you bastard? I've wasted enough time on you. I'm not asking again.' The man aimed at Dave's chest.

'OK, OK! But you can call your man out of the water. The white powder's under the tarpaulin. Back there on the grass where we built the raft.' Dave tilted his head.

'Show me.'

Dave took a step.

'And you, all of you. Walk in front where I can see you.' He jabbed the gun at Nick.

Seth shuffled forwards and Nick followed. The movement seemed to ease the tension.

'Shift it. I haven't got all day.'

Nick's thoughts raced ahead. Each step carried him up the slope and through the gap in the hedge. He saw the expanse of rough grass, the tarpaulin, the cars; he heard the splashing in the reservoir behind. Another step and he wouldn't be able to see the swimmers anymore. He slowed his pace.

'Just keep walking,' the Cockney snarled.

He wanted to fan out from the others, make it more difficult for the Cockney to control them. It wasn't a plan, just instinct. He angled away from Seth.

'Where d'you think you're bloody going?' the voice growled at his back.

'The tarpaulin. I'll take the far end; the others can take this end. It'll be easier to lift it.' Nick kept walking.

'Don't get any clever ideas, or I'll shoot you in the knee. Cripple you for life. Got it?'

Nick felt his chest tighten and nodded. He fumbled as he grasped the corner. He glanced at Dave and waited. Oh God, he thought. What'll he do to us, once he's got the drugs?

'Nice an' slow, now. Let's see what's under that.'

Nick lifted and pulled. The material started to move and then the weight dragged at his arm. The others had already dropped their end of the tarpaulin.

275

'Hold it right there. Now back away. That's right, nice an' easy. That's far enough. Kneel!'

'Oh shit.' Nick felt the blood drain from his head. Everything around him swayed. His knees gave way.

'Good, someone's learning. Now the rest of you, lie face down.'

•••

Matt swam closer to the raft. This time he manoeuvred to the side of a blue drum and lunged upwards. He scrabbled at the blue plastic, but his hand slipped.

He shrieked as his elbow crashed down onto the outer board of the raft frame. Pain burned through the coldness. He held on, kicking the water as the raft drifted further into the reservoir.

He blinked water out of his eyes and focused on a swimmer powering towards him. Was it Tom? His mum had always said, 'Finches don't swim. God would have given you fins not feathers if he'd meant you to swim.' If it was Tom, then his brother had fins.

The face took form. 'Andy?' Matt yelled.

Andy kept swimming. 'Get on the raft, Matt.'

'I can't. I've tried.'

Another stroke and Andy was alongside. 'I'll get on first and then give you a hand. Here, hold these.' He thrust the paddles at him.

Matt watched as Andy held the footrail, took a deep breath and somehow propelled himself upwards like a dolphin. His leg swung sideways as his arm reached over a drum. He was on the raft.

'Hand me the paddles, Matt. Quick.'

'Shite, there's someone else swimming out here.'

'It's one of the gunmen. Come on, let's get you up on the raft. Swim round to the end. The drums aren't in your way there.'

The cross-frame looked high above the water. Matt eyed it with suspicion. 'Oh no,' he moaned.

'Come on, Matt. Hurry. Now!'

Andy's voice cut through the fear. Matt grabbed the cross-timber and stretched up his arm. He felt Andy's grip and heaved himself higher. Andy pulled. His wrist hurt, his shoulder burned and then he was slithering upwards.

'Get your leg over the bar. Quick!' Andy let go of his hand.

Matt felt his life jacket tug as Andy yanked the strap. And then he was up, sitting astride the cross-frame, legs dangling in the water.

'Good,' Andy muttered and shoved a paddle into his hand. 'Now start bloody paddling, unless you want company.'

The swimmer was closing on them. 'Shit,' Matt yelled as he looked directly into the eyes of the gunman. His stomach flipped; it was Tom. Matt shifted along the board and struggled onto one of the drums. He needed to get higher and away from his brother.

'Matt? Is that you? Hey stop.' Tom spat reservoir water.

'No-o-o!' Matt plunged the paddle as something gripped his foot. Clawing hands worked up his leg. 'Get off, Tom!' He began to slip. 'Let go, Tom!' He swung his paddle, hard. Whack! Tom let go.

Matt lost balance. He flipped backwards, over the drum, and downwards into the gap between the cross-timbers. His head hit the water. It filled his nose and stung the back of his throat. He dangled upside-down, shoulders and life jacket wedged in the gap. He wanted to cough. Instead he took a mouthful of brackish water and spluttered and choked. His arms were above the frame and he thrashed about, trying to clutch something - anything to grab to pull himself up and ease his head back through the gap.

Hands tugged again, dragging at his foot, forcing it over the drum. He guessed it was Tom, but this time he couldn't resist. His head was about to burst, his chest explode. A pulse hammered in his ears. His world became speckled. He lost focus.

'Matt! Matt!'

He heard Andy yell his name as his chin broke through the water. He coughed and spat as he carried on rising, pulled up by his life jacket but anchored by someone hanging onto his foot.

'You're a bloody weight, Matt.'

He felt himself rolled and flipped across the wooden boards onto his front. Thwack! Andy slapped him on the back.

'My f-foot,' he coughed. 'Let go my foot.' He retched, spat and puked. Pain shot through his knee and ankle. His ribs ached; his throat flamed as he tasted acid and bile. He rubbed his eyes.

'You OK, Matt?' Andy's anxious voice broke through again.

'Yeah, but get 'im off me.'

'Let go of his foot, you bastard?' Crack! Wood connected with flesh. Andy raised his paddle again. 'Let go of his foot. Don't try and get up on the raft, or I'll smash your bloody head in. Hold onto the board on the side and we'll paddle you to the bank.'

Tom grunted. Matt felt the grip on his foot ease, and then release.

'Thanks, Andy. Thanks, mate.'

'Can you paddle, Matt?'

He coughed again and sat up. 'I dunno.'

•••

Chrissie grabbed Clive's arm. 'There must be something more we can do than just watch.'

'I'm not following them through the gap in the hedge. The safest place for us is back in your car. Come on. They're busy on the water, so let's make our move now.'

'But….'

'The armed unit, the police dogs… they'll be here soon. Believe me; we'll be safer in your car.'

Chrissie started to move. Her muscles ached, still stiff from crouching. 'But what if…?'

'Keep low and keep moving. I'm right behind you.'

She concentrated on the ground underfoot: brambles, rough grass, clay-heavy earth, dead leaves. Her muscles loosened with each step. Stealth or speed, she wondered. *Both*, her inner voice answered.

She stooped as she moved, quickening her pace, picking her way along the side of the reservoir. She didn't give herself time to think or feel beyond the act of moving. She kept one thought in her mind – to reach her car. If she pictured her rafting team left behind, she knew she'd break down.

•••

Nick opened his eyes. His light-headed mist cleared. Blades of grass blocked his view where he lay on the ground. He turned his head, pulling his thoughts together as he watched the Cockney grab the cellophane snake of drugs.

'All of you stay where you are. Understand?'

'Oh God,' Nick moaned, as the memories came flooding back. A distant rumble seeped through the silence. For a moment he thought it came from the Cockney. He raised his head to get a clearer view.

'Head down, you bastard. Nobody move.'

Nick held his breath and waited, one cheek pressed to the ground. He heard footsteps resound through the dry earth. They distanced, and then there was silence, apart from the low rumble. Little by little, he dared to lift his head again. The Cockney had vanished.

•••

Matt grabbed his paddle and scrabbled back onto the drum. The effort forced him to suck air to the bottom of his lungs. He coughed and hawked. His sodden tee-shirt clung to his skin, fine silt covered his trainers.

'Paddle, for God's sake,' Andy yelled.

He thrust the blade into the water. 'I am.' His breath came in sobs.

A distant rumble filled the air, the sound reflecting off the water.

Matt knew the resonance, recognised it immediately He'd heard it often enough at Clegg's. 'It's a 'copter.' Something on the bank caught his eye. 'Look! He's going to shoot.' His guts twisted.

On the far bank the second gunman stood, waving something. Cockney tones carried across the water. 'I've got it,' he yelled. 'Get back here, Tom. I'm leaving now.'

'Yeah, I'm on me bloody way,' a harsh voice snarled from the water.

Matt froze.

'Paddle,' Andy shouted.

Matt lunged and pulled and strained. He thought his chest would burst.

'Can't you paddle faster, you idiots?' Tom clung to the side of the raft. 'You always were useless, Matt. You can't hide from me behind a beard.' He spat the words like poison as the low rumble burst into a crescendo above.

Matt looked up as the helicopter appeared over the trees. It flew low, the rotor blades giving a beat to the pounding thunder. He felt the reverberation. He put his hands to his ears. It was deafening.

'It's the police,' Tom shrieked.

The surface of the reservoir broke into ripples. The gunman on the bank spun around, ducked and disappeared into the trees.

'Hey, wait for me,' Tom screamed.

Matt couldn't move. The noise, the surprise, the exhaustion, it stunned him. He sat astride the drum, bent double and hugging his head. Somewhere down in the water, beside the raft, Tom let out a primeval howl. He splashed and crashed around, breaking into a rudimentary crawl stroke as he headed for the nearest bank, at a right angle to the trees. It was less than ten metres away.

'He's going to make it. Look!' Andy yelled.

Tom emerged from the reservoir and clambered onto the bank. Matt watched as his brother stood, Gollum-like in his dripping clothes. He started to run, turning once to make a jabbing two finger sign at Matt and the raft, and then he was gone.

•••

Chrissie felt safer now that she sat in the driver's seat with Clive beside her in the car. The TR7 was largely hidden from the water by the bank. She supposed they must have made the reservoir by digging a hole in the ground, an area larger than a football pitch, and then piling the earth on the edge. It created a bank. On one side it contained the water, and on the other it sloped down to the natural ground level. And that was where she'd parked, on the slope leading up to the bank.

She heard the distant rumble and recognised the helicopter engine immediately. 'They've got it up in the air.' Relief made her voice light. She beamed at Clive.

'It should be overhead in a couple of minutes.' He checked his watch and got out his phone.

Chrissie waited, all her senses tuned to the rumble. It was like waiting for a kettle to boil. Would it ever come? She heard some shouting and then it materialized above the trees. It shattered the stillness with the power of its motors, thumping out sound so loud it was palpable. She automatically ducked. It slowed and hovered above the reservoir. It was mind-blowing.

The commotion seemed interminable and Chrissie pressed her hands to her ears. A movement on the bank caught her eye. It took form. A sodden figure appeared, water dripping as he ran, crouching and ducking as if the helicopter blades might slice him apart.

'It's Tom,' she yelped, but her voice was drowned by the din. She turned the ignition key. She couldn't hear it, but she felt the engine leap into life. She slipped it into gear. 'Clive, it's Tom.' He didn't seem to hear.

All the emotion and frustration of the day bubbled up. Tom, the architect of so much trouble was about to run past her car. He looked as if he was heading for the cover of the trees. He was about to get away. She gripped the steering wheel, ready to drive. In an instant Tom was alongside, sprinting for the wood. Now was her chance. She let out the clutch with a jolt, the engine engaged and the car surged forwards.

The sudden movement spooked him. He jumped sideways, caught his toe on a stone, went over on his ankle and fell, sprawling to the side of the track.

'Drive on,' Clive shouted. 'You didn't hit him.' Clive turned in his seat and stared behind. 'No, he won't be going far. Looks as if he's sprained his ankle. Keep going, Chrissie.'

'But shouldn't I stop if he's hurt?'

'No. He's dangerous. He won't get far before the police pick him up. Drive on. We need to get away from under this bloody helicopter. It's so loud I can't hear on the phone.'

'I can put the hood up. Would that cut out some of the noise?' Chrissie shouted, as the car bounced over the ruts.

'No. Get into the wood. The trees will baffle the sound.'

Chrissie drove fast. Adrenaline powered her body. Her vision had never felt sharper, her reactions never faster. She saw every rut and pothole before she reached it. She steered and changed gear like a rally driver. She felt on top of her game, aware only of the trail, and her car, an extension of herself.

'Hell, what's that?'

A black Audi saloon accelerated onto the track ahead.

'Slow down, Chrissie. We don't want an accident'

Chrissie positioned her car for the corner. Deep grooves rutted the surface, loose stones littered the track. The Audi ahead took it at speed, accelerating and then at the last moment braking. She watched as its back wheels slewed out sideways. The driver corrected for the slide. Stones scattered. Its front wheels caught in a deep rut. The driver lost control. The car spun. The tail crashed into a tree. Chrissie, a few metres behind, braked and stopped.

'Woah,' Clive whispered.

'We must've come far enough into the woods because I can hear you now.' Chrissie took her hands off the wheel. She couldn't stop them from shaking.

Somewhere in the sky the helicopter rumbled, but the sound was more distant, bearable.

'No, don't open the door or get out. I need to make a call.'

Chrissie waited as Clive spoke into his mobile. She wanted to scream, to release the tension, burst into tears. She thought her head might explode. She knew she hadn't caused the accident. The Audi was already accelerating, well before the driver saw her in his mirrors, but that didn't make her feel any better. She bit her lip and rested her forehead on the steering wheel. 'Oh God,' she moaned.

CHAPTER 28

Matt slept like the dead. When he awoke he was in exactly the same position he'd curled into when he'd gone to sleep the previous evening. He opened his eyes. There'd been no half-waking dream-sequences shepherding him into consciousness. Nothing. Just a blank. He took in the fading blue of his bedroom walls and his brain collided with the day. He fumbled for his mobile and coughed; not much, just some sticky mucous.

The memories came flooding back. Some of it was a blur, but other things stood out like beacons. Tom being taken away in a police van was one. He almost grinned when he pictured it. There'd been lots of questions of course, and the obligatory visit to Ipswich A&E department, but Tom behind bars; that was the main thing.

Matt focused on his mobile. A message icon caught his eye. He fumbled with it as he sat up. 'Ouch,' he wailed. His elbow hurt, the graze on his arm smarted and his abdominal muscles cramped. He already knew his ribs would feel sore from coughing. It had been explained to him by the doctors in A&E. They'd also said he'd been lucky. At the time he hadn't understood the bit about his luck. Where was the good fortune in being thrust into the hostile environment of a reservoir?

He read the text message. 'Shite.' He'd forgotten all about it. Sunday had driven it out of his mind. He was meant to be meeting Mr Blumfield today, Monday at twelve thirty, sharp. He still had a couple of hours.

Matt rolled out of bed. He landed on the floor with his nose in his armpit. 'Ugh.' Stale life jacket, reservoir water and sweat didn't sit well together. It reminded him of the raft and caught his breath. He struggled to his knees, grabbed the bed frame and staggered to his feet. Would he ever be free of the images?

His mum's shower didn't even smell like the reservoir, but the water still made him anxious. He had to force himself to control his breathing as he stood under the warm cascade. It was OK, he kept telling himself. He was the right way up and he could breathe through his nose. The doctors had told him he was lucky. He needed a shower and the interview would go well.

Twenty minutes later Matt towelled his head dry. He smelled of his mum's rose scented shower gel. He'd even used it on his hair. He positively reeked of country garden wholesomeness. He reckoned old Blumfield would be impressed.

He reached for a clean pair of jeans and the special tee-shirt. Chrissie had ordered six. One for each member of the rafting team, and that included Dave and herself. She'd handed them out the week before. 'To be worn at the race,' she'd said. He took his out of its cellophane packet now. Across the front was written: UTTERLY ACADEMY CARPENTRY DEPARTMENT, and across the back in even bolder lettering, **RADIAL-ARM BANDITS**. He held it up for inspection, looked at both sides, and made a decision. He preferred the bandits bit and put it on back-to-front.

He pulled the tee-shirt over his head. The *XL* label scratched against his throat and he fiddled with it until it poked up above the neckline. 'That's better,' he murmured and reached for his trainers. They felt cold, heavy, and still oozed reservoir. 'Yuck.'

The Piaggio responded to his touch and started first time. He sat on the saddle, his stomach all of a flutter. He hadn't decided exactly what he was going to say to Blumfield. He knew what he wanted, but how to find the right words? The wind caught the cotton fabric. It flapped around his elbows, plastered **RADIAL-ARM BANDITS** to his chest and trailed the material out behind. He had a feeling the day was going to be epic; he just hoped the doctors had been right about his luck.

Matt sat outside Mr Blumfield's office door and stared at his hands. Cracks coursed across the tips of his fingernails, making mosaic patterns with the missing chips and flakes. 'Bloody blue drums,' he muttered. He remembered clawing at them, trying to get a purchase. He shook his head, trying to dismiss the memory. Tom must have thought him an idiot. 'Pheasant feeders, my arse,' he whispered. Drugs were much more in Tom's line. He should have realised.

The door opened and Mr Blumfield's round face beamed at him. Matt noticed how sweat glistened through his thinning hair.

'Ah, Matt Finch. Please come in.'

Matt stood up, heart thumping, and stepped into his office. It looked much the same as he remembered it, with the large desk and the Mackintosh style chair. He turned and closed the door, hoping Blumfield would read the back, or rather the front of his tee-shirt and be impressed.

'Sit down, Matt.' Blumfield gestured towards the elegant wooden chair near the door. 'I'm glad we're having this opportunity for a chat. We have several things we need to discuss.'

Matt sat and waited while Blumfield settled in a swivel office chair behind his desk.

'I understand you were in the rafting team... that dreadful incident at the reservoir, yesterday.' He looked pointedly at Matt's chest. 'I can see you've called yourself a bandit, but did you really have to use drums containing drugs?'

'We didn't know, Mr Blumfield, least not till it were too late.'

'Pity, because the police have impounded the raft.'

'But why?'

'As evidence.'

'But we'll still be able to race it next week?'

'I'm afraid not, Matt. They'll need it for forensics. For all I know, they may not release it until the trial.'

'The trial?'

'Yes, the trial for the drug dealers, Matt. And that brings me to my next point. This is very bad publicity for the Academy. As I see it, I have no choice but to pull the plug on the whole project.'

'Pull the...?'

Blumfield leaned forwards. 'Yes, cancel our entry in the race.'

Matt stared at the floor. Disappointment weighed heavy. He sighed and noticed how dirty moisture leeched from his trainers. Faint footprints led to his chair.

'I heard you were in the water a long time, Matt. Are you all right now?'

'Yeah, reckon so.'

Silence settled in the office. Matt's head reeled. This isn't how the interview was meant to go, he thought. This isn't supposed to be about the raft race. I want to change courses. He stood up. 'I want to change courses,' he blurted.

He met Mr Blumfield's unblinking eyes.

'I want to change courses, Mr Blumfield.'

'Have you any idea what you want to change to, Matt?'

'Yeah, Computing an' IT.'

'Have you really thought about this, Matt? I mean, are you absolutely sure?'

'Yeah, been thinkin' 'bout it for ages.' He watched as Blumfield glanced down and leafed through some letters on his desk.

'I've got a report here from Hepplewhites. They say you've been a good worker but not a natural carpenter. And of course there's the sickness record. You started with them late. You'd broken your....'

'Wrist, Mr Blumfield. I bust me other one when the oven exploded. Remember, in the Academy canteen?'

'Yes, yes, Matt. I recall.' He breathed out slowly, not quite a sigh and pulled a spreadsheet from the pile of papers. 'I've got your sickness record here. You've taken over four, no... closer to five months sick leave, if we count the physiotherapy. Yes, I know it was through no fault of your own, but you injured your wrists and... well obviously it's affected your ability with the carpentry.'

'I spent loads of time in the library with the computers.'

'Yes I know, and you've contributed to carving the totem pole since you recovered. I've spoken to Ron Clegg. He said you're a good lad. We had a long chat.'

'But can I change courses?'

'I think… well, I had been considering having you repeat a year.' He paused and smiled thinly. 'But I've spoken to Administration and it seems changing courses would be an alternative. As long as you do it before this summer term finishes and the academic year ends. That way we can get around the question of funding. Being absent through illness for the best part of an academic year of carpentry might also help, in this instance. I know a chunk of it was because of an accident here… and that's a bit of a grey area as well, but I think we can do it.'

Matt stared at Blumfield. 'Are you sayin' I can change courses?' He didn't dare believe it. Tom had played tricks like this on him as a kid. He used to pretend he'd teach him snooker. 'You mean it? Honest?'

Mr Blumfield nodded. 'And I'll recommend you as well, do all I can to support your transfer to the Computing and IT course, if that's what you want.' He patted the stack of paper on his desk. 'I've got enough here to make you look good enough in the reports.'

'Really?' Visions of Tom faded. 'Really? That's awesome. Thanks, thanks Mr Blumfield. They said I were lucky.'

'Lucky? What are you talking about? Now try to concentrate. I'll speak to the head of Computing and IT this afternoon. We may be able to get you started with them before the end of the week. Now off you go' He waved his hand dismissively.

Matt stood up to leave.

'Just one more thing. Sorry to ask again, but you are quite sure you're well? You look… well that tee-shirt seems very… roomy.'

'Yeah.' Matt fingered the *XL* label digging into his neck. 'It's so I can paddle. It's what we rafters wear, sorry, wore.'

'Yes, of course.' Mr Blumfield pursed his lips. 'Why don't you drop in to speak to Administration at the end of the afternoon? They may have some news for you by then.' The words followed Matt through the doorway and out into the corridor.

He couldn't believe it. 'Yeah,' he whooped and punched the air.

He hurried to the canteen, his stomach rumbling like Mount Vesuvius inside the voluminous white cotton. He knew he'd chosen the right tee. It was his lucky day. Students jostled at the service counter, banged trays down onto tables, shouted and laughed. He'd hit the lunch hour rush. He spotted Chrissie and Nick sitting at a table by the window. They were already eating. He queued up and then made his way to join them, his plate heaped with chips.

Nick looked up. 'Hi, Matt. Are you celebrating or eating for two?'

Chrissie paused with a sandwich part way to her mouth. 'I should've got a smaller tee-shirt for you. What size is that, Matt?'

'Well, there's something sticking up at his neck. It says *XL*, from here. Why are you wearing it back-to-front, Matt?'

'I like the **RADIAL-ARM BANDITS** across me chest.'

'Hmm, but when you're wearing your life jacket, that would be covered. Our...,' she seemed to search for the words, 'buoyancy aids sit round your neck and over the front of your chest. Hence the bandit bit was for the back, where it can be read.'

Matt forked some chips into his mouth and chewed. No one said anything for a while.

'Are you OK, Matt?' Chrissie broke the silence between them.

'I'm a bit stiff.' He coughed. 'How 'bout you? Heard you did some ace drivin'.'

'Yes.'

He watched her drop her sandwich back onto her plate.

'Come on, Chrissie. You and the yellow peril, sorry the TR7, as good as rounded up Tom and Ruby Ring.' Nick swigged some water and smiled. 'You did bloody well.'

Matt frowned. 'There's somethin' I still don't get. What happened to Highland?'

'Who? Who's Highland?'

Matt explained how he'd taken the left track and followed the Audi. He repeated what he'd overheard. 'See, I thought they were talkin' 'bout pheasants and blue drum feeders, not drugs. I'd 've warned you when you found that stuff in the blue drum if I'd realised what they were really after. We could've called the police straight 'way.'

'It wouldn't have made much difference. Tom and Ruby Ring were already on their way and they'd still've pointed guns at you,' Chrissie murmured. 'Highland, you say? And a strong Cockney accent?'

Matt nodded.

'Ruby Ring, Highland fling,' she chanted. 'It rhymes. You know it could be… Cockney rhyming slang.'

'You mean Highland as in Highland fling?' Nick put his bottle of water down. 'It's one of the rhyming pair of words, isn't it? Highland – yeah you could be right, Chrissie. Classic Cockney rhyming slang.'

'And it was Ruby Ring who smashed up the black Audi,' Chrissie added.

'So are they the same bloke?'

'Yes, Matt. The same bastard who ran Mrs Hinton down and it seems may also have had something to do with Sobell's killing.'

'Woah!' Matt sank into his own thoughts. Clive had said something about Hoxton. That was Cockney territory wasn't it? He shook his head.

'What's the matter?' Nick asked.

'I was just thinkin', that's all. You know the raft's being held? Taken for evidence.'

Chrissie nodded and bit her nails.

'Well, Blumfield says we've got to pull out the race. Says it's bad publicity, being tied up with a drugs raid an'all.'

'Well he would, wouldn't he?' Chrissie almost spat the words.

'How come you know so much about what Blumfield's saying, Matt?'

'Probably the same reason he smells of roses and is wearing his new tee-shirt back to front, Nick.'

'Oh right - your interview with Blumfield. It wasn't.... Was it today, Matt?'

Matt nodded. He tried to pull a grief-stricken face, but he couldn't hide the grin. 'Yeah, it went OK. Blumfield says I can change courses. It were touch an' go. I think wearin' the raftin' tee swung it for me. And the totem pole might've helped.'

'Epic! It's awesome, Matt.'

'That's fantastic news. When do you change?'

'Could be this week.' Matt couldn't stop smiling.

'So how will you fund yourself? Have you thought about it? The money you get for being an apprentice will stop. You do realise that, don't you?' Chrissie bit into her discarded sandwich.

'He could always do the Saturday all-night supermarket shift. What d'you think, Chrissie?'

'Probably meet a nice kind of girl at one in the morning, Nick.'

'Yeah. It's a well-known dating venue.'

'Is it?'

'Reckon you'll have to find out, Matt.'

He closed his eyes and for a moment tried to picture Jo, her pink streaked hair fluorescing under the strip lighting as she selected tins of baked beans at one in the morning. She'd be just the kind of bird to shop at an unconventional hour, he figured. 'It could be cool,' he mumbled.

'There's something I've been wanting to ask you guys. This may be the right moment.'

'Ask away, Chrissie.' Nick shifted in his chair.

'The raft. There was an unusual piece of wood in the cross-frame. It was so unusual and so distinctive, it caught my eye immediately. Now, correct me if I'm wrong, but it wasn't there the first time we built the raft was it?' She paused and scrutinized Matt and then Nick.

'Yeah, I mean no.' Matt felt uneasy.

'And I'd have noticed if it had disappeared from the workshop during the week. But you were at Clegg's on Saturday, weren't you Nick? So I guess that's when you cut it off. So tell me, which bright spark came up with the idea to use the top of the totem pole?'

Matt heard the bright sparks bit. 'Me,' he said. The word just popped out.

CHAPTER 29

They'd all gathered inside Ron Clegg's workshop: Nick, Matt, and even Clive. It was late Saturday morning and the transporter had finally driven away with the totem pole on board.

'Well, this is nice,' Chrissie murmured, and sipped her mug of tea. 'Thank God it's gone at last.' She glanced around the barn workshop and smiled.

'I'll raise my mug to that.' Ron's voice carried over the benches. He was checking on a drawer, glued and clamped since the end of Friday.

'It's like the elephant in the room,' Nick said. 'The totem pole's been here so long. I still feel its presence.'

She watched as Matt ambled up and down, tracing patterns with his foot in the fine cedar dust. It covered the concrete floor where the totem pole had lain, stretched out on blocks for the best part of a year. Fine specks of paint bore testimony to a final coat of reds, blues, greens and white. Woodchips and shavings littered the ground near one end. That'll be the chain saw incident, she thought, and smiled as she remembered their red faces in the canteen. Secretly she was relieved they'd chopped the top off it. She would have just liked to have been told about it, that's all.

The cedar had gone, but the memories of the previous Sunday weren't going to leave so easily. Chrissie knew it would take far longer than six days before the sudden flashbacks to the crashed Audi started to fade. She was pleased when Clive had offered to give her a lift. Her rally driving attempt at the reservoir came at a price and one of the TR7's track-rod ends attached to the steering arm had been damaged.

Hints of linseed oil and cedar filled the air and she breathed the scents in deeply.

'I think you're going to miss working on that totem pole, Chrissie.' The twinkle reached Clive's eyes. 'It loaded onto the transporter OK. At least it wasn't as difficult as I'd imagined. I think it's going to look pretty damn impressive when they've put it up in the Academy gardens.'

'Yeah,' Nick checked his watch. 'I'm going to drive over soon. I want to see how they're going to unload it. I suppose they'll try and swing it into the hole they've dug.'

'That could be interesting. God, I hope they don't damage it.'

'It'll be OK, Chrissie. It's survived Matt.' Nick paused and then grinned. 'At least there won't be a great audience of students around. You can imagine the headlines: *Caterpillar Tread Nudges Student into Hole as Giant Pole Planted.*'

Chrissie shook her head. 'I can picture Blumfield's reaction. *More bad publicity.*'

'Hope they dig a bloody big hole,' Matt mumbled.

'Are you going to come and watch, Chrissie?' Nick asked.

'Yes, why don't you? I've got to go into Ipswich and finish some reports.' Clive sipped his tea. 'Nick can take you to the Academy with him, can't you Nick? I'll catch up with you this evening, Chrissie.'

'That sounds good, if it's all right with you, Nick?' She glanced at him. He had a faraway look. 'Is everything OK, Nick?'

'I've been thinking about Sunday, can't get it out of my mind.'

There was a long silence. Chrissie blinked away the sudden image of buckled, torn metal, scraped black paint-work and an Audi's smashed rear wing. Nick's voice broke into her thoughts.

'So where did the drugs come from? Was it really from the manuscript place at Bucklesham? Lia was so damn careful about those drums. I mean, she never let them out of her sight when we were near them. But then I thought it was just her way, you know meticulous with everything. I can't believe she was involved in drugs.'

'I'm afraid it's not looking too good for Lia at the moment, Nick.' Clive sounded matter-of-fact. 'We've handed it over to the Serious Organised Crime Unit, but it seems there was quite a sophisticated set up – importing, supplying, dealing and money laundering.'

'It must be a mistake. I was working there for a few weeks. It just seems so....'

Chrissie watched Nick's face as he frowned and stared at the floor.

Clive broke the silence. 'You know, we even had one of their Dutch suppliers?'

'Was that one of the blokes you picked up hare coursing?' Chrissie asked, pleased to move the conversation on from Lia. 'Didn't you say you released him? Sorry, I shouldn't have said that. God, no wonder they had a slick city lawyer. Makes sense now.'

'Yes, I'm afraid so. It doesn't make us look too clever, but at the time we didn't have any grounds for holding him.' Clive shrugged.

'You can't win them all,' Chrissie murmured.

'No, like the raft race. Sometimes things are beyond your control.' He smiled, and then pulled the angles of his mouth down in a mock attempt at contrite.

The raft wasn't a laughing matter, but then neither was letting the Dutchman go, she supposed. She dug him in the ribs.

'Ouch!'

'But why'd you take away the whole raft?' Matt abandoned his toe-tracings and heaved himself up onto a work stool. 'We should've been racin' Needham Lake, tomorrow.'

Clive held up his hands. 'Not me. It's still undergoing forensics. Sorry, but maybe it's for the best, Matt.'

Chrissie glanced from Matt to Nick. His eyes were closed. 'Are you OK, Nick?'

'Yeah, yeah.' He seemed to shake himself. 'I was just remembering... the supercar I saw at the units in Bucklesham. The Audi A8. It was striking, yeah... beautiful. I thought at the time it seemed a bit out of her league. Now I suppose....'

Clive nodded. 'The Dutchman drove an A8. Probably his. It turns out he's an important contact. That's why he was being entertained. Blood sports were very much his thing, it seems. There's nothing like seeing a living hare torn limb from limb, apparently.'

'Don't, Clive. I can't bear the thought.'

'Sorry, Chrissie. Look, I really must be going. There's a pile of reports waiting for me in Ipswich. It's been one hell of a week.' He stood up. 'Sorry I can't come to see the totem pole being planted, but I've got to be on my way. Bye, everyone. Bye Ron.'

Chrissie followed Clive out into the courtyard.

'It's difficult to believe Matt's brother could've been mixed up in anything so grim. I mean, Anne Blink, and then Sobell's killing?'

'We don't know all the details. We're a long way off finding Anne's killer. As for Sobell, I expect he was well known to them. Probably a supplier, or part of the gang... in which case different rules applied.'

'As if that makes it any better. Will Len Carter - the Ruby Ring, Highland fling man, be OK? Was he shaken up much in the accident?' She shivered in the sunshine and took his arm.

'Well, put it this way, it'll take him a while to get over the whole episode.'

The echo of a heavy thud filled her ears as she re-played the crash.

'Are you OK, Chrissie?'

'Yes, yes I'm, fine. Thanks for being here, and for everything, Clive.'

'My pleasure. As they say in the movies, I was just doing my job.' He smiled and kissed her lightly. 'Now, I must go.'

She watched as he drove away, weaving between the potholes on the rough track. Clive was right; it certainly had been one hell of a week.

CHAPTER 30

Nick lay back on the meadow grass; Friar's Meadow, to be precise. Small wispy clouds laced the sky above. They seemed to be as still as a picture, but if he closed his eyes for a minute or two, and then opened them again, they had definitely moved. The air was warm, but the sunshine was already losing its strength and the sounds of picnickers and Sunday strollers played out gently in the background.

'Sleepy?' Kat's voice interrupted his thoughts.

He smiled as she threw herself down beside him. She settled, half propped-up on her elbows and looked across the flat expanse of lush grass and towards the river Stour, its banks dotted with alder, ash and white willow. 'You know, Nick, it's turned out well, bringing the canoes here. When Chrissie suggested Sudbury, I thought she was mad. But now that we're here, I think it's lovely. We could be in a Constable painting.'

'Chrissie's one of life's movers and shakers.' He grinned. 'And anyway, we were all fired up, ready to race a raft, so yeah, the inflatable canoes have kind of fitted the bill. I don't know where Seth got them from… genius. ' He pulled at a blade of grass. 'I think we all needed to let off steam. It's been a few weeks now.'

He rolled onto his side and watched her face. She didn't look at him but gazed into the distance. Twenty yards away on the river, Andy flicked water with his paddle at Seth's girlfriend, Ali. Something between a squeak and shriek rent the air.

'You told me Ballingdon was nearer, Seth.'

'No excuses. I knew I'd beat you two back from the bridge,' Andy yelled.

Kat frowned.

'What is it, Kat?'

'Did you read that stuff in the paper, yesterday? I know you'd already told me about some bloke called Dard being behind everything, so I hadn't thought for a moment he could be a she....'

'I know. Matt said he was a vicious bastard. The *she* aspect is a bit of a shock.'

He pictured the headline. *Amalia Dard slips through Police Net*. He remembered the picture of a serious faced Ms Dard printed below, followed by an article tracing her roots and background: the Dard family history, the Hoxton connection, the proximity to Clerkenwell and associated crime syndicates. The police wanted to interview her in connection with drugs and money laundering, but apparently she was proving difficult to trace. Nick didn't know how he felt about it all. Confused. Disbelieving. Stupid. All of those things and more.

'I can't believe it. I actually spoke to her. I talked to someone who, if you can believe what they print in the papers, ran a drugs empire. A woman. The head of a syndicate and at the top of her game. What I don't get, Nick, is how she seemed so ordinary.'

'I know. She often spoke to Dave and me, and... well, it never crossed our minds. Never in a million years.'

'I guess we were all just naïve.'

Nick shook his head. Before he could say more, drops of cold water splashed onto his head. 'Hey, get off! Ugh, Matt!' He shot out an arm and grabbed at a pair of chubby legs. Matt, encased in a soaking tee-shirt and wet life jacket, landed heavily on Nick's chest. Chrissie stood behind, grinning.

'Brilliant. This looks like a photo opportunity. Parachute fails to open,' she hooted.

Nick looked up into Chrissie's smiling eyes. 'Have you just crept up on us? Just get him off me, will you?' He pushed as Chrissie yanked at the life jacket. 'You're a liability.'

Matt sat up and coughed.

'I couldn't help overhearing, but…,' Chrissie caught his eye. 'Lia, or should I say Amalia, was a killer too, Nick. I know there's all the drugs business but… Tom's come clean and, well he said it was a woman driving the car. He'd never seen her before, didn't know her name but… he recognised a photo. It was Lia in the car outside the night club.'

'Clive told you?'

Chrissie nodded.

'But Lia said she hardly remembered Anne. She sounded so plausible.' Kat touched Nick's arm. 'You remember, don't you?'

'I do.' He also remembered the entry in the visitors' book. Oh God, he thought. Anne had written warmly about Lia. She'd probably considered her a fantastic role model. No wonder she'd have got in the car with her. He shivered. God, what a cold, ruthless bitch. It was difficult to take it all in. 'They think Lia killed her? Are you sure it wasn't just a simple overdose? An accident?'

'It was Tuinal, remember?' Chrissie murmured.

A pulse started to throb in his head.

Kat broke the silence. 'If Anne was an art student, she'd have been much closer to the manuscripts and chemicals than you guys were, Nick. Maybe she discovered it wasn't all purified wheat powder, or whatever they use at the place. Perhaps she saw something dodgy and was stupid enough to ask too many questions. They might have thought she'd guessed what was going on, or spotted a forged manuscript or something.'

'Then why not recruit her? They didn't have to kill her.' Nick rubbed at his temple.

'They were professionals tidying up. For all we know, Dave could have been next on their list.'

'Oh God, Chrissie. Don't say that.' Nick didn't know if he could take any more of this. It was starting to make his chest feel tight. He took a deep breath. 'Have you been over to check out that pillbox yet, Matt?' He pointed at an angular low structure on the opposite bank of the river. Out of the corner of his eye he noticed Chrissie and Kat exchange glances.

'The pillbox? Not yet, mate. Are you goin'?'

'Yeah.' Nick scrambled to his feet. 'Do you want to canoe across or swim?' He watched Matt's face for an answer, but the beard made it difficult to pick up the nuances. He made a guess. 'Sorry Jo didn't come today, Matt.'

'It's OK, mate. We're textin'.'

'Not regretting changing courses?'

'Nah.'

They walked in silence. Ahead on the banks, white willows stretched branches upwards, their silver-grey foliage catching the sunlight. Nick led the way through some taller grass mixed with common comfrey on the bank.

Seth paddled towards them, radiant blue reflecting off the water near the inflatable canoe. 'Are you getting in?' he called.

'Shite,' Matt yelled as his foot slipped between some reeds and into the water.

'There's no point hanging onto the reeds, Matt. They won't hold you. Just get in the canoe.'

They splashed and laughed, and nearly capsized the canoe, but Seth got them to the far bank. Nick waded, and then half hauled himself out of the water. 'You don't need to pull all the plants out of this bank, Matt. Leave the flowering ones,' he said as buttercups and water crowfoot brushed close to his face. He lay on the grass for a moment and listened as Matt struggled up the bank.

'It's awesome. I looked this pillbox up on the internet before we came. Yeah, brick outer skin.' He pointed. 'Rifles an' light machine guns can fire through them gun slits, and on the top... yeah, a mount, or more like a well in the roof for an anti-aircraft or anti-tank gun.'

'Well, you're sounding more yourself, Matt. I thought back on the other side you were looking a bit..., that something was wrong.'

'Yeah, well it's Tom aint it? How was I t'know they'd go an' kill Sobell?'

'Suppose it was a brutal gang message. This is what happens if you mess with my dog, sort of thing. But why'd they give the dog to Tom in the first place? And then you? Why not leave it with Highland?'

'Chrissie says Highland kept 'is dogs as killers. Lurchers for hare coursin' an' Rottweiler-cross-mastiffs for guards and... to kill Sobell. She reckons he didn't 'ave the dog lover's handlin' skills for a Labrador with a sensitive nose.'

'And you did?'

'Nah. Course not, but they must've thought Tom did. Trust a bird to want a sniffer dog.'

'Perhaps Lia just liked Labradors.'

'Who you kiddin? More likely the leotard bird wanted 'im to track where suppliers hid the stock. Find out who'd been cheatin' on her.'

For a moment Nick couldn't place the leotard bird.

'Leotard?'

'Yeah, Lia Dard. That Amalia bird. Italian weren't she?'

Nick nodded. 'Well she, or someone, made a mistake when they chose Tom.'

'Yeah. Bloody Tom.'

'I wonder if they'll ever find Lia,' Nick murmured as he followed Matt to the WWII pillbox.

'Bloody Tom.'

The End.

Lightning Source UK Ltd.
Milton Keynes UK
UKHW021146030420
361293UK00005B/83